# ETHEREAL

# ETHEREAL

# LOIS WOOD

TENTH STREET PRESS

# THIS EDITION

Copyright 2018  Lois Wood

Published by Tenth Street Press
Cover design by Axel

ISBN10: 0-6481676-6-6
ISBN13: 978-0-6481676-6-2

TENTH STREET PRESS Ltd.
MELBOURNE LONDON
www.tenthstreetpress.com
Email: contact@tenthstreetpress.com

"Big thanks go to the many cafes and the university in the Inner Mongolian city of Tongliao, China, where the majority of this book was penned in 2014. Being an English teacher at the university there afforded me lots of non-teaching time to get Ethereal out of my head and onto paper, and then later: onto the laptop. Particularly when it was -30 degrees Celsius outside. Also, massive heartfelt thanks go to my very sexy fiancé who painstakingly helped to get Ethereal fit for your eyes by diligently proof-reading and going through the book with a proverbial fine-toothed comb. I love you Wil."

# CONTENTS

# CHAPTER ONE

Sheena Stapleton lived by two simple rules: 1) don't do anything that hurts anyone or anything else (otherwise known as 'universal law') and 2) always be honest and true to herself, even if having to shield others from that truth, or keeping it closely under wraps. It wasn't always the case with her second rule, and has only been actually put into practise for the past two years, but she's never felt freer or happier than when she realised honesty (with herself, at least) really was the best policy. She's not sure how or why such a stark realisation and abrupt change of heart, life and mind, came about, but this much is certainly true: one morning, a warm, everyday kind of Spring morning, Sheena Stapleton (or Sheena Doyle, as she was known at the time) drew in a deep breath and quietly and calmly told her then-husband over their steadily growing cold coffee at their oversized, heavy dining table:

"I'm moving out. We are going to separate and get a divorce."

She hadn't waited for his reaction or even glanced back in his direction, but had, equally calmly and quickly, gotten up, taken her coffee cup over to the sink where she'd no doubt rinse it later on, and then she'd floated out of that kitchen, out of that stifling suburban prison that she hadn't realised she wasn't *really* trapped in until that final moment, and she set about truly telling herself and revealing what she *did* want in life. She'd had quite enough for now of being and doing what she definitely *didn't* want. Time to get real.

She'd sat in front of her dressing table mirror and stared at herself, in wonder and amazement. How had she lived this life of a lie for so long? As she sat staring at her ivory pale face and dark chocolate waves of thick, silky locks (never been touched by the hair stylist except the very occasional trim) she felt a kilo of weight lift off her usually hunched over shoulders with every statement as she revealed her home truths to herself. Starting with simple statements she began:

'I am not currently happy.'

'I haven't been happy for a long time.'

'I am beautiful.'

'I have tired-looking eyes.'

'I have no real friends anymore, except those through my husband.'

'I need to leave my husband.'

'We got married far too young.'

'I love him still.'

'I love myself too.'

'I cannot subject myself to his verbal drunken abuse and aggression for even a minute longer.'

'I want to heal and be healthy and happy.'

'I want to go to university and train to be a teacher.'

'I am not trapped here with his disease.'

The last two surprised her the most: the first one with its clear directive, telling herself that this is what she wanted – where had that come from? It seemed like a brand new idea, but had clearly been hovering in her vicinity for some time, for it to suddenly seem like what she was *meant* to be doing; and the last thought, because, well, it just seemed so simple and obvious now: she *wasn't* trapped. She could just leave. That would be the answer. The key to leaving this humdrum melancholic life and relationship behind her: physically leave the insanity of her alcoholic husband and all the lies and emotional turmoil that went with it. A visceral wave of relief literally rushed through her and she straightened her shoulders and looked directly into her hazelnut coloured eyes, a small smile appearing in the corner of her full mouth for what must have been the first time in months, if not *years*. No exaggeration.

She shut her eyes briefly and breathed out slowly, feeling her tension and stress exit her body and lungs with the breath, whilst feeling…. Something: what was it, hope? Optimism? Desire for a different life? …fill her lungs with the following incoming breath. It felt such a rush to her and she was suddenly bursting with possibility. Her eyes flicked open and there she was: her beautiful, honest, open self, still staring directly and brazenly back at herself. She took this time to *really* look at herself, to really assess herself and not just (finally!) take her soon-to-be-ex-husband's word for it that she was 'a fucking ugly bitch', or had 'evil eyes, you fucking moron' as he went off on one of his drunken, slurry, angry tirades directed at her.

Her eyes were tired, yes, and still slightly bloodshot from the earlier sobbing, due to yet another countless (but hopefully, the last ever) raging drunken verbal attack on her the night before. But, putting that aside, she noticed her mesmerising, sparkling hazel eyes that seemed to glow almost amber at times, as she gently moved her face left and right in the morning sunlight streaming through the bedroom window. During this thorough examination, she honestly revealed to herself that she looked about ten years younger than her 35 years, thanks to her youthful skin and classically beautiful face and bone structure: she reminded herself that she had been blessed with amazing cheekbones. She continued her assessment, moving to her eyebrows: the same dark chocolate shade to match her thick, shiny hair, they were naturally sculpted and perfectly symmetrical, and they now drew her attention down to her straight, slim, pretty nose, nothing to report there, she thought, no kinks, or freckles or anything interesting of note, she'd always been told, but now, as she moved her head left and right at an angle, she started to see it for what it probably had been all along: a classically beautiful nose and profile. Continuing her thorough facial self-assessment she reached her lips, and now stared at her full, slightly parted lips, naturally a light cherry hue, which usually sat in a straight line or with one being subject to being bitten nervously; she now saw something entirely different: a pout to be reckoned with, she had the kind of lips she now realised that other women would get lip-plumping injections for or would apply venomous or bee sting lip balm in an attempt to manipulate a reaction and get that desired, full, thick pouty effect. At this realisation, those said lips turned upwards into a wide smile, she couldn't help herself. It was as if she was looking at a different woman, or a long forgotten version of 'her', her teenage, happy self who'd gotten lost or held hostage these past 19 or so years. A sudden image of her full, plump lips enveloping a large, rock-hard, dark chocolate coloured cock as she flicked her eyes teasingly upwards had come thundering into her thoughts. What the? She'd hurriedly looked back into her own bemused, quizzical eyes, although noting her now aflame, burning cheeks at the all-too-brief risqué image. Where did *that* come from? She'd asked herself, though continued to smile lovingly and giddily at herself as all these honest thoughts flooded her brain and she made some honest deals with herself. Statements of the truth, the first of her dawning, and deals with herself were those two simple rules that would continue to guide her as she went out and back into the world aiming to: 1) never harm anyone or anything and 2) always be true to herself.

She slightly confused herself with regards to the first rule, and the impending separation and divorce, as surely that *would* harm her then husband, seeing as he hadn't expected nor requested the divorce? She quickly reassessed this train of thought though and came to realise that probably, she was in actual fact, causing him *more* harm at present, by enabling him and continuing to put up with drinking and the abuse, by pretending to ignore his drunken slurs when they were out with friends (no matter how rare of an outing this had become lately) or even, making excuses for him as to why he'd passed out or fallen asleep at certain shindigs. Surely she was hurting him *more* by staying put? As he clearly wasn't going to get better with her there. As he'd often told her, although, yes, of course, under the influence and when wasted: *she* was the reason he drank so much, or was the reason he was so *depressed* and therefore drank so much subsequently, or that her constant badgering *drove* him to drink. Whichever reason he picked at whatever time, the answer was clear: she was making it worse and not helping his problem. She'd read so many times when googling such choice phrases as 'what should I do about my alcoholic husband' or 'is it ethical to leave an alcoholic': you can't force an alcoholic to get help, and nothing you say or do will make a difference. They have to, not only really *want* to get better and change, but they have to actually realise that, yes, they do have a problem. So, it seemed her two simple rules would be her saving grace after all, and she went on and applied her 'always be true to herself' rule, deciding she really wanted and needed to follow this seemingly sudden calling of going to uni and becoming a teacher.

Which is why, on that particular morning, some year and a half or so after her morning epiphany of leaving her husband, she found herself sitting in a cavernous lecture hall, surrounded by hundreds of nonchalant, wholly unimpressed, first-year students, all fresh-faced (even if as a result of carefully applied, precision, 'natural' effect make-up) and around eighteen or nineteen, blithely playing with their smartphones, as their philosophy professor continued his talk regardless, although intermittently sighing and displaying his annoyance. Her world had not only been turned upside down over the past year and a half, but had been turned upside down and then spun around vividly, as if being a pair of wooden die shaken in a large, warm, confidant hand. Her truths to herself had led her here: she'd followed her honest desires, left Sydney and her old life behind and had moved practically the other side of the world, well the other side of the country at least, to Fremantle, Western Australia, which may as well *be* another country, according to both Sydney-siders and Western Australians alike. She felt, not only geographically free from her previous prison, but mentally free too. She'd honestly fronted up to how she would be able to get into university there and had soon found herself on a bridging access course available to those who hadn't gone on to higher education back when they were of age, and who, maybe, like herself, stupidly got married to her high-school Year Ten formal prom-date, who'd promised her an extremely comfortable life of luxury thanks to his family's considerable wealth and fortune that was, of course, to be passed on and shared with their number one (and only) son, their 'golden boy' and who was to be her husband for the next

14

nineteen years: Peter Doyle.

Upon arriving in Fremantle, she'd logically and carefully assessed her financial situation, and took the first job that she could find, that luckily was extremely flexible with regards to her studies and allowed her to swap shifts at short notice if she needed to get to class or lectures: waitressing/helping out at a local café, one of many that lined the friendly, carefree streets heading down to the Port. Then later, when news of how she'd be liable for the *joint* debt from their life back in Sydney (which, at first, honestly caused her blood to boil, as she internally raged at the injustice and how and why *she* should get lumbered with *his* debt caused by too many years of secret binge drinking and his smokes that went with it, and how the hell did they even acquire so much debt anyway, his salary from his family business was *huge*!?) she'd panicked quietly and then took a *second* part-time job which became available just at the right time in her financial crisis, and honestly told herself it was just a means to an end: it did not define her, and, as long as she kept it to herself and was discreet about it, then it wasn't hurting anyone (satisfying her rule number one: Universal law, as she liked to think of it). She *truly* knew it wasn't the making nor ending of her: it was just a job and a role she would play (thus satisfying her rule number two). No one had to know. Her private life was her business. She wasn't hurting anyone or anything, after all. Universal law. How she lived her life.

Which is why on that particular morning and during that particular lecture, her ears literally pricked up as Mr Goodwood, her relatively new teacher (she was about four weeks into the her first term of the first year of her undergraduate degree she was proudly and happily enrolled in) who delivered his philosophy lecture each week, along with the prescribed lengthy list of things they were required to read, told the large class:

"So, you see, my eager and alert throng of faithful studious subjects here before me, we are all subject to Universal Law. That is: everything we think, we see, hear, feel and experience in this reality – it is all to do with *sex*."

Sheena frowned slightly and cocked her head to one side, pondering his last statement (they each seemed to have a different definition of what 'universal law' was) as she stopped rapidly trying to jot down notes as she followed his extremely interesting, as always, lecture. It seemed up until that point however, it was only Sheena who had really been listening, the other students either preoccupied with their phones or with whispering and murmuring to each other throughout Mr Goodwood's talk. But now, at the mention of the word *sex*, there was a stirring in the room. A couple of coughs. Squeaks in the chairs as some students straightened up and leaned forward now.

"Yes, that's right, my avid people," Mr Goodwood continued, smiling mischievously, as if he had a secret he was about to share. "Everyone and everything is connected and we are connected at a very primal, sexual level: we are *all* about sex. *History* is sex. Our daily lives are a scam: just a front, a façade for our true reality and purpose: *sex*. We are *here* to procreate, to create reality, to orgasm and to ultimately have sex. There are subliminal messages and cues everywhere in this world that reinforce this. Once you are aware of this, you'll see them everywhere." He paused and smiled around the now avidly attentive lecture hall filled with students, before continuing: "Or, will you? Are you seeing these sexual stimulations and cues, or are *you* creating them? As we've seen last week, *thought* forms *entities*. What we see or believe in our minds, becomes our reality. We are living in an electric holographic universe: the only truth there is, is this: vibrations and frequencies form everything. So, everything is an illusion. Everything is consciousness. Everything comes from the ether. Everything is illusion: your daily world around you is nothing but an illusion. Your daily routine, nothing more than wavelengths and vibrations. Vibrations *form* your reality, and *you* form the vibrations with your thoughts, therefore, it stands to reason that *you* shape your reality."

Sheena had tuned out momentarily to assess his latest mind-blowing nugget, now scribbling her notes once more to keep up with him. When she flicked her awareness back to him he was telling the hall:

"There is no original thought. Ever. Period. All that is created or thought of today, every 'innovation' or invention or 'original' idea – they have all been done before. Everything comes from thought yes, everything is simply a vibration in this holographic, electric universe, everything is ultimately to do with sex, but furthermore, and this is your take-away point from this lecture today, *everything* is consciousness and has existed for all time and before time: it is from the ether that we tune into or receive our ideas from. There is no original thought. All that is done has been done before. Thoughts, anyone?"

He quickly scanned his mute, baffled looking audience before continuing:

"Thank you everyone. The hour is nearly upon us. I am drawing this talk to a close. I'll see you next week, where we will continue along our lines of 'everything is sex', with my next lecture: 'The Big Bang Theory' or, as I like to call it: 'The Big Gang-Bang Theory'. You don't want to miss *that* one. Stay peaceful, stay creative, stay loving, folks."

With that he packed up his worn, leather satchel (being a post-modern, ironic statement perhaps?) and made for the exit, leaving his students free to hurriedly grab their own belongings and raise their previously hushed whispers to a much louder level as they chatted and laughed amongst themselves, some loudly asking themselves and their peers 'what the fuck was *that* all about?!' or for some: 'I told you! It *is* all about sex! The meaning of life ay, I knew it...'

Sheena sat there quietly gathering her own thoughts and seeing if they aligned with the mind-fucking theories Mr Goodwood had just blasted them with. She smiled to herself, as it washed over her and she realised that they had a lot of thoughts and opinions in common. Particularly that life, this world, this universe, was all to do with sex, but also that resonating reality of there being no original thought.

'Hmmm, ain't that the truth' She murmured to herself, smiling (or cringing more like) inwardly at her semi-ironic choice of a second job being the clichéd, most unoriginal job in the world. After all, wasn't it known as the world's oldest profession? It also tied in nicely with the theory of everything being about sex. She'd always wholly agreed on this point, even if her stifling husband of nineteen years had refuted this fact.

'Don't dwell on him and the past right now,' She reprimanded herself lightly. "Focus on *you* now."

That did the trick and she managed to smile, as she slowly and calmly gathered her notepad and pens and started to leave her mature-age-student persona behind in that lecture hall. Two days later, all last remaining signs of 'Sheena' would be gone (for a few hours at the most, anyway), as she began to carefully put on her mask of 'Ruby': part-time, high-class/premium (whatever you wanted to call her = expensive) escort, working a total of about two to three hours per week at the discreet and classy (she thought, anyway) gentlemen's club, 'Secrets'. On that Friday night, after a full day of studying and highlighting interesting things in the bid to retain the information in her head rather than the paper in front of her, she carefully stored her notepad in her files on top of her well organised, neat desk, in the corner of her equally well organised, neat bedroom, one of two in the cosy rented townhouse she shared with one other student, and turned to her dressing table mirror to apply her make-up (mask) and get ready for her short, be-over-before-you-know-it shift. She reminded herself:

'It's only a job. It doesn't define me as a person. It's only a means to an end.' She paused and smiled to herself, before adding: "Mr Goodwood agrees. Life's all about sex anyway. I'm definitely not the first or last student to have had this very unoriginal thought of supplementing my studies there. It's not that big of a sin.'

Another, wider, smile this time, as she applied her signature, glossy, deep red shade of lipstick that officially turned her from demure, serious, studious, mature-age yet still young looking and fresh-faced Sheena, into 'Ruby': stunning and wicked looking buxom brunette; yours for the hour or the night for a very decent (for her anyway) price.

'After all, sometimes it can even be an *enjoyable* job,' and she continued to smile as a recent paid (wholly surprising, at the time) encounter flashed back in her mind, causing a natural blush to appear.

She had been working there for three weeks or so. She felt like she'd got the hang of it now, the routine: and routine it was, just like any other job. (However with the added bonus of a trusty panic button she could use to summon George, their beefy, imposing security guard, should she ever feel even the slightest hint of a dodgy customer. Luckily, so far, so good.) Far from the glamourous job that books and TV shows, such as 'Confessions of a Call-Girl' had led her to believe: for the most part it was mundane, mechanical, (usually) quick sex, performed as service either to those who were either a) drunk and at the tail-end (quite literally) of their best-mate's stag do, or b) older or single clientele, that would form the majority of her client-base, who'd be (again, quite literally) in and out before she knew it. However, on this particular Friday night, a character that she'd nicknamed Mr X walked in. As soon as Mr X strolled in, sober as a judge without even the slightest hint of a whiff of stale booze (a welcome change for Sheena that evening and a usual huge hazard of the job, making her silently retch and recoil at the smell) and confidently perched on the leg of the room's leather sofa, she knew things would be different. His eyes, dark and brooding, for one thing, bored into her own, as she went through her usual spiel of services, extra and prices, while he was apparently listening intently. She'd started to blush under his direct and obviously completely sober gaze. Not for too long though, as he'd then made his selection and began to slowly unbutton his crisp, black shirt. She let him, stunned into an unprofessional silence as she openly gaped and gawked at his bronzed, ridiculously chiselled and toned, perfect chest and abs that came into view. Quickly catching her breath, she resumed character and 'Ruby' sauntered over and began slowly and sexily removing her own black satin robe, revealing her red and black, extremely skimpy and barely-there, lingerie, as his eyes burned into her. She was stumped as to how or why this veritable Adonis had ended up here: he wasn't usually the 'type', especially the sober part, but more so, the fact he was extremely attractive, and had a calm, patient, completely alluring and seductive manner to him. She'd asked the usual questions and it turned out he was there on a buck's night after all, but amazingly enough, he didn't ever drink. He was just there for 'moral' support for the groom next door. (Ahem...)

"But, well," He'd told her, as he unbuckled his thick, black leather belt, "You never know what's in store for your evening, so why *not* try something different."

The something different for his evening was clearly Ruby, and with that being said he'd calmly dropped his tailored, creased down the centre, obviously quite expensive trousers, to the floor, stepped out of them casually and lent forward to Ruby, where he firmly placed each warm, large hand on either side of her still a little quizzical face. He slowly and gently moved his lips to hers and kissed her, obviously in no hurry nor in the market for just a quickie. The kiss grew into a long, hot passionate one, his tongue invading her wet mouth, caressing her own, now equally inquisitive one. It was a myth that prostitutes don't kiss clients. At least, Sheena had realised it that night anyhow, as 'Ruby' kissed Mr X back hungrily, drinking in his heady, but not overpowering or sickly aftershave. She recognised it as Joop. One of her ex-husband's brothers used to douse himself in the stuff (causing Sheena to keep her distance when at family parties). But, on her mysterious, expert kisser client here before her, it had a completely different effect: she couldn't get enough of it, inhaling deeply and becoming almost intoxicated as the kiss continued. He pulled away and Ruby tried to elegantly catch her breath and stay in control and in character, but it was no good: her burning, blushing cheeks, swollen-from-the-intense-kiss red-smeared lips, and her obvious, standing-to-attention nipples, piercing through the thin, barely-there gauze fabric on the openings of her peep-hole bra, all serving to give her game away: she was, right now, heavily in lust with this mystery client, Mr X, and clean forgetting this was just her paid, part-time job.

She moved closer to him, now removing his open shirt, as he stood there in his colourful, tight briefs, gasping audibly as she did so when his large, muscular, ripped biceps and manly, covered in soft dark hair, forearms came into view. She ran her fingers up and down those arms, noticeably impressed with how wonderfully toned, manly and hard they were. As she moved her hands onto his warm, chiselled, equally hard chest now, his hands casually moved to her hips and firmly pulled her closer to him. She could feel him pressed hard up against her. She bit her lip suggestively and widened her eyes in a bid for mock-horror at his rock-hard member currently pushing into her through the spandex material of his briefs. His hands still in place around her hips, his large fingers all-but burning their way through the lacy, negligible non-material of her g-string, he leant forward and slowly but surely pushed his tongue into her mouth again, gently not-so-subtlety pushing his cock poignantly into her hip too, as he did so. As they kissed, Ruby moved her hands down his chiselled chest and over his picture-perfect, wash-board abs until she reached the seam of his briefs, and his straining against the material, engorged cock, aching to break free. Again, he subtlety thrust himself forward, gesturing that, yes, now was the time.

Breaking free from his delicious, deep kiss, she began to trail a line of light kisses down his perfect chest, past his perfect stomach, and ended up at his soon-to-be-removed briefs. She was briefly reminded that this was definitely not her usual sort of client, where they would generally either instruct her to 'suck this, darlin' (smooth talkers hey) or would simply nod or point her down there. But Mr X seemed in no hurry. Again, odd.

Perfectly calm, perfectly toned Mr X turned out to be perfectly proportioned too, as Ruby gently slipped his briefs down and off, allowing his fully engorged, impressive member to bounce up in her face invitingly. She'd then wasted no time: she grabbed the condom from the back of her bra, peeled it onto him, all the while he just watched her with that calm, brooding, sultry manner of his. As she took him fully into her hot, wet, ruby-red mouth, she finally got a response from him as he moaned and half-closed his eyes. And being honest with herself? She'd moaned too. This man was so incredibly hot and she was so turned on. Feeling how hard and big he was in her mouth and hand, as she worked her way slowly (at first) up and down his magnificent shaft, was making her so wet. No need for any acting tonight. She grasped his thick shaft and pumped up and down in-time with her full, wet lips sliding up and down his cock, as she sucked a little harder now. His broad, warm, strong hands had found their way onto the back of her lustrous, brunette waves and were now firmly clasped around her head, as she worked up and down his beautiful cock. For once, she had no inclination to shake those hands off, as she did with all her other clients, and she'd let out a tell-tale groan as she all-but gagged on his massive member.

He released her head and pulled her up by the shoulders, his smouldering eyes back to boring into her own sparkling amber, dish-plate-pupil eyes. She caught her breath a little, biting her bottom lip again, no mock anticipation this time: she was honestly aching for him, burning for his touch, needed him. Inside her. Now.

Silently he moved her backwards to the hip-height four-poster enclosed mattress and pushed her back onto it while simultaneously grabbing her hips closer to him. He deftly pulled off her lacy, tiny g-string and plunged his full, hard, throbbing cock deep inside her while his hands found her waist and firmly held her in place. She'd cried out as he entered her again and again. All she could see, as he stood there, confidently and expertly taking her on the edge of the huge bed, was his amazing chiselled chest and strong, manly arms as they rigidly held her in place and he drove into her, deeply and surely, again and again. She was so fucking wet. And hot. And was losing her mind with each deep, hard thrust.

Her hands found his chest hair, and roamed around his perfect, hard chest, as he continued to pummel her and drive her home, to the sounds of her cries and groans of pure pleasure. She didn't know what he was doing to make this feel so unbelievably fucking good, but she knew that if he kept it up she would come. Soon. And hard. And all over his beautiful cock. She briefly entertained thoughts of etiquette of all things: *should* she tell a client that she was going to come? After all, it was all about him, surely? Who cares if she was coming? But all thoughts or ability to think were soon out the window as he ploughed into her mercilessly, all the while, his strong, manly hands were tightly wrapped around her little waist. She had no idea whether she'd cried out 'ohmigod, I'm gonna come' or whether she'd just thought that in her head, but soon after she'd gushed all over his glistening throbber he'd noticeably picked up his pace anyway, driving faster and harder, urgently into her, again and again. She struggled to breathe as he slammed into her, faster and faster, reaching his own climax with an understated and slightly clenched-teeth groan as he plunged one last deep time inside her and finally paused, both Mr X and Ruby shuddering and panting, as they both caught their respective breaths.

That experience, Sheena had noted later, had been her first and last time that she'd come whilst working, but she was always hopeful for a similar shift or client. 'You never know', she told herself, as she sprayed on 'Ruby's' signature J'Adore perfume and hurried out of the door (whilst her housemate was safely occupied in the shared bathroom upstairs) to walk the twenty minutes down to 'Secrets'. 'This could be another *memorable* shift tonight.' She really hoped it would be one of *those* nights, or at the very least, at least if she could keep her lucky streak going by having so far, never used the panic button installed in every room.

'Yep: bring on another Mr X night!' She smiled to herself, mentally geeing herself up before she reached the non-descript building.

# CHAPTER TWO

Brendan was having one of *those* days. Somehow his usually pretty cruisy Friday arvo had gotten away from him and he had found himself with not just the few 'Philosophy 102' classes' essays to mark and write semi-encouraging yet extremely vague and mysterious comments on as he sat sipping his usual Merlot in his favourite spot at the Corner Bar, conveniently just down the road from campus, but had somehow been summoned into a staff meeting at the university instead. As the Dean droned on regarding the new IT software program that was being implemented and some sort of roll-out, Brendan couldn't help but check his watch repeatedly, and semi anxiously. Damn! He was surely going to be running late now! This meeting had now overrun it's 'about halfa' that they'd been casually informed that it would run for and was now invading rudely into his 'marking' time.

'Shit, if she keeps on, I'll be late for Jess and Jo too,' he frowned and coughed impatiently. He did *not* want to miss *that* meeting. Nope, not at all. The girls would be so disappointed, not to mention Brendan himself, the main organiser of the extra-curricular, private tutoring session, to be held exclusively at his home, or more specifically, on his sofa, or his desk, or perhaps in his bedroom. He'd see how things would go and how they would pan out.

He'd been organising these 'after class activities' for almost as long as he could remember, since joining the university faculty some six years ago, and he'd never failed to be impressed with the new, eager students each year, usually just certain females that responded to his specific cues and remarks made during his lectures would be invited, but occasionally he'd made an exception and invited along some of the

27

more curious male students too. They (his students) were each just so beautiful, so seemingly unique and 'different' and each one wanting to stand out (in their aim to please him, to explain, and somehow in the way they set out to prove something to him: their maturity or uniqueness perhaps?). However, one after the other they were all so *very* similar and predictable when it came down to it. He really did believe his spiel he taught them in all his classes: 'we are all one. We are all connected. There is no original thought'. Certainly, he sometimes saw them all as one: one face blending into another in his memory: the Emmas, the Stephanies, the Amys, the Megans: each one beautiful and young and fresh. Sooner or later the class was more 'all connected' than some of them were even aware of, with the common link being that of Mr Brendan Goodwood himself, offering them extra, private study sessions with himself, to discuss in finer detail some of the ins and outs of his theories, and usually with the aim of turning theory into practical experiments; his favourite private lessons being those that centred on his lectures on 'Universal-everything's-about-fucking-Law', and 'the Big Gang-Bang Theory'. These subjects seemed to work almost effortlessly for him and his not at all original thought (he knew, he was a cliché) of 'wooing' his new students, and quite often (almost every time, in fact) it was *them* who made the first move, with Brendan happy to sit back and let It happen.

Like something of a sociological experiment he was deeply interested in seeing how long different women would take before making their move: did the blondes react to his subtle come-ons faster than the brunettes? Did their environment and surroundings play a part? (He routinely moved rooms for their study sessions, aiming to see if the soft light of his moderately cluttered lounge was more arousing to them than the brighter, downlights of his small, but cosy kitchen.) Did their *age* play a part? (He found the slightly younger students, those of just eighteen or nineteen, to be both quicker to put it on him, and then, pleasingly, more outrageous and risqué in their sessions once it was clear that this was the go.) Interesting. He'd have thought long ago, that it would have probably been the other way around if anything, but no, his older students tended to actually be more focused, on well, the *study* part of his study sessions. (Much to Brendan's disappointment.) He found it all quite fascinating.

He was well aware that his 'special study sessions' could easily lose him his job, and possibly cause him some sort of grievance with the police (he imagined there would be some sort of fine involved for fucking your students?) however, as he saw it: they *were* all adults after all, and free to choose whatever they wanted to do with bodies (and usually with his too. He was a very willing and flexible participant in these arrangements). He wasn't hurting anybody.

'No,' he often mused, 'I am opening their minds!' (Conveniently he was also opening their legs and mouths too, if things went accordingly, which they predictably, usually, did.) He wasn't about to let something so arbitrary as 'I teach them a first-year, introductory philosophy class, once a week' cause him to lose sleep over the ethics that he may or may not be plundering, along with their beautiful, enthusiastic, lithe bodies. It wasn't like he was their guidance counsellor or some sort of father-figure. Being just shy of 32, nor did he feel even that much older than his students, and he knew they mostly regarded him as a slightly mysterious, slightly older peer of theirs. He got the feeling he was more like some sort of 'cool' older brother or friend for most of class.

It wasn't like he was fucking them *all* either. No, no. Only a select few would ever make it to his house and to his 'extra classes', and this was purely based on their timely reactions during his lectures: their curious, inquisitive looks, or sometimes their downright filthy, lascivious lick of their lips while he was addressing a key point during a talk. None went so far as to write 'love you' on their eyelids to flitter at him, Indiana Jones style, but their coy smiles and blatant, sultry stares were obvious enough to him, and he'd casually mention to said students about some post-class discussions he was holding at his house. One on one. That night. Bring a bottle and an open mind. That usually did the trick.

Of course, not every invitee was straight into it either. There were some quests who would take two, maybe three, evening sessions to adequately warm up to the idea. Brendan would never hurry them. Patience was a virtue, and he was confident in good things coming to those who wait. In his vast experience, better things would surely be coming his way with those who *weren't* so forward and forthcoming on their first or second visit. Case in point would be the delectable Jess and Jo, who would be gracing him with their sweet, vanilla-scented presence in just over an hour, if this damn faculty meeting would just hurry the fuck up and come to a close (why did things always seem to crop up on a Friday afternoon? For fuck's sake…).

Jess and Jo were in his new batch of this year's students, taking his introductory philosophy class. They were two of about twenty or so out of their larger class group of about a hundred students that he'd noticed to be a particularly high and fine calibre. He'd smiled to himself as he'd similarly smiled, mischievously yet warmly and broadly, as if sharing a joke, around the large hall during their first lecture of the term. 'Yes, this term's going to be a good'un' he'd mused, raising an eyebrow back in return to one of the bustier redheads seated towards the front of the room, who was grinning at him. He'd made a mental note to be sure to offer her *any* extra-curricular help that she needed.

Jess and Jo, his would-be guests for this evening however, he'd officially 'met' a few weeks later and into the term, when Jess, your typical curvaceous, busty blonde (all round arse squeezed into tight jeans and a low, v-neck top) had called his name after class one sunny, Wednesday afternoon. She'd been suitably coy and giggly, nervous, he'd thought, yet her intention was clear as she asked him if he had time to go over what he had just said, about 'coupling the mind to the body'. She said, slowly and deliberating, that she was having trouble *grasping* it. She emphasized the word 'grasping' and looked into his warm, dark coloured eyes, her own emerald green ones sparkling back, as she, this time, held the gaze, no giggling. The gentlemanly thing to do was obviously to schedule a time when they would both be free to discuss the conundrum in greater detail. Conveniently and as luck would have it, he was free that evening and recommended that she join him at his home for an in-depth (he assumed) and private session.

Contrary to what he'd assumed *would* occur, Jess was a lot less forthcoming or direct when she'd arrived at his townhouse later that night. If anything, she seemed somewhat *very* shy, and it turns out, actually *did* want to discuss his lecture a bit further. She wasn't about to make any move on him at all, it seemed. As the night had drawn on, he was puzzled. Had he misread her signals? He didn't often get this wrong. As he'd poured the last glass from the now empty bottle of

Pinot Gris out and into her outstretched chalice, and smiled charmingly down at her, he'd assumed he'd probably got this one wrong, and would simply chalk it up to experience. However, she'd then lifted her lips to his face and delivered one long, slow kiss of 'thanks' to his hovering, three-day –growth stubbly cheek. She'd then pulled away again, opened her previously closed eyes, and whispered,

"I want to kiss you, Sir. *Properly.*"

Who was he to object? Flinging the empty bottle carelessly to one side, Brendan, of course, had obliged, and she turned her attentive, full lips to his own, now expectant, ones, kissing her teacher hard and subtlety testing the waters with her tongue. Again, he obliged, opening his mouth to her inquisitive, wet tongue as their kiss deepened, and he smiled to himself.

'Of course,' he thought. 'She's a tease. Craves the suspense.'

Their deep, probing kiss had continued for quite some time, it seemed to Brendan. Long enough for him to have barred up completely (ok, perhaps not that long at all, in real time) and for him eager to see what her next move might be. He was a patient man, no matter how hard and ready to go he was, and he too liked the suspense.

However, her next move had been to abruptly *stop* kissing him, and she stood up, telling him breathily, she 'had to go'. Go? He wondered. They were just getting started. As she left hastily in a blur of flying blond hair and amidst one last lip-smacker and a flirty smile, he'd reminded himself, 'oh yeah, she definitely likes the suspense', returning her cheerful 'let's do this again soon Mr Goodwood!' with a raised eyebrow and a similar flirty smile.

True to her word, 'soon' was apparently the very next evening, as luck would again have it, he was also free (and would have made himself free, regardless) and on this occasion, Jess had appeared at his door, arm and arm with a near replica of herself, introducing the semi-mystery girl to Brendan as

"Jo! You know – also in our class! We sit next to each other."

"Of course, of course," Brendan had ushered them in, cheering inside and not quite believing his luck.

It was clear from the way these two amazingly hot, lithe young things were playing with each other's hands and stroking each other's arms and strands of hair, that they were *very* good friends, and up for being more than just friends tonight, if they hadn't already been. He had retrieved a bottle of Stolli from his well-stocked freezer (where he always kept a couple, in case of such an emergency), a few shot glasses, and then asked his guests to think of a way to combine any drinking game that they knew with his recent discussion on 'one-ness' and how everyone is connected. He gave silent extra merit to Jo for editing the infamous game of Never-Have-I-Ever, when she made it relevant and in keeping with his instructions, where instead of simply skulling your drink when you were not in agreement with the statement (i.e. when you *had* done the deed in question) you also had to demonstrate how connected you were with your fellow players by, ahem, *connecting* with them, quite literally. Brendan, initially, feigned ignorance and asked Jo for a demonstration.

"Ok, Sir. Here we go. If I say 'never have I ever… kissed a girl!' which I reckon we all have, yeah? Am I right? Ok, so down your drinks, Team, and then I'm going to connect with you Sir, *here*." She put her hand around his wrist. "And with you, Jessie dear, *here.*"

She cupped her other hand gently around Jess's left breast, over the top of her tight, white, singlet. Jess returned the 'connection' by sliding her right hand around Jo's bare midriff (she was wearing a kind of crop top together with loose ¾ length trousers, both in a floral, chintzy pattern that was making something of a come-back amongst the early twenty-something generation). Her other hand casually went to rest on Brendan's thigh and gave a gentle, cheeky squeeze. Brendan, seemingly cottoning on quickly, chose to 'connect' with Jo's neck and Jess's other, free breast, causing her to gasp and giggle under the weight of his hand while Jo smiled at him confidently.

"There Sir, you get the idea. Now it's your turn to speak…"

"Never have I ever…" Hmmm, let's think, he mused. "Never have I ever – enjoyed going down on a woman."

He watched them both intently, as everyone moved to pick up their shot glasses, refill them and down them all together. They then surveyed each other and worked out where they might connect with next.

'Hmmm,' He thought to himself. "Very interesting.'

Brendan decided to take the lead with this round and ever so slowly delved his left hand down and under that flimsy white singlet and slid his hand under Jess's push-up (and unnecessary) bra, cupping her hot, handful of a breast with his cool, confident palm. Jess involuntarily let out another gasp, at his cool hand, and her nipple instantly reacted, hardening and grazing his palm. She immediately responded by moving her right hand further up his jeans from where it had been resting and now directly groped over his engorging-as-we-speak hidden member, while her free hand slid into the back of her good friend Jo's trousers, bringing all three players closer together in their triangle. As for Jo, well, her left hand had connected with Brendan's right hand, and she was guiding it over to Jess's fly on her own jeans, while her right hand had flown to the back of Jess's head and was guiding her head forwards to her own waiting lips. And just like that, the 'game' (or the speaking and drinking part of it, anyway) was forgotten.

Jess and Jo's faces and lips mashed together roughly, their two different tones of blond hair merging like some kind of beautiful, exotic sunflower, as Brendan attempted to pull himself back a little to be able to watch this magnificent show that he was both a part of and apart from. One of his hands continued to massage Jess's perfect, full but perky, tit as his other diligent hand following Jo's order slowly unzipped the top of Jess's tight jeans, revealing a patch of black satin material covered in cherries. Jess's hand on Brendan's crotch remained in place and she began massaging him confidently. Being the polite gentleman that he was, he thrust his hard-on further into her palm through his jeans. He used his free hand to deftly pull down Jess' jeans a little further, then when all was revealed he slowly began stroking the outside of her g-string, as Jo continued to play with her breast and, it looked like, suck her face off. Jess has moaned and grabbed Jo's arse tightly through her trousers, and simultaneously rubbed at Brendan's crotch harder and more ferociously than before. As patient as he was, he thought it was time to get rid of the offending jeans and trousers that were slowing this trio down; they weren't doing anyone any good.

He removed himself, reluctantly, from their triple embrace, and ripped his own jeans off first, immediately releasing his rock-hard cock which sprang forth, not being a fan of men's underwear at all. He gestured that the two girls continue on with their hot and heavy passionate kiss and grope, while Brendan went to work at sliding Jess's jeans all the way off now, and then equally expertly doing the same for Jo's trousers. The two friends obliged and didn't miss a beat and stop: Jo's tongue wildly thrashing with Jess's equally fervent one, both of them moaning as they did so. The only reference they made to the fact they now had nothing on their lower halves but their *matching* cherry printed g-strings, was for Jess to now hook a leg over Jo's and grind into her in a sort of scissor-like fashion, grabbing Jo's luscious, tanned, toned arse as she did so still, as Jo returned the sentiment by firmly grabbing Jess's equally grabable tits.

'My, my,' Brendan thought to himself, sitting back on his heels to simply watch and stroke his cock appreciatively at the sight before him. Then, just as quickly as things had turned passionate and were 'on' the girls had randomly stopped, finally catching their breaths, each one panting and flushed. They pulled away further to get some more air, both smiling back at each other. Brendan, one hand on his engorged cock, coughed, looking at his students, who now both looked up at him, startled, like they'd almost forgotten he was there. The three of them (two of whom were rapidly trying to catch their breaths) flicked their eyes back and forth between them. Jess's flushed face grew as deep in colour as Brendan's cock, and she broke the silence and stillness by suddenly lunging for her recently ripped off jeans.

"Come on Jo, we should really be going." And as she left, just as hurriedly and rushed as the night before, dragging an also still-flushed Jo behind her, she'd uttered those same parting words to the now horrendously horny, waiting, stunned Brendan: "Let's do this again soon, Mr Goodwood!"

That had been a whole week ago now, and Brendan had received nothing more than a text message five days later asking if he was free to 'go over some points' again with her and Jo that Friday night. She finished the text with: 'we want to finish where we left off'.

Brendan, instantly barred up at the thought of what was surely, *surely* on the cards this time, had responded eagerly and confirmed that he'd be waiting for them.

Now, stuck in this damn faculty meeting, that was, what the hell, nearing its second hour? He was feeling all hope slowly drip away from him. He wouldn't want to keep the girls waiting (lest they may change their mind, yet *again*) and, my god, he definitely didn't want to postpone it either.

Like he was having some sort of out of body experience, he finally felt like he was rising up, standing up and leaving his body that sat there, leaving the long, tedious meeting, and, oh no, wait, he *was*! Finally! As everyone got up to leave the stuffy boardroom to shuffle out and he got in the queue, amid multiple groans and grumbles, which echoed his own thoughts perfectly, of '*why* a Friday afternoon?' his spirits began lifting once again. Another forty-five minutes or so and he'd be out of his hum-drum, melancholy end to an otherwise ok ish work week and into Jess and Jo alternately or simultaneously, he assumed. And envisaged this eagerly.

A vibration in his jean pocket alerted him to the fact that he'd received a text message, and he retrieved his phone, expecting to see a message from either blond companion for his night, perhaps saying they were running late, or even asking if they could bring a third friend, perhaps? He semi-barred up again at the thought. Then promptly halted that thought when he looked down at the screen and the sender. The name 'Scott' flashed up and Brendan both smiled instinctively but grit his teeth and groaned as he knew what the message would be before he even looked at it.

Sure enough, when he scrolled down, there it was:

'Are you busy this evening? Really need to see you and get out for a bit.'

Breathing in deeply before closing his eyes and releasing a huge sigh of both disappointment and regret, and of quiet resignation, he still with his teeth gritted together, began typing out a guilty, apologetic text message, as he already knew what his answer *had* to be, of course:

'You don't know how sorry I am to do this. Going to have to take a rain check on our study session, Girls. Something has come up.'

Another deep breath in followed by a releasing, calming sigh, and Brendan was ready to ungrit his teeth and reply to Scott, a wry smile now firmly in place on his handsome, slightly stubbly face.

'No probs mate. Be there in about halfa.'

'Oh Scott', he shook his head to himself, 'This is how much I love you, bro!'

# CHAPTER THREE

Hearing low grunt after low grunt, in time with his rhythmic, monotonous, heavy thrusts, Sheena stared up at the gaudy mirrored ceiling and thought to herself, 'nope, this definitely isn't one of *those* nights' as her semi-geriatric client kept up his tedious work. She hoped he'd finish soon and then she could clean up and get the hell out of there: she had some coursework she wanted to make a start on and some laundry to put on. Oh, plus there was that big grocery shop she'd been meaning to do. Sheena ran through her mental to-do list, otherwise occupying her mind so she was less than focused and present in her actual present situation, which, if she was being totally, brutally honest with herself (as she always was) was this: currently a fairly inebriated, but otherwise harmless, old fellow named Brian, one of her less than thrilling regular clients, was giving his best straight-faced, military version of that old classic 'the missionary position', lying flat on top of her, not looking at her face or into her eyes of course, but staring, almost contemplatively straight ahead, lest he got distracted from his arduous task of pumping steadily away until he would, finally, reach some sort of climax, holding out one single, longer grunt this time (Sheena's only real indicator that he was finally there) before he would roll off and would calmly go about putting his trousers back on, leaving her be with a ginger 'same time next month, Ruby love?' and chucking her a wan, embarrassed smile.

Occasionally a gust of stale whiskey or some other spirit would be blown Sheena's way from Brian's cracked, dry lips and she had to turn her head from the physical revulsion she felt and to be able to keep up the act. It was nights like these that she practically had her mantras on

39

repeat just to get her through the shift:

'This is just a job. A temporary job. It's only for a few months at most. It doesn't define who I am. It's only a means to an end.' And repeat.

Brian wasn't even a horrible client or actually even repulsive or troublesome: his main offences were simply his monotony and length of time it took him to finish, and his whiskey breath. Which, well, just took her right back to her old life in an instant. It's funny how strongly smell is linked to memory, Sheena would often muse, usually after a blast of stale booze hit her olfactory nerves and caused her stomach to flip-flop and that feeling of dread to threaten again.

She couldn't really even solely blame poor old Brian either: the booze stench was a hazard of the job, she supposed, and it was unusual for clients *not* to be reeking of it in some form. However, whiskey in particular, well, it just did all kinds of bad things for Sheena, conjuring up her worst memories in an instant. Memories she'd tried so hard to leave behind in New South Wales for good.

'Not tonight!' She quickly reprimanded herself and changed tactics, averting the memory crisis that was heading her way. Instead, she forced herself to breathe slowly through her mouth, as she lay there, deathly still (at Brian's initial instructions, some months back now). Again, she took her mind to her busy schedule: she felt overloaded at the moment. As a full-time student, she was currently enrolled in four modules, each one vying for her precious time and clamouring for her to complete various essays and pieces of coursework, all due at strikingly similar dates and with ominous imposing deadlines. The Foundation of IT course and her Statistics course were currently competing in her mind for 'least favourite' AKA Arrghh-why-the-fuck-am-I-spending-my-time-doing-this-bullshit subject, each one giving her a similar, regular headache and sense of tedium. However, she *was* enjoying the other two: that mind-fuck philosophy class that commanded she be there for just *one* lecture a week, while the rest of her time she was supposed to be reading and studying herself for the same cause (the self-study was actually, usually *done* by Sheena, or aimed to be anyway. Something she was quietly proud of, as she was pretty sure all her other classmates regarded the 'own study' gaps in the philosophy classes' schedule as 'free pub time', not that she minded what they did really); and her fourth module: Intro to Psychology, which, she felt complemented the interesting philosophy course, although in no way did it mirror or match in the case of the required workload or class attendance. She grimaced slightly at the thought of the three seminars, one lecture, and four lab sessions she was required to complete each week for this particular course.

'It will all be worth it!' She regularly reminded herself. This, this business, this struggle to get every assignment and essay in on time, to attend as many classes (punctually of course) as she could, and her weekly and monthly financial balancing act combining the meagre pay from her café shifts with her weekly night work, in order to keep her head above water: it would all be worth it. She *knew* it. She had that *feeling*. Along with her 'always be true to yourself' law, she supposed, was her sense of intuition: her gut feeling. Since she'd told her then husband that she was leaving, this intuition, her gut instinct, had had a dramatic awakening, or she had suddenly developed one, she wasn't sure which. Whichever it was, Sheena used this gut feeling all the time, and it had, so far, never been wrong. From simple things like, should she order Chinese take-away tonight or should she cook, to slightly more important decisions such as, who's flat she chose to share and take up their ad for a housemate. Since leaving for Fremantle, it had never served her wrong.

She smiled now, as Brian quietly hammered away still, as an image of her pretty housemate (and best friend she supposed) came clattering into her head. Yes, she had definitely made the right decision there: on ya, intuition!

Sheena currently resided with a gorgeous girl of twenty-two: another student at the same university, although not on her course: a bubbly, vivacious, stunning, fiery redhead named Gabby. They'd clicked from the very moment that the pine-effect door to the available apartment had swung open, and in walked Sheena, welcomed by a set of wide, sparkling blue eyes and a quick squeeze (yes, Gabby was a hugger, even to a random, potential housemate). It turns out both their intuition was on fire that day, as both Sheena and Gabby got *on* like the proverbial house on fire. Sheena took an instant liking and immediately formed a deep affection for Gabby, and the feelings were obviously mutual, as noted by the frequent texts they would send each other throughout the day: from the mundane 'oy, roomie, do we need milk? Love you xxx' to the sentimental and emotional: 'where would I be without you in my life, Miss Morning-Train-Beauty-Sheena?!' and by the way each of them felt like they'd always known one and other and could tell each other *anything*. Well, almost anything, Sheena corrected herself. Of course, she hadn't gone so far as to tell Gabby about her extra income work down at Secrets, this being purely on a need-to-know basis, and well, no one would ever need to know *that* except herself. ('It's only a means to an end!' 'It doesn't define me.' 'It'll all be worth it in the end.' She trotted out a few mantras to herself.) However, she *had* all but shared practically everything about her ex-husband and marriage break-up, including the ongoing insanity and nightmare to live with that was his drinking problem, to the ever non-judgmental and surprisingly wise ("for my age, right?" Gabby would quip, jokingly) and beautiful, young Gabby, who always knew just what to say if Sheena was having a rough day.

'God knows how she got so wise, and especially knowledgeable about this kinda stuff', Sheena would wonder to herself, again feeling a fool for it having taken *her* so long to figure out herself, 'I mean, come on, nineteen *years* of marriage to that man?!'

This was a common question she had for herself, and although she knew the answer really, she did still like to pose it to Gabby some days, when they were having a D&M chat over tea, or, very occasionally, wine. (Sheena was gradually 'healing' herself and getting to know and learn that it's ok: having a couple of wines with a friend *doesn't* mean it's later going to turn into an ugly and quickly down-spiralling argument complete with disgusting name-calling, and that she *can* drink socially again. Quite the novelty for Sheena.)

"But why, oh why, did I stay with him for that long?!" She'd whine, usually rhetorically.

She'd made peace with the answer mostly. She knew that she stayed so long because of those 'good' moments, the times of clarity and his sober days, and because of all the fun, loving memories from their early relationship. Ahh, a bit like that old nursery rhyme she supposed: when he was good, he was *very*, very good, but when he was bad, he was *horrid.* So lately, instead of hash it all out again and repeat her same excellent advice and consolation as before, Gabby had taken to simply ignoring all of that and saying:

> "Thank fuck you left him when you did and came into *my* life last year! I wouldn't have it any other way, my older-sister-from-another-mister!"

and with that she'd somehow managed to always have a copy of Morning Train by Sheena Easton on her laptop nearby, which she'd then start blasting as she'd twirl and move a now laughing, happy again Sheena around their living room, tripping over various strewn shoes and little quilted bags that Gabby had a penchant for.

That had been the moment Gabby knew she'd found her new housemate, and not only that, her lifelong best friend and soul mate even: when Sheena first introduced herself, Gabby had let out a squeal and told her of her own lifelong passion with Sheena Easton's song 'Morning Train'.

> "Fate, that's what this is: bringing you and me together", vivacious Gabby had bubbled over to her, her eyes wide and shining.

She reminded Sheena something of the kind of girl *she* might have been, had she not gotten married to Peter all those many, many years ago at the tender age of just sixteen.

Sheena felt guilty for not having told her flatmate, and self-appointed (but heartily concurred by Sheena) best friend, of her recently acquired second job, but true to the two simple laws that Sheena lived by, she felt she could not only be damaging their friendship by coming clean, but would more than likely deeply offend and would scare away her dear, happy Gabby (judging by some of the things she'd said in passing about her cheating, deceitful exes and various visits to gentlemen's clubs) and she would *never* want to hurt her. Nope, best keep it just to herself, and hopefully she could retire her role as professional escort for good in the not too distant future, when '*her*' portion of the debt with her ex-husband was finally paid off. ('Huh!' she frowned again, feeling the injustice of the debt that existed to pay off his years of alcohol purchasing and abuse. 'Let it go!' Another favourite mantra then popped out to help.) Then nobody gets hurt and she can eventually erase it from her memory and focus on the 'good' bits of her life: her uni course, her goal of becoming a teacher, her beautiful friendship with Gabby, her lively workmates at the groovy, bustling café where she worked (her reputable day-job that took up about 15 hours of her week) and the cruisy, bohemian, laid-back vibe and feel she got from quirky Fremantle. Life, in general, was good. Very good. She just needed to keep her mind focused on these things, as Brian kept up his monotonous plod ('Surely he's going to get there sometime soon!' She exasperated.)

Ok, back to thinking about her coursework and studies, as she looked up into her own hazel bored looking eyes staring back at her from the ceiling's large mirror.

'I need to come up with something good for my psychology coursework. Really want a distinction if I can swing it. Something *original.* But wait, according to my philosophy teacher, what's his name again… Oh yeah, Mr Goodwood, haha, what a name, ok, c'mon focus, a bit of maturity here! That's right: there's no original thought. Ever. All that is happening has been done before, infinite times and will happen again to infinity. Oh ain't that the truth.' She sighed and her thoughts flashed briefly back to elderly Brian still grunting away on top of her. 'This has definitely happened before, no original thought there, not with his monthly booking block-booked for the next year, yuck....' She grimaced and grit her teeth. 'C'mon, focus, for fuck's sake! Ok, so there's no original thought, ever, and everything is repeated, then surely, it shouldn't matter *what* anyone does? It's all just ideas and situations repeated, yes, simply being pulled out of the ether? Out of consciousness? Was that what he had said?' She felt herself getting confused and her thoughts were getting jumbled.

'Wait,' She attempted to reorganise her stream of consciousness: she really *did* find his class fascinating. 'So, there's no original thought ever, and, what else was it? Oh yeah, how could I forget *that* one. Everything, every single thing in life: it's all about *sex*. Something we definitely agree on, Mr Goodwood. And as there are no original thoughts, ever, then I'm sure he wouldn't be particularly surprised that a student of his has this as their part-time job: hardly original... Duh! Come on, remember, there *is* nothing that's original. I'm sure he wouldn't be surprised either that I'm thinking about him right now as I'm getting fucked. I'm sure I'm not the first woman to think of him while another man is floundering and hammering away.'

She smiled back at herself now, suddenly gaining increased endurance and a sense of patience for the task at hand, as an enticing thought entered her slightly scattered, flowing train of thoughts.

'He has got that mysterious, deep-thinking, hot philosophy professor thing going for him, plus he's pretty fucking attractive,' She remembered, picturing his always slight three-day stubble growth and

46

wry, slightly dirty smile, his dark, probing eyes and equally dark, shoulder-length hair, pulled back messily into something of a casual man-bun. He was tall, but not gangly, with just the right amount of broadness to him, with what appeared to be large, strong arms, perfectly sculpted and crafted and hinged to his strong, broad, manly shoulders, although who could tell too much of what was under his usual 'work uniform' of a black shirt, so now she truly let her imagination run wild, having a very non-original thought of her *professor* pressing her down, and driving her into the hard mattress, not Brian: his stubble grazing her neck as he ploughed his, what felt like an impressively big, fully engorged, hard cock, into her own tight, hot pussy.

She continued her own version of completely unoriginal thoughts about her handsome, knowing, and yes, fascinating, professor, while Brian *finally* ('thank god' she thought, as his non-impressive groan departed from his whiskey hazed mouth) finished up with his own very unoriginal act.

Sheena lay back smiling as Brian gathered his things and left. She breathed out a long sigh of relief and a small giggle of surprise. She was very glad for that help from the ether or consciousness or whatever it was: a great, unoriginal way to get through it. Although, it seemed original for Sheena, she thought, having never have previously pictured Mr Goodwood fucking her. She would definitely be plucking him from the ether again.

'Oh Mr Goodwood...' She mused to herself. 'How interesting...'

# CHAPTER FOUR

"Scottie!" Brendan cried loudly, as the large, red door swung open, revealing his near-clone, a sheepish smile on his handsome face, as he let Brendan give him a hearty back-slap mingled with a manly hug.

"Oh shit, I didn't ruin your plans of student-seduction like a couple of weeks back, again did I?" Still smiling sheepishly, he now blushed furiously and coughed a little.

"Nah, it's all good, Bro," Brendan reassured his brother. "Actually, prefect timing: I'd just bid a fond farewell to the delectable 'Apple' when you called, so don't you worry about that Big-Bro!"

"Apple?" Scott shot Brendan a quizzical look, his face now resuming its usual colour, as they made their way carefully down the hallway and into the living room.

"Yes, Apple," Brendan had a coy smile and a renewed sparkle in his eyes again as he revisited his still oh-so-fresh images in his mind of his latest après-class student, a bright young thing, on an exchange program from China.

"She was appropriately sweet and juicy, if that's what you're wondering." Brendan winked at a now deep scarlet Scott, who lowered his eyes and coughed again. "Yes, she's a lovely student of mine, all the way from the People's Republic of China. Very interesting girl."

An image flashed up in Brendan's slightly weary, content mind of said girl and of her slender, petite hips as he grabbed them confidently while she sat astride him in his leather armchair, wearing nothing more than a mischievous smile. His eyes had travelled down her perky, small but perfectly formed tits, along her taut, tiny little waist and down to her soft, dark, surprisingly afro-like bush, standing stark and unapologetic above her perfect, little pussy. It made such a welcome change, he thought, from all the waxed to within a millimetre of their lives, Brazilian snatches that seemed to be the trend with pretty much *all* his other students. This young woman was *all* natural, and he found it extremely hot.

Scott attempted to mock-scold his brother and told him:

"You're going to get into serious trouble one of these days!"

"Nah, don't worry about me Big-Bro." He ruffled Scott's hair playfully and gently slapped him on both cheeks. "Remember Universal Law? This life's all about sex and pleasure, and we are all *one* anyway."

As if that explained things perfectly. Scott's blushing resumed and he looked away again.

Scott was, correctly stated by Brendan, Brendan's 'Big-Bro', his older brother. However, he was only older by a mere twenty minutes. As identical twins though, they couldn't have been more different in personalities and life choices. Where Brendan was confident, Scott was shy and nervous. Where Brendan was a real people-person and an extrovert, Scott was very much the archetypal introvert. Brendan preferred hiking and outdoor sports, such as cycling, whereas for Scott: reading and watching documentaries absorbed most of his time. Brendan: always liked a few drinks, while Scott had never been big on having more than a couple of light beers. Where Brendan was very much a charming, charismatic, flirtatious ladies' man, Scott, well, he hadn't had much success, as far as Brendan can tell, with the fairer sex. Whenever Brendan would describe his latest sexual escapade, down to the most intricate detail, which was often, Scott had no choice or power over the fact that his whole head would blush a furious crimson in response, and he'd usually cough with embarrassment or awkwardness. Some days Brendan found it hard to believe they were even *brothers*, let alone identical twins, but there was no mistaking their joint good looks: the same dark, long, slightly tousled hair; those dark, probing eyes (even if Scott's tended to probe the floor or the carpet in response to a juicy morsel from Brendan); and those same broad, strong, manly shoulders and large, strong arms. Identical clones of each other, that is, until the end of their torsos and start of their legs, and here's where they have one major difference and part of their bodies that they don't share: Scott's legs have been out of action since the tender age of just fourteen. A somewhat cruel consequence of actually having, for once (and at his brother's behest) 'got off' with a girl, one of the many there at the gathering they were at, who had left him with a couple of months' reminder of her: he had caught a bad case of glandular fever, also known as 'the kissing disease'. In Scott's case this seemed particularly unfair and cruel as his glandular fever was so intense and prolonged that it led to nerve damage and total paralysis of both of his legs. Luckily enough, and he was thankful for this, everywhere else was unaffected ("Yes, it works fine!" He'd stammer out flushed and red-faced, of course, to Brendan, over the years as teenagers) but the end result of his first (and Brendan hoped, for his brother's sake, not *only*) foray into the tempting world of females, was that he was to spend the rest of his teenage and then adult life either using crutches on each arm to get around (his preferred choice) or by wheeling himself around in his, not often used, wheelchair.

Scott wasn't bitter or even mildly annoyed about the situation: it simply was what it was. It didn't change who he was.

"If anything," He'd joke. "It's given me an advantage hey: check out how big my arms and shoulders are compared to yours, Little-Bro!" Flexing his impressive biceps and grinning.

However, Brendan *did* worry about Scott. As independent as he was, or tried to be, he couldn't help but worry about, not only his brother, but his absolute, I-fucking-love-you-and-I-would-die-for-you best friend. Scott received a disability allowance each month, which wasn't too generous (not at all) but which allowed him to live fairly comfortably, in a semi-assisted living apartment complex in Cottesloe, not far from Fremantle: a private, independent apartment, essentially, but with the added bonus of a 24-hour on-call nurse on the property, in case of an emergency, and he had a lady who came in once a week to help with the cleaning and laundry. He *seemed* happy enough, most of the time, but Brendan still worried. He worried about Scott's lack of friends, his lack of a girlfriend, and his 'safe' routine. He knew it was none of his business ultimately , and that, yes, they were very different people, but Brendan couldn't understand how Scott wouldn't go mad if he was cooped up in that little apartment mostly all day every day. *He* sure would, if things were reversed.

However, Scott assured him that most of the time he was fine. Happily researching things online. Happily reading new novels and travel books. Extremely happily cooking and trying out a new 'foodie' idea or recipe, one of his recent passions. He had no job, and not many friends, other than Scott and his regular cleaning lady, Sheila, as far as Brendan could tell. So: Brendan worried about him. Probably more than he should as a brother. He just couldn't help it. The lack of a job, was not down to any physical or mobility issue however, but, as both the brothers knew: it was down to Scott's crippling shyness and introverted ways. So again, Brendan worried.

He'd do anything for Scott: he would always be there for him, and hell, if Scott needed him or wanted to get out of his apartment, well he only had to say the word and Brendan would be there. Even if it meant blowing off a potentially mind-blowing threesome with two busty, flexible blond students, as per a few weeks back. Scott came first to Brendan, and always would, and Brendan knew this worked vice versa too.

"So, you got your invitation then?" Brendan smirked knowingly at his brother. "I mean, come on, his fourth wedding in just over a decade? That's gotta be some kind of record. Why bother?"

Scott nodded, blushing, but smiled and rebuked him:

"But Brendo, apparently this one is *the* one!"

Promptly breaking down into guffaws as Brendan pulled a face in response.

Ridicule was the only way Brendan could as tactfully or subtly as possible even mention their far-away, estranged father, who skipped town (no, wait, skipped the entire *country!*) over twelve years ago. Pretty much the second the twins turned eighteen, he was gone. Admittedly he was in love and engaged (to a lovely Pommie chick, no less) at the time, so maybe it wasn't as calculated as Brendan often felt and joked about. Sometimes he even felt sorry for his father: widowed when his twin sons were just five years old, he'd had to carry the brunt of parental responsibility, to which Brendan and Scott both thought he was never particularly suited. So, it seemed natural for him to flit off almost as soon as he could, not looking back, when they were both 'of age'. Leaving Brendan, he very rarely thought, slightly bitterly, to take sole care of Scott, if only emotionally. Sure, their father did keep in touch via yearly Christmas cards and updates: he was a fan of those long winded, printed essays enclosed with said Christmas cards, detailing the many successes of his 'new' family at the time (which would then be routinely updated and altered with each new, subsequent wedding and marriage. The brothers almost lost count.)

At least he always *invited* them, if only out of politeness. Never mind the fact that it was always extremely last minute (no time to plan time off for Brendan or book flights etc) or that Scott had never travelled by plane or out of the country before, or that they never actually received a phone call about the said upcoming nuptials. Brendan could feel himself getting riled up all over again as he thought about it. No one seemed to rile him up quite like his estranged father did. Taking a leaf out of Scott's book, he reminded himself: 'it is what it is.' Plus, he did at least, still provide financially, well, to Scott anyway. Brendan was pretty sure that Scott's meagre disability benefit was quite heavily and regularly subsidised by their long-lost father. A fact that Brendan *was* very glad about. Scott had tried to bring it up once with Brendan, red-faced and mumbling, about the 'ethics' of accepting his money, being a grown man and all. In his wise, esteemed approach as a philosophy professor, Brendan had had no qualms in telling him outright:

"Accept it. No questions asked. Even if it *is* guilt money." He had given his brother a loving, reassuring slap, and continued: "Spend it on yourself, or on spoiling a new girlfriend of yours hey!"

Wink wink, nudge nudge. Directly resulting in Scott's blazing face to increase its scarlet hue and his gaze to be suddenly averted to the floor. Oh yes, and a change of subject would complete his 'as soon as you mention women I'll clam up' routine.

"Yeah," Brendan now looked down at the white and gold embossed square of card in Scott's hands. "He's going *all* out with this one too. Check it out: open bar until midnight hey…. Maybe it's *not* too late to fly over there, to let's see, where is it? Faversham, Kent."

He sighed. When would his father ever stop irritating him? And how did he do it so easily from such a distance? Still, it didn't seem to bother Scott, who just shrugged and smiled back at his 'Little-Bro'.

"Ok, come on then, mate." Brendan took charge again. "We're going out. What do you fancy? Pizza? Fine wine? Tequila shooters? Name your poison and we're on it."

His enthusiasm rebounded off the nearby walls, making its physical presence know, and Brendan's enigmatic, wide smile spread contagiously over and onto Scott's own ever red face.

"How about coffee?" Scott replied. "Somewhere different to the usual place?"

"I like the cut of your jib, Sir! Yes, somewhere 'different' and new it will be! Let's go then. After you, Scottie."

# CHAPTER FIVE

"You're the ugliest woman I've ever met."

Followed by a snarl. His bloodshot, glassy eyes were boring into her.

"The *ugliest* woman I've ever met." He repeated. "Ugly. You're a nasty piece of work. You fucken arsehole. You're just a bitch. I don't know why I let you do this to me, every time. You're a nasty piece of work and you need to grow up, you fucking teenager. You just love starting drama, don't you, you arsehole. Your night wouldn't be complete without it. Grow up you ugly teenager!"

His tirade was a particularly nasty and hurtful one that evening. Sheena couldn't recall what exactly she had said or done to provoke him, she thought it was probably just a look or a frown that crossed her face, or it could have been her accidental glance at the empty bottle on the floor that set him off. It's strange how most of her memories, the happy ones anyway, of her now ended marriage are all blurred into one mid-length movie montage; the details fuzzy and unclear. However, the finer details of each and every thing he'd ever said to her when he was wasted (which was often) seemed to be forever burned and etched into her long-term memory: always there beneath the surface, waiting to punch her in the lungs once more, when she was undertaking a deathly slow, quiet shift at the café where she worked, for example. All it took was one overheard argument taking place between a couple of patrons there, or one raised voice or someone getting mildly irate talking loudly into their phones, even if just in jest, and she was right back there, everywhere, feeling the raw pain once more as if it had just been freshly delivered, his words slicing into her as she stood there in shock and resignation. The shock was usually from wondering how he'd gotten so far along so soon (Why was he blind already? It was early even by his standards) or at the unfairness of his reaction if he'd twisted her words or misjudged her intention (which was often) or simply seen something on her face and didn't like the look she was apparently giving him. *Resignation*, as she knew how things would unfold: a disgusting verbally abusive argument (yes, usually complete with her own, less drunk retaliation too) followed by no acknowledgement of all the things he had called her the next morning, and back to him being the kind, loving gentle man she remembered, whom she was seeing less and less of as the years went by.

She had *tried* not to retaliate. After all, what was the point? Everyone knows it's pointless trying to reason with a drunk. A fact he would even point out to her, whilst drunk of course. Exasperated she would think to herself wildly, 'well, when the fuck *can* I talk to you then?' being that he was then usually drunk most of the time. 'And am I not allowed to defend myself *during* his tirades??' It made no difference though, whether she fought back or not. Sometimes the silence only seemed to anger him even more.

> "You think you're so much better than me!" He would accuse her. "You're so fucking superior and fucking perfect aren't you, Miss Fucking-Perfect, you arsehole, coming in here and judging me? Well, you can fuck off."

She wouldn't though. Hating herself for it, she would always stay for more. Always stayed, right till the 'end' of the argument or his abusive speech, no matter how much she was arguing at a brick wall, or how awful it was. She was mortified and ashamed of the times when, not only did she stay put, but even went back into the room he was in, for more, time and again.

'Why? Where was your self-respect?' She'd berate herself later, once she *had* finally left. But at the time, each and every time, she'd stay, even when he was shouting at her to go and would forcefully try and close the door on her. Almost like she had to, once it was happening, receive the full, painful treatment from him, in shock (still shocked every time, despite it being a very regular occurrence) at how quickly an afternoon or night could go so horribly, painfully shithouse. Almost like she *couldn't* get up and walk out of the door, as if she just *had* to stay and argue the point with this very drunken, angry man and see just what cruel things he would come up with next. She later thought that perhaps she got addicted to the pain and hurt; was that even possible? Perhaps he was right – did she crave the drama? She obviously provoked him in some way and caused him to be so depressed and angry that he *would* binge drink and then go off into an angry tirade taken out on her.

'Stop right there, Sheena!' Her own guiding intuition stirred and forced her to wake up and she shouted at herself, but it sounded more like Gabby's voice than her own. 'You did *not* cause his disease, nor are you responsible for *any* of that man's actions, for fuck's sake, please *stop* thinking about him! It's over!'

Easier said than done however, especially on this super slow, tedious Sunday evening, where Sheena found herself leaning against the till of the usually more popular than tonight apparently was, 'Café Noir'. She didn't usually work on the weekends at all, and this was severely intruding into her studying-slash-study-break-chatting-with-Gabby-over-giant-mugs-of-tea time. However, her boss, Margie, had called her in a panic: she was away looking after her mother and one of the regular Sunday girls had gone down with a stomach bug apparently. (Hmmm, Sheena had wondered if this stomach bug was anything to do with the all-day music festival that was held in Perth the day before, and perhaps the young girl in question had 'caught' it there?) Sheena didn't really mind though, and being honest with herself *and* with Margie:

"I'd love to. I need every bit of extra cash I can earn at the moment."

She hoped it wasn't always this quiet on the Sundays there. Both she and the only other staff member there, Jerome, were spending most of their day twiddling their thumbs. Jerome was a fairly new addition to Café Noir's team: he looked about twenty and Sheena though he could be described as one of those 'hipsters' judging from his man-bun, 'hipster' beard, checked shirt, and his extremely nonchalant, brooding-esque, but otherwise pleasant, attitude. He was a man of few words and gave the impression he was always deep in thought, even whilst inspecting his nails and leaning against the counter that housed the impressive, industrial-sized coffee machine. This was fine by Sheena. She didn't want to pry into others' lives, or even pass the time making idle chit-chat or small talk. *Usually* that is. However, on this particular evening, her demons and memories were back and haunting her with a vengeance, and she would have gladly welcomed some mindless breeze shooting, wishing that Margie were here too. Although, then she supposed, *she* wouldn't get to be here making this extra cash…

Glancing at the clock, she saw she still had a full two hours left to go, and surveying the near empty room, bar a couple of teenage girls in the corner booth, she sighed heavily.

'Think about something else!' She ordered herself.

Her 'something else' mental subject change these days seemed to always be: sex. Was this a hazard of the job? Or a side effect of being newly divorced and single, perhaps? Not that she'd even actually gone out and 'picked up' since leaving her old life well and truly behind, but the thought that she *could* (and might, soon) made her face light up with a smile every time. After years of extremely less than satisfying, infrequent sex (thank you again, side effects of alcoholism!) Sheena had surprised herself by remembering her libido actually existed. Which, despite having to fake her enjoyment during client participation every Friday night, was definitely reawakening, if her usual daydreams were anything to go by.

Forcibly blocking any last vestiges of one of her memorable (for all the wrong reasons) encounters with her ex from her weary mind, she straightened her shoulders and threw another look over to Jerome, who was still giving his fingernails a thorough and lengthy inspection, while they both continued their metaphoric thumb-twiddling, waiting for the next customer or for closing time, whichever came first. Closing her eyes, she took her creative mind to the cramped storeroom at the back of the café, adjacent to the staff bathroom there: She's checking inventory, box of sugar after box of sugar, it's a particularly hot, stifling, late afternoon and the café's air conditioner is broken. She thinks she's alone, that they've shut up for the day, save for her slogging away doing the monthly check for a bit of extra cash. Stopping for a breather, after having just played giant, 15kg per box, Tetris around the cupboard-cum-room, she stands up puffing and wipes her sweaty forehead with the back of her hand. Knowing no one is around, she then roughly pulls off her turquoise-blue camisole top and flings this to the floor, feeling the slightly cooler, fresh air on her glistening, bare skin, apart from her full, voluptuous breasts which are still trapped in her hot pink, satin bra.

"Need a hand?" Comes a breathy, low, male voice from the direction of the doorway.

Sheena spins around suddenly, caught completely off-guard by the quiet, contemplative, smouldering look young Jerome is giving her, as he's leaning casually against the doorframe.

"I thought no one was here." She starts and smiles at him. "How long have you been standing there?"

Jerome shrugs and says nothing. He straightens up, all the while staring at her. Then he slowly begins to unbutton his checked shirt, button by button, as she watches him, speechless.

"It's sweltering in here"

Are his only words, and he strides over to where she's standing waiting for him. His arms are surprisingly strong-looking and his shoulders are broad, with a fine grazing of soft looking, dark brown curls forming a diamond on his own lightly perspiring, hard, sculpted chest. Reaching towards her hips he begins to stroke the material of her tight black jeans, shaking his head.

"Let's get you out of *these* too, it's much too hot and sticky in here."

His fingers gently fingering the seam and then snaking around to the zipper, where he confidently pulls it down quickly. The tight jeans miraculously fall away and to the floor, with none of the usual wiggling and coaxing (hey, this was her fantasy, after all) and she's now standing there before him, his intense green eyes (wait, *were* they green? Or blue? She wondered) slowly looking her up and down as he began to unbuckle his belt and push his own jeans down, revealing his tight, black briefs connecting with a taut, hard stomach and another line of that dark, soft hair drawing her eyes further down…

'Wait, this isn't working!' She berated herself, and her eyes flicked open, feeling annoyed at herself for ruining her own damn fantasy. But, and no offense intended to Jerome, who seemed nice enough, but he just wasn't doing it for her, not even in her very active imagination and all-too brief fantasy while standing paralysed at the invisible, tumble-weed strewn cash-till.

'Hmm, let's see." She closed her eyes again and she's back in the storeroom once more, standing there in a short, black summer dress, again wiping her brow from the heat and exertion. Feeling a sudden fatigue *due* to the heat and exertion she decides to take a little nap on the boxes she's just rearranged. She awakens a short while later, a bit dazed and confused and feels a pair of large, confident, manly hands upon her: one is currently pushing up her dress's hem and is exploring inside her lacy, black g-string, whilst the other is clamped down over her mouth. Her eyes widen in alarm as she realises what's happening and she tries to stand up, or at least shake off this unidentified man at least, but he's too strong. Moving her arms upwards to push him off she realises why she has no hope of doing so: her hands are securely fastened by packing tape to the edge of the aluminium shelves, as are her ankles. In horror she realises she is completely trapped: vulnerable and unable to move and spread eagled for this stranger. Her shock grows when she realises this man is making her very, very wet. She is incredibly turned on, but she can't move, nor can she speak or even see who this heavy handed perpetrator is, as his face is turned away to one side. His fingers continue to explore her: probing her, now unbearably wet and hot pussy, drenching through the flimsy black g-string material as he proceeds to finger-fuck her vigorously. She wants to yell at him to stop but he's still got his other hand clamped firmly over her mouth. She manages to lick it though and she gets his attention. Moving his face back to hers, he positions himself directly on top of her now, and immediately she recognises his face. Her eyes widen yet again.

"Don't scream or I'll tape your mouth too."

He warns, as he goes to remove his hand from her face. After a few deep breaths, all the while he continues to finger her, now at a slower, less frantic pace, but still deeply, very deeply.

"Mr Goodwood!"

She gasps breathily up at her philosophy teacher's huge, chocolate eyes, his tousled brown hair falling in sweaty clumps around his stubbly, handsome face, but mostly, she's caught by his intense look probing her as deeply as his two fingers are.

His response to her shocked statement is to rip off her wet thong, revealing all of Sheena, and he begins to slowly lower his face down towards her aching, throbbing, soaking wet pussy, moving his wet, hot mouth and his three-day stubbly chin lower and lower, closer and closer, as Sheena, trussed up and unable to move a muscle, watches him, helplessly feeling herself getting hotter and hotter, as his mouth begins to close around her...

The bell atop the stained glass panelled door to the café tinkled annoyingly, momentarily alerting Sheena to that fact that, yes, she was still very much just standing behind the till, fully clothed, and not tied up about to be devoured in the storeroom. More's the pity. Jerome was still studying his fingernails intently, and the two BFFs in the corner were still taking endless selfies before analysing them, deleting them, and repeating this process (getting that duck pout, *juuust* right). The only apparent noticeable change was Sheena's flushed face and tell-tale smile (or so she felt). Swallowing and shaking off her recent, very vivid daydream, she assumed the position (needing only to stop slumping over and she stood up straight and alert) at the till, ready to greet whoever was about to grace them with their presence and actually give them something to do for the remainder of their shift. The door was held open as if the next customer wanted to build up an air of suspense (yep, that's how dreary and tedious this particular shift had become. It's the little things…) and a few minutes later, the very star of her recent fantasy slowly hauled himself inside on two sturdy looking crutches, carefully but skillfully, as Sheena just gaped at him.

'What are the chances!' She wondered, her flushed face now aflame as she wondered if he'd be able to tell just by looking at her that she'd not long finished having some very inappropriate thoughts about him. 'And what's with the crutches? What happened?'

She waved over at him causing him to blush and look immediately down at the terracotta tiled floor. Hmm, maybe, actually, he didn't even recognise her? He must have hundreds of students.

'How stupid of me! Egocentric much…' She chided herself. But then, it was an unusual response from the usually extremely confident, whilst simultaneously being quite vague and mysterious, teacher.

He was shortly followed by another man, and they made their way to an empty table at the far corner by the window.

'Bloody hell!' Sheena marvelled. 'There are two of them!'

She smiled at the thought that, of course he didn't recognise her – *they* had never met, and as she scrambled about pulling a couple of menus from the rack, whilst attempting to compose her still blushing, facial features ('Come on, poker face, Sheena!') and started to head over to greet them, as per Café Noir's protocol, her smile widened as the correct Mr Goodwood (*her* Mr Goodwood, at least) waved to her in recognition.

Taking her time to saunter over, she took a good look at the twins: two fine specimens of broad, strong manhood, more suited to being stars in a Western than of sitting there casually waiting to order a coffee or a sandwich or whatnot; their equally broad, strong shoulders straining against their jackets, their dark tousled, semi-long hair, and the stubble of approximately three day's growth (on her Mr Goodwood's face anyway): she could just picture a cowboy hat atop each one and a matchstick or toothpick in their coy, smiling, beautiful mouths. A sudden, more explicit image of the two brothers also popped into her head, with her starring, unimaginatively, in the middle of them, one strong, broad brother on either side, simultaneously kissing her bare shoulders and grazing her soft, white flesh with their manly stubble.

'Not very original,' She scolded herself mildly. 'But then, just like he was saying: nothing is!'

"Hello there!" Mr Goodwood greeted her warmly, and as a long-awaited friend might. His double quietly surveyed the floor,

66

cheeks aflame.

'Oh,' She smiled again at his confirmation. 'He *does* remember me.'

"Haven't seen you in here before, Mr Goodwood! And hello there."

She directed her attention quickly to his brother, who in turn went an even deeper shade of pink, before briefly flicking his eyes up to hers and bleating out a quick: "Hi."

"This is my brother Scott." Mercifully Mr Goodwood took charge. "And please, we're not in class at the moment – call me Brendan."

She smiled back, noting the name for the next time she may use his image for her other part-time job and as fantasy fodder to get her through the more difficult, tedious clients. 'Brendan, Brendan, oh god, Brendan!' She could picture herself picturing it already, quite liking the ring to it. As her face grew slightly red again at the thought, Brendan continued:

"And I'm terribly sorry, but I don't yet know *your* name. But I would *never* forget your face."

He gave her a poignant look and a broad smile. Scott coughed and began to examine a different spot on the floor tiles now.

'Is he flirting with me?' Sheena wondered. 'Surely not – he's my *teacher*! It probably hasn't even crossed his mind! Not that I would want him to, or anything... What can he tell from looking at my face exactly, I wonder?' She suddenly felt exposed and glanced hurriedly over to Jerome who, nope, was still standing there, passively, unalerted by any inappropriate behaviour from her, or none the wiser.

'Calm down, Sheena – it's all in your head. And Mr Goodwood –

*Brendan* – here, *can't* tell what you were just vividly envisaging happening.' More's the pity.

"Sheena." She replied, her confidant smile back in place once again.

"Sheena?" Brendan tried it out. "Were your folks  big fans of Morning Train then? I do love that song." He smiled encouragingly at his brother now, who smiled too, but at the floor tiles where his line of sight was still being focused on. "Ahem, sorry, you probably get that all the time. Not very original, I know." He apologised. "But then, nothing *is*, is it?"

Sheena's eyes snapped back abruptly to look at his, where they both held the gaze, comfortably yet inquisitively. This was uncanny. It was as if he *could* read her mind after all. Now it was her turn to drop her gaze to the floor, as she resumed flushing, and she felt that hotness and familiar ache from her reverie before creep back over her. Brendan continued to look at her, and she could feel it: felt her body burn under his watchful, inquisitive eyes.

'Come on, Sheena!' She warned herself again: 'This is your teacher, for god's sake. Pull yourself together!'

As she hurried back over to begin counting up the day's takings (or pretend to anyway, suddenly needing a task to occupy her hands) his words from a previous lecture of his reverberated in her mind: 'All this, everything you do or see: it is all about *sex*; sex is the meaning of life.'

# CHAPTER SIX

Brendan had looked over to their brunette waitress-cum-hostess and felt a welcome jolt of recognition. As they exchanged smiles, he had a feeling of coming home or that they had met somewhere before.

'Previous life perhaps.' He pondered, as he'd waved cheerily over to her approaching form. And *what* a form it was: she was fucking gorgeous, head to toe. As he watched her come closer and closer to their table, he quickly (and expertly) surveyed his nameless (as yet) student (oh yes, he had seen her before: she was one of his attentive, studious ones: yet to corner him after class on something or other, a wholly disappointing fact to him now). Her long, waves of glossy, chocolate coloured curls gently bounced and swung this way and that past her toned shoulders as she walked their way. Her full, curvy hips obvious beneath her standard issue black work pants, emphasised by her petite, flat waist. Her curves then reappeared with gusto as his eyes travelled further up her impressive physique, now resting on her equally curvy and full cleavage, or would-be cleavage if she'd just pop open one more button on her crisp, white, sleeveless and nearly sheer shirt; although there was no denying their generous, more-than-a-handful size, even whilst clamouring under wraps. He found it so refreshing, and so alluring, to be looking at the beautiful specimen of all woman coming further into his line of sight, and he savoured every moment of her slow approach.

'Such a nice change from all those skinny minnies,' he thought vaguely. Whilst he *did* appreciate the feminine form in *all* shapes and sizes, regularly, he had to admit there was just something about the more pronounced and obvious curves on a woman. He never felt he was at risk of breaking them when fucking them all sorts of sideways, nor did he usually expect any of the standard insecure comments about their weight and bodies (a common grievance with some of the skinnier, petite female companions of his. Why?? Another of life's great mysteries).

He noticed she wasn't wearing any make-up either, nor had she been during his lectures either, he was pretty sure. Nor did she, of all people, even *need* to wear make-up. 'Well,' he corrected himself. 'I suppose no one really *needs* to, but there you go…'

No, this beauty was all natural gorgeousness personified: she looked fresh and glowing even; a classical beauty of brunette, with the most intriguing, sparkling amber coloured eyes, he realised now. There was a look about her of, what was it, oh yes, some kind of *innocence*. She had a certain demureness about her, yet at the same time: well, he couldn't quite put his finger on it. All at once he found her to have a sense of purity, of wholesomeness, but then again, her smile, *that* smile, and those full, luscious lips of hers, were conjuring up an entirely different image of her in his mind. Such a pity he hadn't had the, ahem, *pleasure* of getting to know her, yet. He would definitely love the chance to probe her *mind* at least out of the classroom: this mystery, beautiful brunette.

After their brief introductions, she'd sauntered away again, leaving the brothers to make their selection from the minimalistic menu. Brendan breathed out a low sigh of appreciation and then looked at his brother, whose face was starting to resume its normal colour. Come to think of it, Brendan thought Scott was shyer than normal, even for him. 'He's taking this extreme fear of women malarkey too far,' Brendan thought.

'Tsk! Looking at the *floor* when he could have been staring into those pools of liquid gold eyes of hers, or running his eyes up the beautiful curve of her hips to her waist, and then up to her…' Sure, Scott was usually shy when women were around, all except for his devoted cleaning lady Sheila, but it was like he was mortified tonight.

"Scott." Brendan commanded.

Scott coughed and looked up. He caught his brothers eyes and Brendan gave him one of his most direct, I'm-sussing-you-out-and-delving-into-the-depths-of-your-inner-most-mind look, that he was so adept at.

"Scott," He repeated. "What is it that you *desire*? What do you *want*? What takes your *fancy*??"

Scott's face grew his custom shade of red, but he didn't break the gaze held by Brendan.

"Umm," He began unsurely. "What do you mean, Brendan?"

Brendan simply stared back intensely for a few extra seconds, before breaking into a grin and waving the menu in Scott's half-frowning face.

"From the menu, of course!" He gently nudged his brothers' resting arm with the long, cardboard rectangle.

Scott smiled, looking somewhat relieved.

"Yeah, course." He looked down again, at the menu this time.

"Umm, I'll have a long black, cheers Bro."

Brendan appeared to study the menu now, but kept his peripherals very much actively clocking Scott glancing anxiously over to where their new brunette friend had just disappeared to. He would then look hurriedly down, and would bite his lower lip, nervously.

'Hmm, interesting.' Noted Brendan. 'Maybe he *does* fancy her? What's not to like though…'

71

"What do you think of the lovely Sheena then Scott?"

Brendan smiled at his now bright red brother, who was currently giving a very bad impression of someone feeling breezy and nonchalant.

"Who, what?" He began coughing, as he did so, his mahogany brown hair swayed welcomely across his face and into his eyes. "Oh, your student over there? She seems very nice."

"That's all?" Brendan was clearly not impressed with his brief response.

"Yeah. Nice." His smile faltered as he began his own awkward question of: "She's not one of your, ahem, 'special' students, then?"

'Not yet.' Brendan immediately thought, feeling his cock stir too at the mere mention of a study session with this particular mystery brunette with the perfectly mysterious (or unusual anyhow) name: *Sheena.*

"Oh come on! Give me some credit! I usually do find out their names and have had a conversation with them first. You saw me Bro, we only *really* just met. That wasn't some kind of act mate."

But he *felt* like they had met before. A warm hug of a feeling that he couldn't quite put his finger on.

"Yeah, but," Scott continued, looking up into his own mirror image brown eyes they shared. "There was all that flirting between you two. It's obvious where this is headed – don't tell me you wouldn't *love* her to ask you for your, ahem, private tutoring or whatnot."

'Ahh Scott,' Brendan conceded to himself. 'You know me too well. Wait a minute, according to Scott she was flirting back? Interesting…'

"You have such a low opinion of me, Bro!"

He chuckled and lightly, jovially punched Scott's solid, strong bicep.

"Nah, Brendo, not low." He smiled lovingly at him. "Just realistic."

'Well,' Brendan mused, 'He's right there. God, I'd love to see her after class, would love to trace my fingers down her collarbone to her shoulders, would love to slowly work my way down to her white shirt's seam to the V-neck middle and gently, or not so gently, pull that shirt clean off of her...'

"But Scott!" Brendan halted his current train of thought. "What about you? Do *you* fancy her mate?"

During the moment's hesitation, while Scott went suitably red and composed his answer (which, for some unknown reason, Brendan was strongly hoping it would be a definite 'no') Brendan thought about Scott, and in particular, his love-life. Or lack thereof, lately. Brendan was sure he'd had girlfriends in the past: he'd had loads of beautiful, equally studious-minded female friends at high school, Brendan remembered. Although Scott was always quick to point out, if questioned, that they were all 'just friends'. Sure, sure, Bro. Brendan never bought it for a second. But, that was Scott's private business, so he usually left him well enough alone on that one: he didn't want to upset him by prying. However, lately, Brendan was worried about the lack of any females in Scott's life, albeit for sixty-something, solid Sheila, who was more of a kind, loving, Aunty figure than anything else. If anything, it seemed Scott was getting shyer and even less confident when it comes to women, if his current behaviour was anything to go by.

'Maybe I should fix him up with someone? Find him a new girlfriend?'

Brendan wondered, as he waited for Scott's denial (he hoped) of fancying Sheena.

"No, of course not." Scott replied, while Brendan gave a quick, relieved half-smile. "Only just met her."

'Thank fuck for that.' Brendan told himself.

"Well, here she comes again, so here's your second chance!" he said teasingly, while smiling warmly at the beautiful figure now reapproaching the two brothers.

Scott coughed in surprise, near choking and spluttering while Brendan hurriedly and vigorously slapped his back.

Sheena looked worried, rushing over to them now. Putting her hand on Scott's shoulder she asked:

"Are you ok? Would you like some water or something?"

He regained his composure, but his face, red from his coughing fit, remained the same colour, no doubt a side effect of the close proximity of the luscious and beautiful Sheena.

"I – I'm fine." Scott said. "Thanks though."

He actually looked up and into her concerned wide, amber eyes. Brendan thought the gaze was held for slightly longer than was absolutely necessary. They wouldn't be having a moment would they, surely not...

'You're not jealous are you?' He berated himself.

"So," Brendan filled the silence with a mock conspiratorial: "*This* is where you spend your time when you're not being extremely attentive and hardworking in my classes then. Who would have guessed."

Sheena withdrew her hand from Scott's shoulder and swung around to

Brendan's smiling face once more, now locking eyes with those same dark chocolate, brown eyes as just a moment before. She laughed, the sound all at once: familiar and exotic, to Brendan's ears. Who *was* this girl? And why were they only just meeting *now*?

"Yep, you got me." She played along. "Caught out: the secret life of the student-slash-waitress. My very exciting, glamourous other life! Guilty as charged."

Her colour grew again, as she smiled back at him, unfaltering. There was something else though. Something behind the wide smile and confident appearance. Brendan couldn't help but feel a pull towards her. He wondered what lay beneath her layers, and not *just* her material, clothing layers. Although those he would most definitely love to delve beneath too. And all this from just a few words from the woman in question?

"I've been meaning to thank you after class." Sheena continued.

"But, you know, you're always so busy and all."

Was he? He thought he'd have definitely dropped what he was doing or stopped rushing off somewhere if *she* was heading in his direction. More likely then, he assumed, that by 'too busy' she may have been referring to the frequent other female students waiting to bend his ear after class.

'Oh shit'. Perhaps she knew about his after class sessions? Then: 'Why 'oh shit' Brendan? All the easier to arrange a get together then.'

But no. No hint of a wry smile or joke being made about his Lothario-esque ways. She seemed completely genuine.

"Yeah, I wanted to thank you: I've found your course and lectures fascinating. Really."

There she went again with the furtive, genuine smile, reaching far into her warm, golden eyes.

"Stop – you'll give him a big head!" Scott interjected, smiling cheekily at Sheena, before breaking immediately into a deep crimson colour.

"Don't listen to him – I don't mind at all! You're welcome!" He played along with the good natured banter and told Sheena: "I too find it all fascinating. A good thing, I suppose. Makes for an enjoyable job."

Scott had continued with his blushing and was now looking around the room anxiously.

'Yep,' thought Brendan, 'He's definitely getting worse.' He was impressed with the joke Scott had made at his expense, however, he could sense how uncomfortable Scott was with Sheena's presence there still. Geez, he could feel him burning like a furnace from where he sat. He thought it must have been obvious, and not just because of that famous twin-thing, as Sheena picked up on 'it', whatever 'it' was, and decided it was time to take their order and make her retreat.

"Well, what'll it be then? Mr Goodwood, I mean, Brendan? And Scott?"

She stood there expectantly looking from brother to brother, her notepad and pencil poised and ready to scribble.

God, Brendan could just *eat* her. She was so fucking delectable. He had a sudden vivid image of her sitting astride him while he sat on his leather sofa: her long, chocolate ringlets bouncing and waving freely over her soft, smooth, bare shoulders; her burning eyes connecting with and looking deep into his own as she slowly adjusted herself and rose up further, reaching one hand down to where his own were holding her hips casually. She grabbed his left hand and placed it over her right breast, her very full, perfect breast, and swiftly did the same with his other hand on her free breast. God, he could almost feel her nipples hardening under his touch as he pictured gently massaging them, and she responded by slowly rising up and then back down, arching her back and slowly moaning what he thought sounded like, 'Oh Mr Good wood….'

"well, Mr Goodwood? I mean, Brendan, sorry…"

He was pulled out of his impromptu reverie, back to Sheena calmly and patiently awaiting his order. His face must have been a picture. His cock was definitely responsive and he could feel himself barring up. He wondered what was written all over his face. After all, Scott wouldn't meet his eyes right now, and was giving yet another terracotta tile a very detailed inspection, while Brendan all but wiped his drool away.

'How vaguely embarrassing' He thought. 'That is, if I was one to *get* embarrassed, which I don't – why? What purpose would it serve??'

He smiled just a little longer at her, before asking for their requisite long blacks, and as Sheena departed again, causing Brendan to instinctively think: 'Hate you to go, but I love to watch you leave, mmm…' His eyes took in the retreating voluptuous arse under those tight, black work pants.

The brothers now met each other's gaze and said nothing for a few moments. Scott was first to break their comfortable silence.

"She's beautiful."

Accompanied by a shy smile, of course.

"She sure is."

Brendan agreed, letting out another deep sigh of his appreciation. Beautiful, innocent Sheena. Where have you been hiding? He wondered.

# CHAPTER SEVEN

"So, you see, or do you," Brendan spoke at a fairly rapid, confident pace. "As we discussed a few weeks back: not only are there a host of different subliminal messages and cues that guide our thought processes, that essentially *create* this reality you apparently see and feel before you, via your thought forming entities, not only this, but, yet, if we *believe* this *reality*, we are really just trusting our limited senses. We all know that us humans can see only a mere teeny, tiny fraction of the colours and wavelengths around us, so why on earth *would* we trust our senses?"

A pause and a look around the hall at his, wholly not too attentive audience.

"Who can tell me who famously said 'I think, therefore I am?' Anyone? No?" Without giving his student body any time to respond, he continued. "Well, look that up, that's step one for your homework this week. Anyway, famous old-mate said that. Have a good think about it. Are you positive that yes, you exist and so does everything around you purely because you are *seeing* all these things (wavelengths, really) and transmuting them into images and your elusive, magical thoughts? Who's to say you are not simply a part of that oft-spoken dog's dream? Or, a character in a computer game, far far away? Perhaps this civilisation and universe as we know them are simply the microorganisms living within a larger organism and alternate universe, which, in turn, is within another larger version, and so on, endlessly, to infinity? I mean, how can you trust your mere senses? It's ludicrous."

Another slight pause as he scanned the room once more, this time locking eyes with Sheena, who smiled and nodded her acknowledgement back at him. He continued, this time, seeming to have changed his focal point in the hall. Now it appeared he was talking directly for her benefit. Or was she imagining this?

"We discussed coupling the mind to the body a few weeks back, and about how some believe there is a dual reality in existence: that we are conscious beings living out our human experience through a material body plugged into the matrix. What do *you* think about this?"

Oh shit. Was he actually asking her? In a lecture? His question turned out to be rhetorical thought, as he then continued.

"What *do* you think, everyone? Can you even explain what you do *when* you think? Whose thoughts are they anyway? Where do *they* come from?"

Sheena felt mesmerised. She had missed his lecture the week before due to another café staff crisis (again? It was becoming something of a regular thing now. Oh well, she needed the money, she kept reminding herself), and she hadn't wanted to miss this lecture too, despite the days having been altered and Mr Goodwood changing it from their usual Wednesday to a Friday due to personal reasons (personal reasons? She hoped he was ok?). She was very glad she had made it. There she was: feeling vaguely mesmerised. His voice and his body language and gestures seemed wholly directed at Sheena and Sheena only. Or was this just her wishful thinking and vivid imagination? It could, she thought, have something to do with the fact that she was maybe the only one, or one of small number of students, who *wasn't* currently fiddling with or playing with their smartphones covertly, or in an attempt to be covert, thus keeping said phone down next to their hips or in their laps. Something like mild annoyance surfaced in Sheena and she felt the usually well hidden chasm between her and her fellow, more youthful students. How inconsiderate and rude of them, she thought to herself, but it didn't stop from being fixed in position and hearing Mr Goodwood's words, ('I mean *Brendan's*) word for word as if they were written for her.

Where do my thoughts come from? She wondered. Who is the person speaking in them? If we create our reality via our thought processes, then why can't I stop thoughts of Peter from resurfacing all the time? Did I *create* his drinking problem? Did I *want* the divorce to eventuate?

Now whilst logically, she knew deep down that no one else was really responsible for causing a person's drinking problem, she did still wonder. Certainly on the occasions when Peter *would* admit to having a problem, she was accused of being the reason behind it in the first place, as he'd directly tell her:

> "Of course I have a drinking problem. It's the only way I cope with living with you."

And not so directly, where apparently anything she said or did on a particular day would inevitably lead him to drink, mostly in secret, of course. Things had seemed to escalate about five or six years before she'd miraculously woken up and gotten out of that stagnant, painful life, when she had come across a stash of hidden empties (mainly vodka bottles) in his rarely used golf bag, when she was tidying up the garage one day. Shocked, she had taken the off chance that there may be more around the place and opened up a few other containers and possible 'hidey-holes' in the garage, where conveniently enough, Peter would often be pottering about, apparently sipping from just the one beer can. Horrified, she had found empty vodka bottle after empty bottle. Hundreds of the things. What was going on? She'd wondered wildly, at the time, but had a sinking feeling of dread. She *knew* really. Had known for a long time, and the bottles had just confirmed it. She'd felt sick to her stomach, and sure enough, when she'd confronted him, he'd shrugged and laughed it off, telling her he was just messy and that the bottles had been there for *years* and he just hadn't gotten round to chucking them away, or (and she loved this next one) that how did she know they were even *his*? They could be hers??

Since that fateful afternoon Peter and his definite drinking problem were *always* on her mind, occupying her daily thoughts and taking up her ample free time. So, she now mused, in that cramped lecture hall while Mr Fricken-Gorgeous-Goodwood's eyes bored into her soul almost, did *she* cause the drinking and subsequent arguments to take place and form due to her thoughts and because of her focusing energy on it all the time? *Was* she the culprit? Maybe he wouldn't have had such a mammoth problem and things wouldn't have turned so hideously sour if she simply had never conjured up all those terrifying thoughts in the first place. Peter *had* been a fan of telling her how exactly how much she'd been provoking him or setting him off: it was usually her face, apparently. So, she wondered if she had inadvertently caused it *all*.

Eventually Sheena had developed the unwanted skill of being able to tell immediately whenever he had had his first drink of the day, regardless of the hour. It was hard to describe, but Sheena would recognise a sort of very slight puffing up of his face, a sort of slight *gurning* look about him, with 'that' look in his eyes and general defensiveness and anger resonating from him. Let alone the smell, which would give him away too, yet he would usually rebuke any accusation of early morning drinking with tales of how that was just fumes coming out of his pores from the previous night.

But *had* she created it all? By thinking and worrying herself sick about it, had she inadvertently caused it to *become* a reality? Careful what you dream of then, no matter how terrifying or negative. Once midweek's hump day or the weekend rolled around, Sheena would routinely physically tense up and feel sick with dread, envisaging and imagining what would no doubt unfold (based on many, many episodes previously) and then, low and behold: the same pattern would emerge and history repeated itself pretty much every week or half a week.

"You fucking nasty piece of work!"

Had she made that happen?

"You fucking cunt dog arsehole."

Did she create this one, too?

"You're a fucking psychopath, you need to see a doctor."

Had she inadvertently created this line too? It was one of his favourites, especially useful to him after she would try and tell him to go and get some professional help and to see a doctor.

Why would she have wished *that* upon herself, even subliminally or subconsciously or however it may have come about. But then, she supposed, like a vicious circle, perhaps her tension and anxiety (palpable as it must have been) every Friday morning and early afternoon or before any party or social event they were both attending, may have, in fact, been the catalyst for yet another binge drinking, verbally abusive episode, rather than having been a result of the last time only a few days earlier. It was a tricky one, much like the old conundrum of whether the egg or the chicken came first. Which came first: *her* tension and angst and hurt over the night before's abuse that then led to him drinking in retaliation, *or* his drinking and abuse which then led to Sheena's subsequent upset on that night and the next few days.

If she did in fact *cause* his drinking problem by focusing on it and attempting to diffuse or curb it, then surely it stood to reason that she could visualise it going away and getting fixed. However, this was obviously not the case, and there she was, almost two years later, *still* wondering as to the whys and hows and what actually went wrong in the first place, no matter how much she thought she was 'over it' and had moved on: independent, both emotionally and financially (at long last).

Sheena noticed Brendan's smile had gone, and although he continued with his speech, yes, still looking directly at her it seemed, he was now frowning and looking concerned. She realised his frown was matching that of her own as she was temporarily lost in her sombre thoughts, and she quickly fought hard to reorganise said thoughts, and *stop* her downward descent into those very pointless and depressing memories. Forcibly relaxing her frowning forehead muscles, she managed to allow a genuine smile to reappear as she realised that his look must have actually been one of concern, directed at her, and she flashed him her gentle reassuring smile along with a subtle nod of thanks.

'What a great teacher,' She marvelled, although most of her lecture hall peers were still otherwise occupied. 'Oh well, I don't mind a bit of one-on-one attention!' she thought cheekily. A sudden longing deep within her reminded her of her various recent fantasies featuring Mr Goodwood and being precisely that: one-on-one performances mostly, and sometimes even two-on-one scenes when she revisited her all too easy to conjure up fantasy of Mr Goodwood (sorry, '*Brendan*') and his identikit (for the most part) brother. Mmm, that had been a particularly spectacular long, hot bath for Sheena.

A low vibration halted her more welcome thoughts re: her sexy teacher. What was it he sometimes ended his class with? Oh yeah: 'the truth vibrates in harmony'. She was quietly pleased with herself for having a go at being 'star pupil', and this course (and the excellent grades she had gotten back already) were a huge confidence boost. After all, she had been out of this education and academic game for a very long time now.

Being her turn to oh-so-subtlety reach for her own phone now, she, as covertly as she could, checked to see what the message was that had caused the phone to buzz.

'Sheena, Stunner-Sheena, you will call in sick tonight to the café and will come out with me and my friends – that is an order!

Your loving housemate, Gabs xx'

Sheena bit her lower lip nervously, wishing for the thousandth time that she didn't have to lie to Gabby about her whereabouts. Sometimes on a Friday she had an essay to finish by a deadline, sometimes she wasn't feeling well, and sometimes she had an emergency shift to cover at Café Noir. For someone whose main philosophy in life is being honest and not hurting anyone, she had found it surprisingly easy to come up with a host of reasons why she was *always* unavailable on a Friday night. She thought wistfully of her gorgeous, vivacious housemate Gabby and of her equally bubbly friends who she would be out with tonight: all girls, of course (Sheena sometimes wondered exactly *what* had happened in Gabby's past or with her ex to make her so completely, vehemently anti-men, but then, she supposed, everyone had their own secrets and baggage and stories to tell). It *would* be a laugh and a nice change to actually go out and have some fun on a Friday night, instead of her usual couple of hours acting out another person's life. For a moment, she was considering following Gabby's order and not getting the ruby-red lipstick out after all, but then remembered  that on that particular evening she was part of a 'duo' booking: her least favourite part of the job, but the one that earned her the most money, unsurprisingly. Duo bookings were usually for a pair of men coming in together and wanting that 'group' experience or sometimes were just the one man wanting to pay extra for the luxurious experience of two women at once, who the majority of these bookings were. They were always booked in advance and they charged them three times the usual hourly rate. The basic outline for such an appointment was this: she and another girl take paying customer into the room, sit him down, dance for him, lapdances, touching each other, lesbi-chic style, then they may start going down on each other or whipping the strap-on out to use on each other, before going down on the customer and giving *him* a double-heady. He would usually finish off the proceedings by banging each of them in turn.

Sheena often mused that it should be an easier booking, right? As they were sharing the workload. But no, guys, when booking their 'duo' services expected more: expected a prolonged, imaginative (tiring) performance, and they were more than happy to pay extras for more extras along the way too. However, this wasn't the reason why she disliked these appointments: they were Sheena's least favourite activity at Secrets because somehow, when she had to act with another woman, *another* actress, in the room, she felt exposed and like she'd surely be picked as a fraud. It was nothing against the other women she worked with, but she'd rather not see their face, and every other inch of their bodies, in such close proximity. It somehow made this secret, occasional part-time income supplement, more *real* and much more degrading and raw for her.

It would then, she mused, be *so* nice to cancel her shift for that night, duo booking and all. However, her partner in crime for the wealthy 'gentleman' was April (Sheena thinks that that *is* in fact her real name too) and hence Sheena felt her spirits lift slightly: with April it wouldn't be too bad. She didn't want to let her down at short notice either. Now her mind, while she was still aiming to look attentive throughout Mr Goodwood's last portion of his lecture, took her back to her first meeting with April:

She had been rushing around Café Noir on a routinely busy Tuesday evening. April had been sitting in the far corner booth and when Sheena approached her with her coffee, their eyes met. Sheena couldn't help but notice this woman's glossy, perfectly styled, long, straight, black hair, her freshly manicured French polished nails, and her cherry pink, shiny lips, as she smiled warmly up at her. They had got chatting despite the busy café being filled with thirsty and hungry patrons, and

Sheena immediately felt like they would be great friends. They just seemed to click. Reluctantly she had left her new friend's table to get back to help with the rest of the café.

When April had gotten up to leave, she came and found Sheena as she was clearing up another table and placed her perfectly manicured, smooth, soft hand on Sheena' forearm, gently enveloping her in a mist of her sweet perfume, as she looked intently at her. She'd told her how lovely it was to meet her and that she had a great opportunity for her that she may be interested in. She gave her a simply printed business card featuring just her name and number, and urged Sheena to call her, that she *had* to see her again. She'd mentioned something about how she could tell Sheena had an open mind and then she'd flashed another winning, warm, wide smile at her being rushing off. "Call me, Sheena, darling!" were her departing words.

Sheena, still being fairly new in town, with only a handful of acquaintances and friends to call her own (mainly the café staff, a few students, and of course, her new house-mate, Gabby) had, of course, called April, intrigued by her mysterious 'opportunity', but also just wanting to chat with her and see her again.

They had met in Benni's: a café by day, nightclub/bar by night, and gotten a table for two, where they shared a chilled bottle of sauvignon blanc. April explained, matter-of-factly, her job and what Sheena could do, if she was up for it. She explained the perks of: the minimal working hours each week, the high security and safety factor they all experienced at Secrets (and the exclusivity of the club, meaning that they only employed the more beautiful women, for their premium clients: i.e. rich businessmen and wealthy bachelors, thus keeping prices suitably high too, and resulting in weekly, regular bookings), and a pretty impressive (extra) income for whoever worked there. She basically sold it as this: low risk, high earning, supplement to your current lifestyle. She assured her that it would pay considerably more in just a couple of hours of her time, than a whole week or more of her shifts at Café Noir.

She was so business-like and down to earth about the whole proposition, but Sheena was still understandably a little (ok, a *lot*) taken aback and shocked. She'd wondered why April had singled her out? 'Why *me*?' She wondered. 'Do I look skint, perhaps?'

Again, there was her beautiful, knowing smile as April then echoed her own earlier thoughts:

"I don't know, I felt we just clicked straight away, and that we could be great friends. I'm guessing that you're not working in that café for shits and giggles and that the extra money would come in handy." Sheena had nodded along. "Plus, you seemed, I don't know: *curious*."

She leaned forward and gently stroked Sheena's soft, pale cheek.

"Not to state the obvious either," She continued. "But you are fucking gorgeous, Sheena. You really are."

Sheena had smiled uncertainly back at her new friend, and had wondered how in the world had her life changed so dramatically in such a short space of time. April had made some very valid, good points about the 'job' (which would really only be a few extra hours of work a week – "how we keep our exclusivity and premium nature," April explained) and she was right. Sheena *did* need the money (again: thanks, alcoholic ex-husband!).

She agreed to go with April and just 'have a look' at where she worked. No promises, just to get a better idea. There had been no pressure from April, nor the bosses at Secrets (unless April *was* the real boss? Sheena couldn't tell. It was all very, well, *secret*, about who was actually running the joint) and Sheena had spun herself out a lot with the reality of hearing herself telling them, "why not?!" and she said she'd give it a go. After all, you never knew where your life was headed and she could at least *try* it and see how she went, thinking of the money and how she desperately needed to just get back on top again (having not long signed her year-long lease and being well into her first few weeks both at uni and at Café Noir when she'd been informed about *her* portion of the debt). Meeting April came at just right time, and April, sensing a lot of nervousness on Sheena's part, even though she'd said she'd like to try it, told her confidently:

"Remember: this doesn't define who you *are*. This is just a
temporary means to an end."

April had made it sound so easy and the obvious choice and solution to any financial difficulty. So Sheena had gone with it. April took her 'under her wing', so to speak, and showed her the ropes and the ins and the outs of what she'd be doing. She didn't sugar coat anything or use vague terms but told Sheena *exactly* what she should do and what to expect. Sheena thought of her as somewhat of a sexy, confident, independent mentor (and friend too) and found her direct, open nature about the job very reassuring. She must have only been twenty-five, tops, but Sheena felt she was wise beyond her years.

'How do all these young women get to be so damn confident and self-assured?' She'd thought, slightly enviously, thinking of her equally wise and confident housemate. Sheena certainly wasn't when she was their age. In fact, April reminded her of Gabby, albeit a raunchier, flirtier, seductress version. She didn't know what she'd done to deserve these two very wise, beautiful, loving women to come into her life, but she was infinitely glad that they had, and at just the right time too. She, quite honestly, didn't know what she'd do without either of them. She knew that they would both surely get on with each other too, if only they could meet.

'Or would they?' She asked herself. Again, she immediately thought that Gabby, no matter how non-judgemental and wise she appeared to be, would have a very hard time understanding their part-time work, and she just didn't want to go 'there' with her, not just yet anyway.

Sighing and wishing that she didn't have to let Gabby down on that particular evening, she responded to her text message, apologising profusely for not being able to join them.

"Next time!"

She promised, lamely. She hoped there *would* be a next time. A mid-week or Sunday 'next-time' would be perfect.

Putting her phone hastily back in her pocket, she now focused on trying to focus once more on what Mr Goodwood was saying. Oh good, he was apparently back to relating everything in life to sex.

'How appropriate.' She mused.

# CHAPTER EIGHT

Well, that had gone better than she'd anticipated. Sheena was sitting on the lime-green, 'vintage', old sofa in their shared, cosy living room, a mug of tea in hand and a contemplative, slightly tired, but happy look on her face. Dressed in a pair of old, black tracky-daks and an ivory, lace camisole, bra-free and very much relaxed, she was savouring this late Saturday morning peace and quiet before she'd have to get focused and motivated and crack on with the humdrum activities of laundry and cleaning up the flat a bit. Interspersed with some online banking (yuck) and the requisite studying she felt she had to get done over the weekend.

The duo appointment the night before had gone on later than she'd anticipated, resulting in a nice, fat payment of cash that was now securely in Sheena's handbag, along with some slight soreness and stiffness. Hazard of the job sometimes. A self-conscious smile made its way onto her pretty, swollen-from-too-much-kissing mouth, as the events of the night before came back to her.

April and the client had already been inside the room when 'Ruby' arrived. She'd lightly rapped on the door before slipping quietly inside. April, her signature long, straight, super-shiny, raven-black hair cascading down her back and around her shoulders, was sitting on the lap of their client, her beautifully manicured fingernails playing casually with his expensive looking purple and blue striped tie. The client, Sheena decided, looked like a 'Justin' or a 'Richard', or perhaps, even a 'Drew': yes, 'Drew' would do nicely.

Drew was sitting there, his custom-tailored slate coloured suit still on, and open at the front, as he was casually sprawled with his legs apart, supporting April on one of his strong, muscular-looking legs. His face told Sheena that he was in his mid-forties, and the expertly closeness of his shaved skin, together with the subtle but obviously-expensive aftershave fragrance, told Sheena that he was clearly wealthy. Well, wealthy enough to be spending at least a couple of thousand dollars on his Friday night there. His calmness and confidence told her that perhaps he had done this many times before and was no stranger to working girls. He was calm, self-assured, and was clearly in no hurry to get things started: he sat there motionless, his eyes fixated on April's impressive cleavage, currently pushed up to its maximum height, thanks to the deep red basque she had on, that perfectly matched her red g-string and suspender belt. Sheer, hardly-there, stockings completed her outfit.

At 'Ruby's' entrance April looked over to her and flashed her a wide, lascivious grin, raising her eyebrows at her in a 'well, whaddaya think?' manner. April stood, her magnificent, extremely large, out of proportion, breasts leading the way, and went over to where Ruby was standing, in her own red and black costume, almost identical to April's, yet with nowhere near the amount of full cleavage April was sporting. 'Ruby' sucked in her own breath and also found it hard not to stare at April's breasts. They never failed to amaze and astound her. Sheena was more than happy when it came to her own generously sized, full breasts (not too big and not too small: *just* right…) however, April's tits were incredible. Before meeting April, she'd have assumed that to have a bust that size it'd *have* to be as a result of surgery, surely, but no; April was her red-hot, living proof of the beauty and wonder of nature. As, here stood a woman, all of five feet four inches, with an athletic, petite, toned body, including a tiny, tight, round arse and the smallest, flattest waist Sheena had ever seen, and then these gigantic, full, magnificent, majestic breasts coming out of nowhere, making her very much top-heavy and quite mesmerising to look at, let alone to be able to play with and fondle them, as Sheena was imagining she was not far off from doing as part of their 'act' for tonight.

"David," April told the solemn, silent client. ('Ahh, so he's a *David* Sheena thought. 'Close enough.) "This is my little sister, Ruby. She'll be joining us for the evening."

So that's how they'd be playing it tonight. 'Ruby' smiled mischievously back at her 'older sister' April, quickly getting into character. Sometimes they would be sisters, sometimes there would be a cheating husband caught out by his 'wife' coming back early, and sometimes they would simply *be*. It all depended on who she was performing the duo appointment with and whether the client had any special requests. Sheena wondered if David had asked for a pair of sisters or if April was simply improvising.

April snaked a hand around Ruby's slim waist and pulled her close for an extended embrace, kissing her cheek in an exaggerated fashion as she did so.

"I love her *sooo* much," She continued. "Don't you think she's pretty?"

She started to gently stroke Ruby's face.

David, still silent, picked up his drink and took a slow sip on it, just watching them.

Ruby responded to April by running her fingers lightly up and down

April's slender, smooth arms, and attempted a butter-wouldn't-melt look on her made-up, pretty face. They made their way over to where David sat and took a seat on each of his still open, outstretched legs, now mere centimetres from his face. April cupped Ruby's delicate chin and brought her closer to her, where she gently pressed her moist, warm lips to hers, eyes closed now. Ruby again responded, shutting her eyes and returning April's soft, sensuous kiss. This lingering, gentle kiss gradually became a deep, passionate one as April slowly pushed her tongue into Ruby's ruby-red mouth, massaging her own hesitant tongue there. Ruby's hands had found April's waist and were firmly grasped around her tiny, flat stomach, whilst April had moved her hand from Ruby's face, to travel slowly down her neck and collarbone area and was now idly playing around the top of her basque, teasing her with a light grope of her breasts every now and then, and stroking one of her nipples hard to attention under the lace and satin material. April's other hand had been casually resting on Ruby's black-stockinged knee, but it now began traipsing slowly up to her inner thigh; slowly creeping up her leg to the top of her stocking, where she began to rub her soft, smooth, bare skin of her upper inner thigh in wide, slow, deliberate circles, all the while penetrating her mouth deeply with her tongue.

David made no move and sat there, silently watching their close-up performance taking place on his lap. With every slow, teasing stroke and rub of Ruby's thigh, April would now tentatively, yet deliberately, brush her thumb, as if accidentally, over the tiny patch of red lacy g-string material barely covering Ruby's pussy, causing Ruby to stifle an early and genuine moan and lean further into the touch and deeper into the kiss. Sheena was actually extremely turned on. This was starting to be not just an act for her tonight, but she had no idea if April was feeling the same way, or if she was just a very good actress. She was a professional, after all, and very good at her job. It was times like these, when she was being kissed so deeply and passionate whilst having her clit lightly stroked and teased, along with her thigh and tops of her breasts by April, that Sheena wondered if she could, perhaps, be gay? Then the memory of just how much she also enjoyed being pummelled and pounded by a very manly man came thundering back to her and she quickly discarded her lesbian theory. Perhaps she was bisexual then? Or perhaps it was just the way *April* touched her. Whatever the reason, she was more than happy for her own arousal that evening. It meant less acting and an easier evening all round.

They had moved back to standing after *finally* being prompted by David, who had tugged one finger gently on each of their basques while shooting them a raised eyebrow each, gesturing that perhaps it was time to take them off. Ruby went to April first, reaching around her to unclip the many metal fastenings and freeing her magnificent, jubilant breasts at last, which spilled free from the basque. Ruby chucked it to one side and took both of April's breasts in her small hands, or as best she could, considering their size. She began to lower her lips to them, hungrily kissing and alternately sucking them while April stroked the back of Ruby's glossy, chocolate waves and pushed her face even closer to the tits she was hungrily devouring, bent over at the waist, her own arse and pussy, covered only by the flimsy strip of her g-string, pointing towards David's watchful eyes, mere inches away.

"Your turn."

April whispered and pulled Ruby up to a standing position once more, where she slowly, clasp by clasp, removed Ruby's own basque, letting it drop to the floor where they both stood. Ignoring her beautiful, round, swinging-free breasts, April went straight to Ruby's neck instead, sucking hard as her hands found their way down and into Ruby's g-string. Ruby and Sheena moaned loudly. Again, no acting. April would, surely, have been able to tell how turned on she was, and she then outed her to their voyeur:

"David, she's *so* wet and hot."

This was no exaggeration or lie.

David seemed content to continue to simply watch them for the time being, his half-full drink still in one hand as his other handed rested lightly on his own upper, inner thigh and the impressively large bulge that had formed underneath his trouser leg, so April manoeuvred Ruby over to the bed directly in front of where he sat on that sturdy leather chair. April sat her down, facing her towards David, and continued her very welcome simultaneous assault on Ruby's neck and down her still-on g-string. This wasn't their usual routine, Sheena noted vaguely, as she closed her eyes and arched her back and breasts towards April and threw her head back, her chocolate waves cascading around her shoulders and back as she did so. They hadn't even danced together for him yet, yet had gone first into this fondling/kissing scenario. Not that Sheena or Ruby were complaining. Perhaps April had just wanted to mix things up a bit, and David remained in place, still apparently fine for them to take as long as they liked without him, his only movement being the rise and fall of his tumbler of bourbon to his lips and back down, and the slight shift of his other hand (blink and you'd miss it) carefully and subtlety rubbing his cock through his trousers. Fine by both women there, as they knew that the longer they could see out this appointment, the more rewarding, financially at least, it would be for them. An added bonus then, Sheena thought, that this was so far, extremely rewarding for her, and not just from a money point of view. As April continued to play with Sheena's hot, wet pussy, gently rubbing her index finger in slow, delicious circles against Sheena's now swollen, aching clit, while her mouth sucked hard and hungrily upon her available neck, Sheena wondered briefly why she was going to all this extra special trouble. Was this just for show? To make David's appointment last that little bit longer? Or was this a 'thank-you' for Sheena having joined her on this duo booking? April was well aware that Sheena was less than enamoured with group bookings. However, she felt her confidence was building up somewhat in this regard.

Or, was April into this too? Sheena wondered. As much as she felt like she'd always known April and that they 'clicked' as friends, most of the time she conversely got the impression that she knew nothing about her really. Other than her name, and she wasn't even 100% sure on that one either. A dark horse, an enigma, was April: mysterious and beautiful. But then, she supposed, the same could be said about herself. April's mouth had left Sheena's neck now and was making its way down her chest in a flurry of small, hard kisses, eventually coming to rest on her left breast, where she slowly, tantalisingly circled her erect nipple with her wet tongue, all the while looking up directly into Sheena's now open eyes, a cheeky glint in her own eyes. Again, David made no further move other than to bring his glass back up to his lips and take a sip. ('Wow, he *really* likes to watch. Or spend his money. Or both.' Sheena debated.) Sheena unwittingly held her breath as she felt and saw April now making her way further and further down past her breasts and down along her own taut stomach, to the seam of her g-string, where her other hand still lay within, still gently stroking her wetness. Using this hand, April simply pulled the material to one side, and Sheena felt the sudden rush of cooler air on her wet, throbbing, red, now-exposed pussy and she instinctively pushed herself closer to April's waiting face, a dirty smirk now in place as April took one last glance up to Ruby's dilated, dish-plate eyes. April bit her own bottom lip in anticipation and to drag out this moment of suspense, before she licked her lips, rewetting them, before lowering her mouth directly onto Ruby's swollen, smooth, shining, hot clit and sucking gently here, causing 'Ruby' and Sheena to moan loudly in unison.

Sheena smiled warmly at the memory of this particular early moment of the evening, taking another sip of her tea at her kitchen table. She'd marvelled at just how fucking *good* April had made her feel. Just how did she get so good at doing that? Sheena wondered. Now, Sheena had been given head before, of course, but her ex's hesitant, brief attempts, where Sheena would before too long, hastily drag his head back up to hers, leaving both of them relieved that the rare action was stopped, was *nothing* like this. She felt like she had just learnt a new language overnight, or as if she'd finally worked out one of life's great mysteries. So *that's* what it's all about, she smiled to herself.

The rest of the appointment, after their excellent start, had been much as she'd expected, once David had decided to join them both, and they had got a condom on him and got back in the swing of their usual performance. But the memory and the after-glow of that initial headjob, well, Sheena kept it firmly in her thoughts that evening (it was hard *not* to) and now, here she was, still smiling and giddy with the feeling some half a day later.

Life was so strange. One minute Sheena was lying back on a firm, satin-enshrouded mattress, April's full, voluptuous breasts spilling into and over her face as she ground her pussy against her own and their client for the evening took turns and alternately fucked one and then the other from the end of the bed as they lay in place, sandwiched together, April pinning Ruby down mercilessly; and the next, she was sitting, demurely as a nun, make-up free and super casually dressed in her comfy tracky-daks and vest-top, lounging at the cheery, homely kitchen table sipping tea. Life could be so dichotomous and surprising. At least, *hers* was at the moment. It made her wonder: did everyone have a secret 'other' life or activity or job or persona, only known to themselves? She surely couldn't be the only one. However, she couldn't quite picture the glamourous and mysterious April lounging around in track-pants and braless on a Saturday morning.

"You look like you had a good night! Something I should know about? You got a secret lover working at the café with you?"

Gabby interrupted her thoughts and caused a guilty, blush to spread across her smiling face.

"Haha." Sheena replied. "I wish. Nope. Just enjoying this fine Saturday morning and loving the peace."

She smiled up at Gabby's inquisitive, round, cherub-like face. They exchanged a look of understanding. Gabby knew what Sheena was referring to when she mentioned 'peace', knowing that this was in stark contrast and comparison with her very non-peaceful past life of her marriage and subsequent marriage break-down. She squeezed her shoulder in encouragement and reassurance.

"There's tea in the pot." Sheena told her, gesturing to the table in front of her. "You look like you could do with one too – good night last night, Gabs?"

Now it was Gabby's turn to blush.

"Yes, it was great! But nothing like that, I mean." She hastily added. "Yeah, it was *so* much fun! Wish you could have joined us. Loads of dancing and shooters. Well, I know you probably wouldn't have been keen for the shots, but the dancing was tops. *Just* what I needed."

She poured a cup of the strong, black tea from the pot in the middle of the kitchen table, and sat down on one of the creaky, bright yellow, cracked-painted chairs next to Sheena.

"Of course, there were the usual creeps out and about on the dancefloor though." Gabby frowned. "I mean, what the hell – can't a girl just dance with her friends and have a good time without being subjected to the filthy, roaming hands of these filthy pervs?! Fuck me, they're all the same, pervs, the lot of them!"

Now, Sheena, knew this *not* to be true, but far be it to point that out to Gabby this morning, seeing her friend's need to get her daily anti-men rant out her system. For the millionth time, Sheena wondered what had happened in her past, to warp Gabby's view of all men on the planet. She supposed that, in good time, Gabby would confide in her. All she had ascertained so far, by reading through the lines, was that Gabby's ex, of many many moons ago, had played up on her whilst out on a boys' night or on holiday or something, but she was yet to get to know the gory, finer, potent and painful details.

As she listened to Gabby go on about the slimy, creepy, 'pervy' advances made by the menfolk of Fremantle the night before and her subsequent claims that they were 'all the same', her mind started wandering and looking for examples of upstanding men who were clearly *not* like that and who didn't fit Gabby's scathing description: who were genuinely *good* men; good, loving people who didn't just think with their dicks, but who were interesting and humourous as well as having the added benefit of being manly and attractive. She knew that they *did* exist, despite Gabby's rant to suggest otherwise, and Sheena's mind came to rest upon an image of Mr Goodwood, '*Brendan*', chatting lovingly with his brother Scott. Now that was a great example of a good, honest man, Sheena thought, her face lighting up again at the thought of her interesting, and yes, very sexy, teacher, as she continued to nod sympathetically along to Gabby's liturgy. She wouldn't have put him in Gabby's harsh category of 'being just a man: they all think with their dick only', however she knew, that really, his own view on the world was that *everyone* thought with their respective genitals (if it's *all* about sex), so where did that leave him?

She would *love* to pick his brain about this and really just talk with him further. She'd found his classes so interesting so far. Wednesday afternoon couldn't roll around soon enough.

# CHAPTER NINE

Brendan stretched his arms casually above his head and just lay there. For how long, he wasn't sure. His view was his faded, off-white, slightly cracked painted ceiling in his bedroom, and he was alone. He hadn't a clue what the time was, nor did he have any pressing appointment or anywhere in the world he had to be in particular. God, he loved Sundays. Rolling over onto his stomach now, he slowly arched his back upwards in a semi-cobra-yoga-esque pose, and fully took his time to assess himself and his surroundings, and that, yes, he probably *was* fully awake now, as amazing as his long, lazy lie-in had been. He now glanced at his bedside clock which flashed cheerily back at him: 12:36.

'Fucken hell!' He marvelled. 'That was some sleep! Must have needed it.'

Ever so slowly rolling back over and onto his back, he pushed himself up to a seated sprawl now. He reached for the glass of water he'd cleverly remembered to leave there the night before, taking a few big, urgent gulps as he assessed the damage. 'Hmm, not too bad.'

He thought he would have been more hungover than he was currently feeling, but strangely enough, he felt fine. Yesterday had been his meant-to-be-weekly-but-usually-ends-up-being-every-three-or-four-weeks squash game with his old school mates Damien, Chris and Anthony. The usual agreed-on schedule for the evening was: play a game or two of squash then retreat to the clubhouse bar for refreshments, and continue the refreshments for quite some time, usually changing venues to another establishment at some stage in the night, and often ending with legendary late-night recovery kebabs. Yesterday was no different.

They had started at the clubhouse, fresh from their après-squash showers, and exorbitantly happy to see each other. It had been some *five* weeks since their last get together, the postponing force majeure due to various family and marital commitments from his three friends, a source of constant ribbing from him, but he didn't mind really. Just meant that when they did eventually grab their squash rackets and meet for a fair few sips together that the three married men would be even more keen to let off some steam. Of course, Brendan would usually be subjected to their venting and ranting about their other halves, and thus when there would be the usual backslap from Damien and accompanying:

"Take my advice mate, never get married. Stay single, you lucky, lucky bastard", Brendan would have no choice but to silently agree with him.

Despite their marital disharmony and obvious stress, all three mates would, without fail, pick apart Brendan's love-life, or lack of it, and would good-naturedly have the gall to rib *him* about when was *he* going to find a girlfriend and 'settle down'.

"Hold on," He'd challenge, although everyone would be about five or six drinks in by then. "Don't you see the irony of this? Married men driven from their homes by stress and arguments to their happily single friend whom they implore that he find a life partner too? What, you want me to be as miserable as you three sadsacks then?"

Smiling wryly around the table. It was all just in jest however. All three knew how very happily single Brendan was, and when it got to the subject of his latest conquests, well, he felt happy to share. After all, so what if they were living vicariously through him and his bachelorhood? A friend in need and all that…

"You lucky, lucky bastard."

Damien had repeated, when Brendan had finished detailing his encounter just the night before, when a charming, young lady named Kelly had stopped by to pick his brains.

Now, relaxing the next morning, Brendan thought the night last night ended in their usual, standard fashion: they'd acquired their kebabs from their favourite kebab and fried chicken shop en route to the taxi stand, then stood in the ridiculously long taxi throng for about fifteen minutes before all deciding to go their separate ways and walk home, possibly sobering up a bit on the way, as an added benefit for the three that had maybe mildly concerned (or, waiting up) wives at home. Brendan didn't actually recall going to bed nor was he sure of the time, but there he was on that lazy early Sunday afternoon, lying on said bed and thinking.

His first thought, after realising the relatively late time of day and congratulating himself on a rare (for him) lie-in, was that of coffee. Keeping the lazy-casual-slow Sunday theme going strong, he ever so slowly got out of bed and sauntered down to his kitchen to put the kettle on.

'Damn. Out of coffee.' He was mildly dismayed. Tea or plain water just wouldn't cut it. He'd have to go and get some, *or*, go out for a pricier, but much better, stronger and more effective coffee. He chose the latter.

Jumping in the shower now with a new sense of purpose, he let the hot stream flow over him as he briskly scrubbed the stale beer smell from his pores. Feeling, and smelling, 100% better, a short while later, he was strolling out of his front door, jangling his keys, as he hummed a tune to himself.

'God, I love Sundays.' He thought again to himself. Everything seemed so full of possibility and optimism. It helped that his hangover was yet to appear ('am I still drunk, perhaps?' he wondered) and that the day was a particularly beautiful one: a quiet, sunny, fragrant, Spring-verging-on-Summer day, not a cloud in the vast blue Western Australian sky.

As he strolled along the street happily, he thought to himself, 'Life *is* good.' He was in a very good place right now: good friends, good job, good health, good and frequent sex, good environment and town where he lived. Everything seemed, well, pretty damn *good*. Why try to change that? His friends' goading and advice came back to him now, about how he should find someone to settle down with. They were just jealous, surely? Plus, it wasn't like there was any one woman who he wanted to settle down with, let alone *marry*. They were all just flirty, young students having fun. And so was *he* (minus the student part). He rarely wanted to see them again or more than once or twice anyway, so what did that tell him?

A sudden, brief image of his student *Sheena* flashed into his mind, momentarily silencing his defensive thoughts. Her hazel, liquid gold eyes in her perfect, pale, ivory face framed by those flowing, shiny, chocolate waves, had an interesting effect on him.

'Now, *Sheena*, I would like to see again.'

He realised that his path to a café to buy a 'proper' coffee had led him directly to Café Noir, the café he went to a few weeks back with Scott.

'Yes,' He concurred. 'I really would like to see *her* again. Let's hope she's there.'

So, come on, subconscious, he'd lightly scorned himself, was this your intention all along? Casually drop by the café where she works, under the guise of 'I need a coffee and I can get this pile of marking done too', and just, run into her again? Good one! He rolled his eyes at his very obvious and completely unoriginal idea.

'Oh well, you're here now.' He wrapped up his internal debate. 'Might as well go inside!'

He threw open the door and strolled inside, smiling confidently. He took a seat in the much busier, hustling-bustling café than the one he remembered from a few weeks back, and scanned the room (subtlety, he thought) for his beautiful, brunette student-cum-waitress-cum-mysterious-dark-horse.

Feeling disproportionately disappointed, he realised she was not there. (Perhaps she's taking her lunch break, or is in the storeroom? His hopeful mind suggested.) A bearded young man apathetically took his order.

Getting his second years' essays out that he'd brought with him to mark ('See? I *did* come to work, not just to speak with Sheena', he thought smugly.) he sighed and got on with the semi-arduous task of marking them, while he waited for his coffee and simultaneously kept an eye out for any change in staff or reappearance of a waitress from the back room.

No such luck, however, and some fifty minutes later, Brendan called it a day. Well, he'd marked over half of the essays safe within his leather satchel, and the dregs of his coffee had grown cold over twenty minutes ago. Time to go. A sense of resignation and disappointment filled Brendan, threatening to ruin his otherwise relaxed and cruisy, happy Sunday. Shrugging this off as best he could (after all, what had really changed from just an hour or so ago? He didn't have plans to actually *meet* her there, so why was he feeling so, well, gutted?) he got out his phone and tapped out a cheerful:

"Yo, bro! Are you at home? I'm nearby. Gonna call round, is that cool?"

Thinking better of it, he then pressed delete-delete-delete and resumed his peaceful stroll. Preferring the element of surprise, some fifteen minutes later he was pressing the buzzer for Scott's apartment complex.

"Hello?" Came his brother's unsure, loveable voice.

"You got company, or you gonna buzz me in, or what?"

Brendan stuck his tongue out at the door's secret camera and rolled his eyes upwards.

"No, no, you're alright." Scott replied hurriedly. "Buzzing you in now, come on up!"

Brendan had banked on him not being busy, with female company or otherwise. He would have been quite taken aback had Scott had a girl up there, and he told him so as soon as the door slid open and his handsome copy smiled back at him. This inspired Brendan and a stroke of genius came to him. Wasting no time, he informed Scott:

"This can't wait. I have some exciting news. I'm going to get you a new girlfriend!"

Scott gestured him further into the apartment and groaned.

"Not this again, Brendan. Leave it out!"

He protested, but he had that red-faced, embarrassed look about him with sheepish smile, so Brendan took that as a good sign: a sign that he really *did* want his help.

"Come on, Scott. You know I hate to think of you brooding all alone up here, when there are hordes of beautiful, sexy, young things out there, ripe for the picking!"

He settled onto Scott's firm, high-backed, velveteen sofa and gestured that Scott resume his own position.

"Come on, mate. You know you want to. I mean, when's the last time you had a girlfriend?" Brendan pressed, looking knowingly at his twin.

Scott, his face flushing a little deeper, retaliated fairly accurately with:

"I could say the same thing to *you*, bro! Pot calling kettle black much."

Brendan frowned. Ok, fair point. He had him there.

"Yeah, but I'm happily single." He protested now. "I'm fine being the bachelor that I am. No problems there, thank you."

Scott raised his eyebrows at a Brendan with a look of 'well, what about me?'

"Yeah, same same no different." He assured Brendan in a deadpan manner.

There *was* a difference. They both knew it. But Brendan let it slide for the moment. He was sensitive enough to not cross that line *too* much; he knew Scott had issues when talking about sex in general, let alone his *own* sex life.

"Ok, humour me, Big-Bro." Brendan reclined back in the large

111

sofa, placing his hands behind his head. "If you *were* looking for a girlfriend, what would she look like? Tall/short? Big breasts? Long legs? Are you more of an arse man? Blond? Redhead? What??"

Scott sighed, realising that Brendan wasn't giving up. After a short silence, he replied,

"Brunette."

Good! Brendan thought. That's a start.

"Ok, tall, medium or petite?" Brendan shot back at Scott, glad he was playing along.

"I dunno, medium or tall, I suppose."

"Describe her for me." Brendan pushed.

Scott appeared lost in thought for a moment, looking up at the ceiling as he mulled this over.

"Ok, she's got pale skin, she's very pretty, she has long, dark, wavy hair, big but not gigantic breasts, she's thin but has a round bum and lovely hips. That do you, Bro?"

Brendan was impressed. Scott had come a long way in a short space of time. He smiled lovingly at Scott who had now resumed staring at the floor and was blushing. Brendan's smile faltered slightly as he realised that Scott had just described *his* student Sheena. Pretty much down to a T.

"Ahem," He began. "Anyone we know?" He probed.

"I thought this was just hypothetical!" Scot replied. "Anyway, enough about *me*, what does your ideal, fantasy woman look like then?"

Scott was embarrassed and Brendan could tell how uncomfortable he had made him.

"Sorry Bro, yeah yeah, just hypothetical, of course. Umm, my ideal woman?"

Brendan appeared to be thinking hard, and ignoring his first thought that had risen of '*exactly* as you've just said' he went with:

"Oh you know, too many to choose from. I really couldn't narrow it down. I'll take them blond, redhead, brunette, skinny, cuddly, big breasted, small breasted, long hair, shaved... Endless possibilities!"

He assured Scott enthusiastically, but he was finding it hard to shake that image of Sheena, so perfectly described by Scott only moments before. He wondered what she was doing right now. What did her Sunday usually entail, when she wasn't working at the café?

"So, here's what we'll do!" Brendan had another brilliant idea.

"We're going to throw a party, at my place, with a host of lovely, sexy, available chicks, and you'll have your pick of the bunch, promise. It'll be great, lots of booze, beauties and good times guaranteed. What do ya think, Bro? You in?"

Scott frowned, looking unsure.

"I dunno Brendan. It's not really my thing. Especially not as some sort of match-making party!"

"Ok, so we'll call it my almost-end-of-term-pre-Christmas party or something. Don't worry!" He sensed Scott's clear reluctance and discomfort. "Look, Bro, how long have I been working at the uni? And how many of my end-of-year bashes have you been to?!"

They both knew the answer was a big, fat zero. After a moment's silence, Brendan leaned back and relaxed his arms, going in for the kill:

"So, it's settled then! A party it is! Can't wait! Who knows – you might meet your ideal woman there too! There'll be plenty of available, up-for-it brunettes, I promise you that."

He thought protectively and possessively, 'but just *not* Sheena please,' and then frowned at his gut response and reaction. Where had *that* come from? He didn't know Sheena any more than Scott did, but instinctively he felt like she was somehow *his* something. 'Why, Brendan? Because I saw her first? Or because she's my student?' He had no logical, rational answer for himself.

'Oh well.' He resolved. 'Worry about that later, if and when she even *comes* to the party.' The party which was, as yet, all simply a figment of their imagination and yet to be put into practice and into 'reality'. 'I'm getting ahead of myself,' he checked himself.

'Still,' he mused, later that afternoon when he was back in the relative comfort of his cluttered living room-cum-study once more. 'A party is just what the doctor ordered', and as he attempted to finish his essay marking once and for all (nearly there! Just ten or so to go!) with an accompanying full glass of Merlot and the Foo Fighters playing in the background, his mind wandered and he thought about the prospect of the party. He would invite most of his students, that's for sure (especially the females, after all, he had genuinely meant it about finding Scott a new girlfriend) but also some of the other teachers and his mates from outside of work. And Sheena. Sheena would most definitely be getting an invite (along with many others from her class group). He hoped he would be able to catch her after his lecture on Wednesday. She was quite the elusive one, it seemed.

Is that what makes her so mysterious? He wondered, sitting back and sipping his Merlot contemplatively. For yet another time that day, he wondered where Sheena was and what she was doing.

# CHAPTER TEN

'This was a bad idea,' Sheena thought to herself, as she and Gabby approached the steps that led up to the front door. She was feeling extremely nervous. Much more so than she felt before her weekly shifts at Secrets. Which is crazy. She would chide herself. 'If you can do *that*' (that being the two-ish hours per week performing and playing the role of Ruby: premium-priced prostitute) 'then you can surely attend your *teacher's* party, no problem'. She would have thought that she would have had much more trouble adjusting to her second part-time job than she did, and quite honestly, at first, she had presumed that after one or two weeks working there that she would find another lucrative, high-paying, short hours job as an alternative, or that she'd be so horrified with what went on there that she'd just quit anyway. This was not the case for either of those possibilities, and unlike some of the other girls that worked there, Sheena preferred to be absolutely stone cold sober when she went to work. She felt safer and more in control that way. But she was well aware that her colleagues had to routinely get pretty wasted just to be able to go ahead and perform their own routine. Must be their nerves, she decided, and then felt the full brunt of her own nerves now that she was there, on Mr Goodwood's doorstep, following the vivacious, confident Gabby through the crowd and into the packed house-party.

She knew why she was so nervous and it had nothing to do with part-time job. No, no, this was safely pushed to the back of her mind, and she didn't expect to run into any clients there either, although this idea had briefly crossed her mind when Mr Goodwood had asked her last week to join him and his guests for a nearly-the-end-of-term party. He had actually run over to her after their usual Wednesday lecture, calling her name. Startled she had clumsily dropped her full notepad and, blushing, she'd had to quickly drop to the dusty corridor floor to retrieve it.

"Sheena, let me help you." He'd offered.

"It's fine, no worries. I've got it."

She straightened back up and felt her stomach flip-flop as she realised she was staring face-to-face with the object of her recent, explicit fantasies. (It seemed she had developed quite a crush on this mysterious but friendly teacher of hers.)

"Sheena, how're things?"

He asked, not breaking their eye contact for even a second.

"Oh, yes, things are – things are good, thanks."

She could feel herself growing nervous. 'Ridiculous!' She scolded herself. 'He's your teacher, get a grip!'

"Sheena, I'm throwing a party next Saturday, at my place, a sort of nearly-end-of-term/pre-Christmas generic house party. I wondered if you'd care to join us?"

His smile deepened, stretching all the way into his dark, sparkling eyes, as he waited (with baited breath) for her response.

She was slightly taken aback as she wasn't expecting this, and her first thought, after 'oh my gosh – is he asking me out?!' (before she immediately squashed this ridiculous sentiment by reminding herself that a) he was her *teacher* and probably had never looked at her in that light and never would, and b) that she had no intention of getting romantically involved with anyone anytime soon, not after having just come out of a messy marriage break-up, or so it seemed...) was to wonder briefly as to his guests and would there be anyone she may have already *met*, say, in the form of Ruby?! She thought it was probably pretty unlikely given the small amount of men that she did see each week (one or two at most) and so far she was yet to see *any* of them outside of Secrets, despite the small and cosy, neighbourly feel Fremantle had to it. This had actually been one of her key reservations when April was first initiating her and showing her around the club. Sheena had had a sudden awful thought of 'what if I run into people I've *serviced* when I'm out and about, say at the café, or at uni??' She'd asked how April dealt with that, and it turned out, April didn't give one fuck. Her exact words. She'd also said she wasn't ashamed or embarrassed by what she did and saw no reason to hide it.

" 'cept from some straight coppers, of course!" She'd cheerfully added. Sensing Sheena's reluctance and discomfort, she'd clarified for her though: "But don't worry Sheena, you're only going to be working as a casual – you'll have a very small number of clients, and I highly doubt that you'll move in the same circles as them or will run into them outside of your work here. I don't reckon your student friends could afford to go to a place like Secrets! Plus, what are they gonna say: oh hi Love, I remember you – we met when I came and fucked you the week before my wedding! It's not gonna happen mate."

Sheena had added her own weight to the argument by reminding herself that she wouldn't be doing the job for very long anyhow – just a few months until the debt was dead and buried. Then they'd be zero chance of any unwanted reunions, as soon, she'd have no clients whatsoever.

So far, so good, and Sheena struck this mild possibility, of running into a client at her teacher's shindig, from her mind. She was just about to remind herself to put her lips together and *speak*, when, obviously sensing her hesitation, Brendan continued:

"I promise I won't play Morning Train if you say you'll come, pretty please Ms. Sheena?"

She laughed, shaking her brown waves delicately over her shoulders.

"Actually," She confided. "I quite like that song."

'Aha!' he mentally noted this nugget of personal information regarding this quiet, mysterious student of his.

"Well, great then! 8 o'clock next Saturday. There'll be other students there too, a few teachers, and some other friends. Oh, and my brother, of course, you remember him? So, bring a friend or many friends, if you like Sheena: the more the merrier!"

Without giving her the chance to actually deliver a definitive 'yes' or 'no, he mentioned that he had to be somewhere and had scribbled his address down on her notepad's cover before dashing off through the busy crowd in the hallway. She'd watched his departing head leave and realised she was still smiling back at him, still in her spot she was apparently frozen in. She'd felt excited. And happy. And confident. Despite knowing that he's inviting other students and that he doesn't think of her in *that* way, she was still unfathomably giddy and happy over the fact that this handsome man had singled her out and come to find her after his lecture, given how busy he was and all.

But *now*. Now she was actually there, at his party, with Gabby at her side, she felt inexplicably nervous, and she couldn't shake it off. Gabby had picked up on it as they'd neared his front door, of course.

"Look, Sheena, I know big, boozy parties must be hard for you, but just try to loosen up hey! Let your beautiful hair down! So to speak… You'll have fun, I promise."

She'd squeezed her arm affectionately and urged her inside.

Was that it then? Sheena wondered. Was she nervous about the party and all the inebriated people attending it? This certainly could have been a possibility, but then, she did alright at Secrets, where the majority of her clients were usually very much inebriated. She knew her nerves were for a very different reason. But she couldn't tell Gabby that. Gabby, who would no doubt respond to her potentially mentioning that she had feelings for her teacher, would be something along the lines of: 'they're all the same, Sheena! Cheating, lying dogs that fuck anything that moves! Don't do it to yourself again!!' Plus, it was only a crush, she would remind herself. Ridiculous to be this nervous. 'You're a grown woman, Sheena!'

But then, perhaps Gabby *did* have a point. Sheena was well aware that, although her marriage break-up and subsequent divorce was almost two years ago now, that she probably had to re-educate herself when it came to social events and boozy house parties, especially. She suppose nineteen years of habitually keeping one eye open and her peripherals trained on that *one* person, to check he hadn't passed out yet or fallen over or done or said something horrendously offensive or disgusting to someone, or of making excuses about *why* her husband was asleep already, was a hard habit to shake, despite her being 'free' now. She had to constantly remind herself that she was *not* responsible for anyone else's behaviour other than her *own*, and that she *could* have a few drinks and get a little bit tipsy, or even blind drunk, if she chose to.

Gabby must have been reading this portion of her thoughts as she chimed in, loudly now, to make herself heard over the noisy crowd they were being swallowed into:

"You're young, free, and single, Sheena! Have some fun! And if any sleazy dickhead gives you trouble, he'll have me to answer to!" A cheeky glint in her emerald eyes as she delivered this last promise. "I'm going to track down the kitchen to put our wine in the fridge. You mingle, Honey. I'll come and find you!"

Her red hair bounced its way through the throng of other guests.

Sheena noticed a few other students from her class and was waved over to join them. She gingerly made her way through the heaving living room and joined their conversation tentatively, although the music was blaring so loudly, she was mainly nodding along politely and exchanging smiles instead of too many words. The place was packed! Mr Goodwood was clearly very popular. This idea made her smile and she thought warmly of her teacher. He was obviously a very *good* bloke, and clearly much loved and well respected. She felt almost honoured, and yes, still nervous, that he had invited her.

A gentle touch on her elbow alerted her to his quiet presence and she swung around quickly, as he exclaimed:

"You made it! Hi there, Sheena!"

She beamed back at him. God, he was so damn attractive. She was giddy again. Ok, this is definitely some crush I've somehow acquired, she reasoned with herself.

"I'm so glad you came." He continued.

'I bet he says that to all his guests, Sheena! He's just being polite. Don't read too much into it.' But she was inwardly semi-swooning and simply staring back at him. Remembering to not appear completely mute, she piped up:

"Thanks for inviting me! What a great party!"

She enthused. He looked at her quizzically.

"Yeah? You been here long? I must have missed you. Sorry about that."

"No, no, it's fine!"

She yelled back louder this time, over the music, only *just* making herself heard.

"You've got no drink, Sheena! Let's rectify that immediately! Come with me!"

He went to take her hand and lead her presumably through to the kitchen and the drink supply. She scanned his eyes instinctively for any trace of intoxication and did a once over of the beer bottle in his hand, wondering how many he might be on. Then mentally kicked and berated herself.

'He's *not* Peter!'

She shook it off and smiled again, taking his hand and allowing herself to be led through the mass of people there. She was mildly surprised when he then opened a near-hidden door under the stairs, which looked just like a storage cupboard but appeared to have steps within that led down to a musty, semi-lit, stone cellar, filled with rack after rack of bottles of wine and what looked like a large bar fridge too. Sheena was impressed. She really *did* appreciate and enjoy good wine and would have loved to have been able to keep some 'good' bottles in the house, possibly in a similar wine cellar set-up, back in her marital home in Sydney, but it would have been destroyed within a week, she just knew it. No bottle had been safe in the Doyle household, not even if it had been a gift for Sheena or to be given from them to someone else.

As Sheena was running a finger casually along the edges of one of the stacked racks, mulling over the amazing wines he had apparently collected, Brendan spoke:

"This section is not officially part of the 'party', and is 'out of bounds', so to speak. But, I thought we'd have a better chance of getting a drink than trying to wrestle through that mob out there to get to the kitchen. Plus, it's much quieter down here. We can talk, if you'd like."

He gestured that she sit on one of the upturned wine crates. Her nerves had disappeared. She felt strangely calm and 'at home' with Mr Goodwood ('I mean, *Brendan*') in his musty, private wine cellar. He set about pouring them each a drink.

"Pinot noir ok with you, Sheena?"

She nodded quickly, taking this opportunity as his back was turned, to run her eyes up and down his tall, muscular body. Again, she was taken aback by just how solid and strong looking he was, especially for a teacher or academic. He looked like he'd be more at home, physically speaking, in the nearest gym, or perhaps under some iconic fireman garb. How original Sheena. This crush was showing no signs of dissipating. She gulped suddenly, wondering if he'd brought her down here to unwittingly act out some of her recent Mr Goodwood fantasies?

'Get a grip.' She yet again reminded herself. 'He's your *teacher*.' She knew he obviously wasn't interested in her like *that* and that the thought had definitely never even crossed his mind. Like he said, he just wanted to talk to her.

"So, Sheena."

He handed her a full glass brimming with ruby liquid.

"Reveal all – tell me about yourself!"

She raised her eyebrows at him, buying herself a bit of time.

"You know." He continued. "Where are you from, what are your hopes and dreams, what's your relationship like with your parents? The usual stuff."

He took a healthy swig of his own drink, waiting for her response.

She laughed amicably and told him, as if reading off a list of carefully prepared bullet points: "Sydney. To be a teacher. To travel the world and be happy. Non-existent: we're estranged."

He raised his own eyebrows now.

"Same same. Well, the parents part. One of them, anyway, the other one died."

"Oh, I'm sorry." She frowned slightly.

"No, no, nothing to be sorry about. I was very young when she passed. I don't remember anything about her." He assured her.

"So, you're a long way from home, then." He continued. "How long have you been in Freo?"

"Coming up to two years now." She told him, sipping her drink again. "Mmm, this is delicious!" Sipping the wine again.

"You're a newcomer! Excellent." He sipped his own wine, and concurred with her. "Yep, this one's a keeper."

He meant the wine, clearly, but her stomach did a very strange flip-flop at his statement.

'Stop it, Sheena! He's just being friendly. More's the pity.'

"No kids?"

He asked, sipping his wine again.

"No kids." She replied. "You?"

"No, no kids."

More sips of their wine. A comfortable silence ensued. Sheena simply smiled at Brendan, drinking the smooth, delicious wine. It had been quite a while, years even, since she'd felt so, well, welcome and warm, and at peace. She felt like they could sit there forever, comfortably asking each other about their lives. With his questions she felt compelled to answer them: she actually felt like telling him *all* about her failed marriage and subsequent new life here in Freo. She got the feeling he was so easy to talk to, and she felt drawn to him, and inexplicably close: like they had known each other their whole lives or something.

'Ridiculous, Sheena!' She scolded herself again, but didn't drop her smile, nor did his falter.

She opened her mouth, intending to start to tell him about herself, really tell him about herself, but then stopped, hesitating, and instead told him:

"Well, Brendan, thanks for the drink. This is amazing down here.

I should really go and find my friend though."

'Really, Sheena?!' She knew that Gabby would be fine; she'd get on with anyone, save for those chauvinistic swine of the male gender of course, but still, put her in a room filled with people and she'd have ten instant new best friends. 'So, why, oh why, Sheena?!'

Brendan looked mildly disappointed ('or am I imagining that?' she wondered) but gestured that, of course, they should both stand and go back up to the heaving party. Sheena would have really preferred to spend a lot longer down in his cellar, and just the two of them at that, but her nerves were biting back at her once more and self-doubt was plaguing her as she told herself: 'he's probably bored being stuck down here with me, he must have friends he's eager to get back upstairs to' and so, in keeping with her gut feeling of telling him her honest answers and thoughts, she told him so.

He stopped moving and looked directly at her, telling her, honestly too, it seemed:

"I would much rather be here with you actually, Sheena."

A moment's silence and the tension was palpable. She bit her lower lip and widened her eyes.

He broke the silence and continued:

"But of course, I don't mean to hold you hostage. You must go and find your friend!"

His smile and jovial manner were back now, and that moment, that brief, awkward moment, yet somehow poignant, meaningful moment (although she didn't quite know why or what it meant) was lost.

An all-too-brief image of him actually holding her hostage in that dark, musty cellar, while he proceeded to do unspeakable things to her, invaded her slightly tipsy and confused mind, and she inhaled sharply as she followed him back up the stairs to rejoin the noisy, bustling party. He stopped at the top and just before opening the door to release her back into the crowd, he turned to her and said:

"Perhaps we can continue our chat sometime?" He asked

genuinely.

Her stomach did that flip-flop thing again and she felt that familiar tingle and ache in her groin.

"I'd love to, Mr Goodwood. I mean, *Brendan*, sorry!"

She blushed and smiled sheepishly back at him. God, he's do damn, *nice* as well as being ridiculously hot, she thought.

'What a genuine, lovely teacher and man. I really need to get it together and stop having filthy fantasies with him as the star. He's my teacher! As if he'd be into that!' Her smile widened however and she thought wistfully of his stubbly chin and wet lips caressing her neck as his large, manly hands invaded her dress, sliding confidently up to her satin, tiny knickers…

'Stop it, Sheena!' She reminded herself to slow down on the wine as she left Brendan at the cellar door and went in search of Gabby through the now even busier, if that were possible, house party crowd.

'Oh, Mr Goodwood.' Sheena sighed to herself. 'It is your fault for being so damn attractive!'

# CHAPTER ELEVEN

She'd told Brendan everything. About all the years of pain and misery, coupled with the ever surfacing and irrational *hope* that things would get better. That *Peter* would get better. That their marriage could be saved. She told him about the name calling; the constant verbal abuse that was *always* forgotten (by Peter at least) the next morning. She told him about their lack of a sex life, which, luckily for all involved (and especially any unborn child) had obviously never resulted in any pregnancy. She told him about the loneliness and solitude she experienced being married to an alcoholic. And she told him just how long it stupidly and regrettably took her to actually realise that he *was* in fact an alcoholic.

He was just so easy to talk to, and not only that, but she felt somehow compelled, almost, to confess all: all about her past life pre-Fremantle. And Brendan? He simply listened. He took it all in. He didn't seem to judge or even seem surprised, but just let her go on telling: listening and nodding sympathetically and empathetically with her tales.

She didn't quite know what had prompted her to be quite so forthcoming with this man, her *teacher*, who, god knows, was probably only being polite in asking what brought her all the way to WA, across the other side of the country, but, she just felt *safe* with him and wanted to tell him. It was a strange sensation. She felt, all at once, so inexplicably *close* to this man, yet, so on edge and nervous around him still, even some five weeks since properly 'meeting' him. She supposed it was the lust she felt, and her wildly inappropriate feelings she had about him and when she was around him. But, true to his word, he *had* apparently wanted to continue chatting with Sheena and had, once again, called her name after his next lecture on the Wednesday following his party. He'd asked if she had any more classes on for that afternoon or if she'd be free to have a coffee or a wine with him.

"Anywhere but Café Noir!"

She agreed, feeling that familiar adrenalin surge rush through her as she tried to remind herself there's no need to be nervous: this was her *teacher*, after all.

'He's probably just being polite!' She'd thought. 'I bet he likes to get to know all of his students.'

A sudden image appeared in her mind of just how much she'd like to get to know him, and she squeezed her legs tightly together and for what must have been the thousandth time, told herself to get a grip. There's no way he'd get to 'know' his students; this was just her recurrent and unavoidable fantasy. Unavoidable because he was always on her mind. And so easy to talk to.

They began to meet each week after his lecture, as if suddenly a part of their schedules, each time with Sheena double checking with him:

"You sure I'm not keeping you from somewhere you have to be?"

"Not at all, Sheena dear." He would reassure her genuinely.

Sometimes they would go to a café and exchange nuggets of information about their respective lives, whilst sipping on steaming hot, long blacks, or sometimes they would simply walk through the park nearby, and talk. Sheena felt as if she had acquired a sort of new best friend. Albeit a best friend who she longed to touch, longed to be touched by, longed to rip his clothes and ravish him at his lecture podium. The only other person in the world she'd ever shared this much about her past with was Gabby, and now, she supposed, this (what was it? Friendship? Student-teacher relationship?) that had arisen with Brendan, had somehow even surpassed her intimacy with Gabs, seeing as she was doing a good job of *not* telling Gabby about it.

There was nothing wrong with what she was doing, nothing at all. No boundaries had been muddied, and no line had been crossed (despite her fantasies and wishes for otherwise), so no *real* reason to keep her chats with Brendan as a sort of secret, by not telling Gabby. Well, *another* secret from Gabs now, she admitted to herself. Admittedly though, it wasn't as if she had even seen much of Gabby lately anyway: she'd be leaving when Sheena was coming, and vice versa, so her new 'secret' had been an easy one to uphold effortlessly.

If she was being honest with herself, as she always aimed to be, she knew that she didn't want Gabby to 'ruin' it, whatever it was, which she knew she would. As much as Sheena *loved* Gabby, she sometimes grew tired of her endless anti-men campaign, and she was sure that not even the lovely, gentlemanly, respectful Brendan would be spared. Gabby would probably accuse him of just trying to get in her pants.

'Wouldn't *that* be nice.' She told herself wistfully. Sheena smiled at how far from the truth that idea would be. Brendan was, to Sheena, quite honestly the most open, trustworthy, genuine and intelligent man she'd yet to come across. So warm too. He seemed to genuinely *care* about her. She reminded herself frequently that this was probably why he was such a great teacher: his manner more than likely got loads of his students confiding in him and fancying him just like Sheena. In fact, she was sure of it, judging by the way certain members of her class-group peers were heavily trying to put the moves on him at his own party. Ahh, bless him, having to turn them down oh-so-gently so as not to break any young hearts.

So, she'd opened up to him: told him so much about herself, her estranged relationship with her parents back East (not much to tell), her young and futile marriage, and wanted to go on and tell him more. Namely those two things that she just couldn't possibly tell him: 1) how much she wanted him and lusted for him (after all, it wouldn't be very appropriate, and she was sure this was definitely  unrequited and not even on the outskirts of his mind), and 2) her other 'secret' life of that tedious, unoriginal part-time job. The latter secret, she reasoned with herself, she would *never* need to tell him anyway. After all, it was *her* business, and plus, she'd soon be done with it. Her debt was almost clear, so no need to be working there too much longer. She smiled at the realisation that she'd be quitting her job at Secrets oh so soon. So, definitely no need to tell Brendan, or anyone else for that matter.

But some days, she did *wonder*. His recent lecture to the class had been all about ethics and the nature of sinning. What would Brendan Goodwood make of her choice of in-between-profession? Would he class it as a sin? As ethical? Would he surmise that this is what she had made happen, with the power of her very unoriginal thoughts and wavelengths? Would he think less of her? Would he not want to continue their weekly talks? Would he be simply offended and disgusted by her? She did not want to find out. And wouldn't have to. She promised herself cheerily:

'Not long now! It's coming to an end.'

This had become her new mantra for her 'work' that week, as she performed her dreaded shift at Secrets that Friday night. As she led the slightly overweight, in his mid-forties drunk client into her room and as he ordered from her wall-mounted list of services, she told herself: 'Not long now. This will all be over.' As he sat back on the leather sofa and lazily lobbed out his semi of a pink knob and slurred at her to get a move on, she told herself again, 'not long now, Sheena!' As she sank to her knees and rolled on the condom, she took her mind elsewhere and her thoughts drifted back to Brendan. What was *he* doing right now? She imagined him to be alone in his wine cellar, thinking hard about which bottle to select. When he makes a decision and is about to pour himself a glass, he's startled by a knock on the door. He yells at the closed door that it's open and low and behold, Sheena is behind the door. As she makes her way down the dusty, fragile steps, Brendan looks straight into her eyes and tells her:

"I've been thinking about you. I wanted you to come."

She goes to him, silently and effortlessly gliding over to where he's standing watching her, his dark, brooding eyes boring into her hotly.

"Come here."

He demands, and she obediently gets closer and closer. When she's within arm's reach he suddenly stops her, pinning her against the wine rack to his left, his strong arms and hand gripping her shoulders and slender frame and holding her in place so she can't move. Still staring straight into her eyes, one of his hands moves to her hip, where it rests a few moments, before moving further down to her leg. He grasps her upper thigh teasingly and pushes his weight gradually, surely, into her. His other hand now moves from her shoulder to her neck, fingering her slender neck, tentatively at first as she surrenders to his touch and instinctively throws her head back, eyes half-closed and her mouth slightly parted. He grabs her neck tightly now, causing her to fling open her eyes wildly, both a little alarmed and very much aroused. His other hand continues its gentle massage of her inner thigh, as he holds her in place and kisses her hard on the mouth, his lips smashing into hers and forcing her slightly anxious mouth to open, where he then plunged his tongue urgently into her hot, wet, still a little surprised mouth.

His left hand roamed further up her leg now, finding her g-string, which he wastes no time in yanking off and straight down her bare legs, his hand now confidently groping her arse cheek, and delicately, teasingly, ever so subtlety sneaking around to finger her pussy every now and then too, all the while his right hand holds her neck tightly, almost *too* tightly, as Sheena struggles to breathe and Brendan continues to plunge his tongue into her mouth. Now releasing her neck, his right hand joins his other and grasps Sheena's other arse cheek, squeezing her tightly while his body presses hard against hers. He deftly picks her up and places her atop the bench surface, shimmying up her tight, black dress and spreading her legs apart roughly. The cool air hits Sheena's exposed, wet cunt and she gasps. Feeling more than a little exposed she'd have possibly been embarrassed by this angle, but has no time for this to occur as Brendan pushes his body, rock-hard and urgent, in between her open thighs, grasping and massaging her toned arse cheeks once again and nuzzling and sucking her exposed, bare neck.

Her hands find the back of his head, running their fingers through his messy, tousled, brown hair, and pushing his face further into her neck, as she groans. God, he is making her so horny, so wet, so *aching* for him. His stubbly, rough kisses and bites travel South now, lower from her neck, and Sheena tries to look down at his face, currently melding itself with her heaving cleavage, as he presses his still clothed, solid body hard up against her own half-naked body and she grinds herself against him, needing him so. She starts to pull at his shirt, needing it off. Now. All but ripping it open, he helps her to take it all the way off his solid, rock-hard chest and broad shoulders and they fling it to the floor. It's just his jeans separating him from Sheena now. She can feel his hard bulge beneath them, pressing into her, rigidly straining to be released. Scrabbling at his jeans fly now, she urgently yanks down the zip and, again, he assists and helps her to push them down and off. He then kicks them aside and moves back to in between Sheena's thighs. His smooth, hard, bulging head is resting on her wet cunt. He doesn't move. Simply rests it there and grabs her hips with his expert, large, manly hands, massaging her more urgently this time. She kisses him hungrily, pushing her hips forward slightly in a bid to tell him: 'now! Take me now!' God, she is so wet, so ready for him. This is unbearable; she *needs* him. Inside her. Now.

He obliges. Slowly. Pushing his thick, hard cock deliciously and agonisingly slowly inside her, filling her up so completely. She cries out and wraps her bare legs around his back, as his mouth finds her neck again, sucking hard; hard enough to leave a mark. His hands still on her hips fixing her in place, he plunges into her again, a little faster this time, her legs still wrapped firmly around his beautiful, muscular back…

Shit. She finished the task in hand with her boozy client annoyingly *before* she reached the end of her own fantasy. Oh well. Save that one for later when she had a lot more privacy so she could really finish off what she'd started.

Is it healthy? She wondered randomly, as she bid adieu to her wealthy client and went about getting dressed and gathering her things to leave. To be this in lust with her teacher? Who was now also her friend and confidante? 'Come on, Sheena, it's *never* going to happen!' She reminded herself. Yet again. Although, she continued her debate and toyed around with the idea that if we create our reality via our thought processes and putting our own energy and vibrations out there into the universe and ultimately creating the electric holographic *results*, then surely, nothing's impossible? After all, they *had* become friends since she'd started *thinking* about him. Thus, which came first, her *thoughts* or his *presence*? Did she think about him as a result of seeing him and hearing his lectures, or was it the other way around: did she think of him and then ultimately *create* his being there, calling her name affectionately after his lecture. She made a mental note to bring this up with him if they went for their walk and talk again that next week, of course, omitting the part about precisely just what thoughts she was having about him. No doubt he'd listen politely thought, she mused, after all, he *did* say that life's all about sex anyway, it's not like he'd be horrified. Perhaps he would even be flattered, she pondered.

# CHAPTER TWELVE

So *that* was it. That was the reason behind her quiet, alluring, yet-to-be-uncovered mystique. Brendan had had his 'aha!' moment only about a halfa into his first 'proper' chat with Sheena, after his lecture on the Wednesday following his party. They had started talking and he'd asked why she left Sydney. Sheena had hesitated for the slightest moment, but then had started to tell him. To really confide in him, he felt. She told him *all* about it: about her ex-husband, his verbal abuse and aggression, his barely concealed drinking problem, and of her years of loneliness and despair.

He listened, nodding in what he hoped was both a sage yet empathetic manner, thinking, '*that's* it!' The reason behind the feelings he got that there was more to Sheena than meets the eyes. Well, he supposed, that's probably true of everyone. But, Sheena? Beautiful, delicate, somehow almost-childlike and pure Sheena – having to go through all of that pain, and still come out strong enough to start again and pick up the pieces of her life? He felt both in awe/inspired and outraged. He quietly fumed as he thought of this man, her ex-husband, what a fucking prick, what a moron, taking her best years away and damaging her, or making her think *she* was the reason behind his disease. He had, admittedly, just met her really, but he had sensed there was a secret she was keeping. She was the proverbial dark horse. Now he knew why.

He had to admit it, he felt pretty pleased that she'd chosen to 'confide' in him, in her words. Did she feel it too, then? This feeling he had that they had met somewhere before, or that they just *knew* each other, well, somehow.

As she went on, telling him about the countless times she'd been labelled a 'fucking moron', 'an arsehole', a 'stupid cunt', 'an imbecile', and a 'teenager', he continued to see the inside. Who was this prick?! Yes, he understood that it wasn't really *him*, or certainly the same bloke that Sheena married, and he knew that alcoholism was a devastating disease full of insanity. *But*, at the same time he had a strong urge to find this man and get all machismo on him and punch him so hard that he'd lose the ability to even form such phrases. And Brendan was *not* a violent man.

He vowed right there and then, whilst they sat in Starbucks, of all clichéd places, that he would *never* let any man or person harm this wonderful woman *ever* again. *He* would protect her and help her get back to her true self. Even if she didn't want him to. He *thought* there was something damaged or broken about her, and a kind of nervousness, a certain eagerness to please, and now it all made sense: she had demons plaguing her still from her ex-husband and her years of suffering in their marriage. It was Brendan's duty, was is not, as her teacher and new friend, to help her in any way that he could? At the moment, that help took the form of meeting with her for coffee or simply walking and talking, usually, conveniently after his (soon to be over for this term) weekly lecture, when the elusive Sheena was fairly easy to pin down. He barred up slightly at the thought that, ideally, yes, what he wouldn't give, to *actually* be pinning her down.

He was dumbstruck sometimes by her sheer beauty. She was smoking hot, but clearly didn't realise this, he thought, probably as a result of the damage inflicted by that prick ex-husband of hers. But Sheena? Well, Sheena was ridiculously attractive, that much was obvious. Brendan had to remind himself to 'be good' with this one, lest he scare her away for good. He knew she was in a delicate state at the moment, even if she thought she was fine and 'over' all of that. He also longed for her to make the usual move he had become so accustomed to from his other female students, but when this didn't eventuate and she didn't, he would remind himself of her 'pure/innocent' and slightly damaged status:

'You idiot! She's hardly going to be looking for anything either, having just gotten out of an awful, painful long-term relationship. Plus, she's shown no hint of thinking of me any other way than as her teacher and friend.'

He felt both protective of her and yet completely floored by her and was hugely attracted to her. Yet he didn't want to ruin what they had and their recently created weekly 'routine'. He actually really looked forward to *talking* with Sheena, and listening, and even looked forward to the quiet lulls in between their conversations.

'God, and she hasn't even *touched* me.' He groaned to himself. This was most unlike him, and he was well aware of this.

What was also most unlike him was a coincidental, self-imposed, female drought. For the last month or so, Brendan hadn't been quite himself. That is, he hadn't been intimate with *any* students, nor had he held any evening 'study' sessions. This was not the fault of his female students by any means. Their requests were coming in still, if anything, thicker and faster than usual. One of life's mysteries, he supposed, and probably where that old wise adage of 'treat them mean, keep them keen' came from. It seemed now that the more, he said 'no', the more they would ask him. The trouble is that, very recently, he just hadn't wanted to keep them keen. *Most* unlike him. He had physically groaned and sighed when he received a text from Jess asking him to pay out on that raincheck he'd given them, astonishing himself by responding with a:

"Sorry Jess. Going to have to cancel that meeting. All the best."

He hadn't received any further soliciting from Jess so he assumed his bland and blunt message had been well and truly understood.

'Why the hell am I turning down sex with these twenty-somethings?' he rhetorically asked himself, but he had a sickly feeling that he knew the answer already. He now even felt *guilty*, of all things, about his previous six years of free-loving, extra-curricular behaviour. He thought he felt ashamed too. Very strange, he mused, as there had been no problem before. Before…. Before *what*?? But he knew…

Even his friends could tell something was up with him, as they'd sat drinking their first beers down at a rapid pace, eager to get on to round two, after one particularly sweat-inducing squash tournament one Saturday afternoon.

"Come on then, you slut," Anthony had probed endearingly.

"Fill us in. make us sick with envy over your latest young piece of poontang. We don't mind really!"

"Yeah, you dirty, old man." Damien had chimed in. "How many notches since we've seen you last?"

Brendan laughed feebly and rebuked:

"Oh come on. That's not *all* I do, fellas."

He resumed sipping his pint, thirstily. His friends exchanged glances, waiting for him to continue and reveal all, telling them the gory details of his conquests that they all knew they revelled in, living vicariously through his much more vivid and exciting sexcapades than their own, long-time married versions. When silence remained:

"Well?" Damien pushed.

Brendan coughed awkwardly and took another sip of his beer before telling them, nonchalantly:

"Well, none, as it happens."

More casual, breezy sips of his pint, hoping that they would leave it at that. He was at a loss to be able to explain his recent behaviour (or more to the point, *lack of* behaviour) so he hoped they'd just give up and change the subject and move on.

"What, none?" Anthony was incredulous. "Not even a sneaky blowjob?! You're shitting me."

All three of his good friends were frowning slightly, looking at each other. In all the six years of his diligent service to the university, this had never happened before.

"Nope. None."

Brendan stated, offering them no further information.

"What happened mate, is the boss onto ya or somethin'?" Chris asked sympathetically.

"Nah, no, nothing like that." He took a gulp of his beer before admitting: "No, actually, I just haven't felt like it, hey."

He attempted a reassuring smile to the group.

His three amigos resumed their worrying glances at each other once more.

"Erm, mate, you're not, you know." Damien began, stumbling over his words. "You're not ill, are you mate? Or you lost your touch?"

He was genuinely concerned, but smirking as he checked.

"Ha-ha. I'm fine."

Brendan was slightly offended. Only very slightly, however.

"Look, there's been the usual requests, but I turned them down,

ok? Just didn't feel like it, and no, I'm not ill."

He huffed a little and did a fairly good job of mock-sulking.

His three friends all took a moment's silence, each one thinking back to Brendan's party just over a month ago, lost in their own private reveries of the gorgeous, young, flirty stunners they'd had the chance to gawk at that night. *Those* hotties were his students and Brendan was turning them down? A stunned silence continued awkwardly, for slightly longer than Brendan would have liked.

"So, let me get this straight mate, for the last, let's say thirty days

or so, however long you've taken up this new monk's lifestyle,

you've not met up with one, single, fair, feminine student

creature?!"

Anthony was clearly, and rightfully, baffled by this turn of events. This just wasn't *like* Brendan.

"Um, oh, well actually, no."

Brendan was starting to wish he had just made something up and told them a more plausible (although entirely fictional) story about Jess giving him head while he fingered Jo, or something of that nature.

"I've met up with one of my female students, once each week, as

it happens. But, it's not like that!" He protested. "We just talk."

The three mates' glances resumed again, however this time with more than a hint of smugness and knowing.

"Oh, I see!" Damien exclaimed. "Well, that explains it!"

The knowing looks continued, accompanied by some head nodding now, and guffawing.

"Good on you, mate!" Chris seconded.

"Yeah, yeah, whatever, you dickheads. Let's talk about something else."

Genuinely sulking a bit this time, Brendan was confused enough by himself: he didn't want to hash it out and analyse it with his friends, as much as they were his good friends. Not yet, anyway. Not when he didn't even really know what he was feeling.

'What's the point, anyway?' He sulked. 'She's your student! She's not going to be interested in *you*, for fuck's sake!' The irony was not lost on himself. Plus, he was well aware that she was really only just out of a relationship; the last thing she'd be looking for was to start anything. But, did he *want* to start anything? He was confusing himself, which, as a philosophy professor, was a rare event in his life.

The only person he *did* want to possibly talk to about this, his strange addictive, almost pull, towards Sheena and his simultaneous (or subsequent? He mused) disinclination and rejection of any other of the many willing, young females, was Scott. Ahh, Scott. As redfaced as he would no doubt turn if Brendan mentioned that he's been turning down random sex with his other students and that he felt these weird, guilty feelings about his past student sexual encounters, and that he felt almost sick with fear that someone from the class might tell Sheena something about his reputation and history, well, despite Scott's embarrassment at the subject matter, Brendan was sure he'd be there for him, and would listen to him, without judgement and unconditionally. Hell, he may even have some gold advice for him, you never could tell. That is, if Brendan could actually get to *see* Scott and bend his ear about it. Scott had been uncharacteristically 'busy' or out with friends when Brendan had called or sent him messages lately. Brendan wasn't offended. He was pleased, sure, loved that his brother's social life was picking up. But he was missing him, and really needing a proper chat with him. He knew Scott would see him right, even if just silently, by listening to him, or maybe by telling him what he should do or what he thought was happening. He had always had a grounding, calming effect on Brendan, even if just on a practical level sometimes, with Brendan knowing he'd have to be sensible and logical enough to always get back home to be there for Scott and help care for him during their teens and into their early twenties.

Surely Scott would be available *this* weekend, Brendan hoped, really genuinely missing his time with his twin. It felt like ages since he'd seen him, but it couldn't have been more than four weeks. He made a mental note and changed that to *five* weeks, when he remembered that the last time he saw him was at their jointly hosted almost-end-of-year house party.

Brendan tapped out a quick text message:

"Scott-bro, what's doing? Fancy a beer? I'm free all weekend. Give me a call Big-Bro."

# CHAPTER THIRTEEN

"The last thought I'll leave you with prior to your philosophy exam next week is this: who are you, *really*? When you peel back those veneers of 'student', 'friend', 'daughter', 'brother', 'barmaid', 'writer' or any other label you've either given yourself or been given – take those away, and who are you? Have a think about it and then complete this sentence: 'I am….'. Metaphorically, that is. We won't be actually seeing one and other for classes anymore this term, so when I say complete this sentence, I mean, to yourself, or better yet! Save it for that exam! Hint, hint, I'll say no more." He smiled conspiratorially around the room full of mostly bored looking students. "It's been a blast, folks. Who are you? I'm Mr Goodwood, and I'll be seeing you…"

With that, Brendan drew his final lecture of the term to an end, and began gathering his papers together, still smiling, despite the vague, apathetic response he'd invoked from the crowd.

Sheena, sitting in her usual mid far-right position, went to gather her own things, feeling mildly panicked and anxious. She thought they would probably catch up again after that class, as has been the case for the previous six weeks, and yes, there he was, looking expectantly her way. But, then what? Term would be over, this module would be finished and completed for her and she possibly might never see him again. Unless she fails her exam and has to redo this class, she pondered. The thought filled her with horror. The former thought, that is: that she may never see this man again, may never get to sit close beside him discussing their lives and the world, burning to reach out and touch him but feeling paralysed by her inability to act on this or say anything due to those pesky circumstances prevailing that he was her *teacher*.

"Well, I'm sure you'll be very glad to know that's the last long tedious talk from me for the year." He joked when he reached her. "Fancy one last post-lecture coffee?"

'Oh god, he even called it our last coffee!' She gulped.

"Of course. I'd love to." She said honestly.

As they sat down with their drinks at a portside, funky arthouse establishment, he continued candidly:

"So, you're always polite enough during my lectures to at least appear to be interested." He half shrugged. "But, the rest of them, I dunno, half of them have that look of quokkas caught out during the daytime. I feel like I'm just talking for my own benefit, half the time. Well, and yours too, perhaps?"

He looked hopeful.

"No, definitely! I mean, *yes*, of course for my benefit." She hurriedly concurred. "I, for one, have really loved your weekly lectures. Honestly."

She looked at him simply, feeling warm and safe, and longing to reach out and touch his cheek, to feel that dark stubble graze her hand.

She turned her head to one side slightly, in sudden confusion.

"Quokkas though?" She frowned. "You lost me there."

"Over on Rotto." He looked at her quizzically. "Tell me you've been to Rottnest Island!"

He was doing a good job of acting horrified.

"Oh, nope, sorry." She laughed. "Guilty as charged!"

146

He loved the sound of her laugh. He wanted to just go on making her laugh, and *never* make her frown or be upset.

"This is outrageous! You've been in Freo for how long now, and you've never been to *Rotto*?"

Mock disbelief splashed all over his face.

She shrugged her shoulders and laughed again.

"Well, I think we need to rectify this matter, most urgently." He continued. "I feel it's my civic duty as a Fremantle-born-and-bred bloke to take you to Rottnest as soon as possible!"

Her stomach flip-flopped. She hoped she didn't have as inane a grin plastered on her face the same as she felt in her mind, giving her away.

"How about, I don't know, this Sunday?" He enquired casually.

She went to protest and started to tell him:

"But you've probably got a lot of other more important things you need to be doing. You really don't have to…"

He was still staring her down with mock stern authority and outrage. She relented.

"Well, ok, then. Yes, Sunday, I'm free. Why not?"

She smiled cautiously back at him now and he returned the smile.

Outside she was all cool, calm aloofness personified. Inside? Well, quite a different matter. The flip-flop feeling was not going away and she felt like her guts were soaring. She felt giddy and buzzing with excitement (and nerves). If she was being honest with herself.

So, she *would* see him again, even after the course had ended. 'Phew, what a relief.' She thought to herself.

She was practically giddy and high from that Wednesday afternoon right through to Sunday: nothing could ruin her good mood. Not even a less than favourable shift at Secrets. Although this came pretty damn close this week. She even used the damn panic button for the very first time. Her client was getting quite a bit too rough and aggressive for her liking, and she didn't think he was just acting or playing a fantasy role. So, she'd called George and Benson in, hurriedly. As her now ex-client was suitably roughed up and frog-marched out the door, (ok, kicked the shit out of and thrown out the door) and Sheena caught her breath, adrenalin surging through her, Brendan's poignant words came back to her: 'Who are you, really?'

Being completely honest with herself, she *knew*, and not even very deep down, that *this*, this other, secret, seedy job she had, as much as she told herself it's 'just a job' and doesn't define her, blah blah blah, that *this* was not *her*. She couldn't do this anymore. Now it just felt, somehow, *wrong* and tainted. Much more so than before. She was thoroughly fed up with it. But, wouldn't let it spoil her Sunday outing that was fast approaching and she'd momentarily shelved her dilemma of 'who am I? How can I go on working at a brothel, for fuck's sake' for later.

She'd met Brendan at the wharf to get the ferry across to Rottnest Island. Her nerves were back, but only slightly, The sun was shining brightly and it looked to have the makings of a perfect day, weather-wise. Brendan arrived and walked confidently towards her. She sucked in her breath as she took him in: black polo shirt, tight-ish over his muscular arms, together with some casual khaki long shorts, pockets-a-plenty, and casual trainers. His hair was in its usual tousled, brown arrangement and his face was uncharacteristically shaved clean and smooth. His smile was wide and contagious and his eyes penetrated her own, looking onto her and they smiled and stared at each other.

'Fuck me. He's even hotter out of his 'work clothes'.' She noticed. All thoughts of her current stressing, her many troubles, her less than favourable, sleazy job that she now realised she hated doing, her essay deadlines and exams to study for: all these simply went out the ferry window as they crossed over to 'Rotto', as he called it. Sheena even let go of her 'he's my teacher!' dilemma. It felt like they were just two people, two good friends, out on a kind of date. A date? She sucked in her breath again, reminding herself not to read too much into this. He's probably just being a nice bloke.

But it *felt* like a date. Had all the makings of a perfect, idyllic date that she'd read about in books and seen in movies and soap operas. They hired bicycles, laughing and teasing each other, as they explored the small island, stopping at the various small, completely isolated and private coves, where they dove into the cool, refreshing water and splashed each other playfully. They lay out in the hot sunshine drying off, and happily forgot about time, having no particular place they had to be right at that point. They wandered into the pub on the foreshore after returning their bicycles and ordered a bottle of wine to share. Sheena didn't even think to watch and add up how many drinks they were each having. Then they ordered a second bottle of wine. She couldn't remember feeling *this* carefree and of having this much fun in, well, forever. Not since she was a teenager, at least. Pre-marriage. She felt, so *happy*, and *right*, being around Brendan. He made her laugh, made her feel safe, and he *excited* her. His words came back to her again: 'Who are you, really?' She couldn't put it into words, in any eloquent way that is, but she just felt like *herself* when she was with him.

Like this was who she really was and who she'd been meant to be.

She also felt like she possibly shouldn't have had that last glass of wine, and she suddenly stood up, feeling hot and flushed, and very dizzy. She needed some air. Abruptly making her excuses and mumbling something of this nature, she rushed out of the busy pub and into the cooler evening air. She could see their ferry waiting there to her left and a few people milling about nearby, waiting until they could board, and she took a sharp right instead, finding herself swiftly on the sand of the deserted little beach there. She sank to her knees and took a few deep breaths in, debating whether she was going to be sick or not. Another few deep suck ins of air and the feeling passed. Phew.

She looked up just as she felt a heavy, warm hand on her shoulder. Brendan was looking down at her, frowning with a very concerned look on his beautiful face. He got down to join her on the sand, and she sat back now, sitting comfortably and closely beside him, their thighs touching, and his hand still resting on her shoulder, his arm now casually draped around her.

"Are you ok, Sheena? I was worried."

He asked genuinely, squeezing her shoulder affectionately.

She turned towards him and smiled in thanks back to him, reassuring him:

"Yeah, I'm fine. Sorry. Just needed to get outside in the fresh air.

But I'm great now."

She meant that. She felt great, sitting there with him, feeling the warmth of his body tightly against her and his hand on the bare skin of her shoulder. He was close enough to touch, close enough to kiss…

She leaned towards him, pulled towards him, needing to kiss him and have him kiss her back. Her lips found his and her eyes closed. The kiss started off delicately, sweetly and softly. He kissed her back, hesitating at first. Then, as if a sudden hunger had overcome him, he moved his hand to the side of her face and drew her in further for a deep, passionate kiss, his mouth now opening and his tongue delving into her mouth to find her own tongue. She felt like she was on fire everywhere. She had never wanted anyone more. She didn't want their kiss to end, and she moaned helplessly as he continued to kiss her deeply and hungrily. He pushed her back now, back onto the cool sand, pushing the weight of his strong body tightly and firmly against her welcoming body, her legs wrapping around his own instinctively.

Suddenly he stopped kissing her and pulled back, breathily. Sheena attempted to get her breath back, as she shouted in her head 'no! Don't stop!'

Brendan was panting slightly and looking completely flushed. He was frowning now.

'Oh shit.' Thought Sheena.

He explained:

"Look, Sheena. I'm sorry. That shouldn't have happened. Not like this. Not yet…" He trailed off briefly.

'Not yet?' She wondered, her breathing still shaky and rapid.

"Look." He tried again. "You don't know how much I *want* you, Sheena. Honestly, I've thought about this so much."

'He has?' Her heart swooned and she sucked in a sharp breath, biting her lower lip nervously.

"But," He looked down, frowning again. "I am a *teacher* and you're a student at the same university. We can't do this here.

151

Not yet. Not like this."

Sheena was confused. Was she hearing correctly? He had feelings for her too? He *wasn't* just being polite and a nice person, and he *did* fancy her right back?

"I've thought about this too." She stated genuinely.

May as well be honest with him as far as this goes, she thought.

"Brendan, I've wanted to kiss you for so long, wanted to touch
you and have you touch me…"

She trailed off now as his eyes bored into her own pools of amber, his body still pressed hard up against her own. She could feel just how much he really *did* want her. Yet, his frown remained in place. He groaned in frustration and repeated:

"You've no idea. I want you, Sheena. But not yet, not like this."

What did he mean? What's with all the 'yets'?

He explained:

"I know I may be jumping the gun here, and I know this may
seem hasty. But, the feelings I seem to have acquired for you
Sheena, well, they're *strong* feelings. I hadn't dared to hope you
may feel the same way… Just give me some time. There's
something I've gotta do first."

He didn't elaborate further. Sheena was confused, but elated. She didn't press him further, just lay there, looking at him, as he looked back, almost lovingly. She took his words to mean that he probably had someone he was seeing to now let down or break it off with, although he'd never mentioned a girlfriend. That didn't help them with their 'teacher-student' conundrum however, but again, she didn't probe or pry.

'We all have our secrets,' she supposed. 'Oh god, *Secrets.*' An image of her Friday night jaunt flashed up unwelcomely in her mind now. 'Fuck'. She couldn't go back there. She'd had enough. How would she ever explain *that* to this wonderful, attractive, sexy man here before her, who has the same deep feelings for her as she has for him? Surely that would definitely change his mind about her? He must never find out, she decided then and there. 'And I can never go back'. She confirmed.

Not much more was said on that day, as if mutually agreed upon. They had helped each other up, brushed the sand off their clothes and from their long hair respectively, and hurried off to jump on the ferry back to Fremantle. They had departed with nothing more than a soft kiss to the cheek and a warm smile each, and now Sheena was back at her flat some days later, the events of that Sunday, and Sunday evening in particular, on her mind on repeat.

She sat sipping a tea contemplatively at the kitchen table. Did that really happen? It felt like a dream. Yet she could still feel his lips on hers, his body pressed up against her own. She could taste the salty, sea air even. She smiled and sighed, sipping the tea slowly. Her smile disappeared though as she realised: a) she didn't know where they had left it at, 'I mean, he's still my teacher and I'm set to be a student here for the next three years', and b) she had to quit working at Secrets. She *had* to, she knew that now. She found it almost unbelievable that she had even worked there for that long now. She knew it was the money that kept her there, but she suddenly felt revolted at herself for the past year's worth of 'work' there. She must have been out of her mind to do that! So much for always being true to herself. She felt like she had deluded herself and felt cheated. Again, Brendan's words from his lecture came back to ring in her ears: "Who *are* you, really?"

Well, she was *not* 'Ruby', and wouldn't be anymore. She'd have to quit, give her notice. April would understand surely, and quite frankly, she didn't care if she *didn't*. Although there was the minor matter of money, the whole reason she'd worked there in the first place. She frowned now, wondering how on earth she would manage without that extra money: she made more in her couple of hours working as Ruby than she did working her twenty-five hours as a waitress in the café. Still, her debt *was* almost paid off and she could almost see the light at the end of the tunnel.

"You look like you've got the weight of the world on your shoulders!"

Gabby suddenly broke her reverie and came into view, as she bounced into the small kitchen.

"Hey, Gabs!"

Sheena smiled brightly now at her friend, her frown disappearing at once. She felt like she hadn't seen her ages.

"Got time for a cuppa? I've missed you mate!" She wholeheartedly meant that.

Gabby hugged her, kissed her cheek and sat down, nodding.

"Would love one. Yeah, we've been missing each other lately. So, what's up? Anything the matter?"

"Oh, just financial crap. Just money worries." Sheena told her honestly. "Nothing serious, all good."

"Anything I can help with?" She looked concerned. "You only have to ask."

God she was so wise beyond her years. Sheena felt like their ages should be reversed and that Gabby was the one in her mid-thirties giving advice to the young, naïve twenty-two year old Sheena.

"Thanks mate." Sheena smiled reassuringly. "I'll be fine, don't worry."

A comfortable silence settled over the pair of friends.

"Actually, I have some news."

Sheena stated at exactly the same time as Gabby said:

"There's something I wanted to tell you."

They laughed, each one gesturing to the other that they should go ahead and continue.

"Go on, Sheena, you go!" Gabby instructed, taking a swig from Sheena's mug of tea.

"Well, I'm not sure what to say, really." Sheena began, blushing and continued apprehensively. "I probably shouldn't even be telling you this, as nothing's happened yet. But, I think I'm in love with my teacher."

'Who are you, really?' His words floated back to her yet again and she answered her own question in her mind: 'I'm Sheena, and I'm in love with Brendan.'

# CHAPTER FOURTEEN

If he could whistle, Brendan would have been whistling up a storm as he casually strolled down the street in the glorious, mid-afternoon sunshine. Unfortunately, he'd never quite mastered this skill, so humming would have to do, which he was doing absentmindedly while smiling and all-but skipping his way down the street, away from the institution he'd come to known as a home of sorts for the past six or so years. He felt a wave of relief and felt surprisingly happier and more excited than he had expected to. Well, he had done it. Given his notice. Resigned. Told them he was leaving. In just four short weeks he would be officially unemployed and would be 'Mr Goodwood: Philosophy Professor' no more. He would simply be: Brendan. *Free*. Free to do…

Whatever he chose to do. He wasn't absolutely sure as yet, or at all actually. Luckily he had built up a fair bit of savings over the years, having been a dedicated bachelor with no car, and therefore most of his salary he had been able to squirrel away for that elusive 'rainy day'. So he knew he would be fine until he got another job or embarked on a totally new path. Plenty of time for all that, for working out *what* or *who* he would like to be, professionally speaking. He *had* always vaguely entertained ideas of putting pen to paper and embarking on that iconic and oft idolised 'becoming a writer' venture. Perhaps he might finally give that a go, now that he was soon to be 'free'.

The department and the Dean had, embarrassingly enough for him, taken his resignation well. Very well, in fact. They hadn't even seem that surprised. Had simply enquired where he was off to next, which university he was moving to, to which he'd vaguely answered that he wasn't quite sure yet, and then they'd reassured him that, of course, they would miss him and would write him a sterling letter of recommendation and do keep in touch etc etc.

In fact, the whole 'I'm quitting' process had been a lot easier all round than he had imagined it would be. When it came down to it, all it took was a few printed words on his official 'letter of resignation', a few kind words, expressing his desire to leave coupled with his gratitude, and that was it: free to no longer be a teacher there. Well, in four short weeks anyway. Free to simply be Brendan. Free to be with Sheena. *Really* be with Sheena. He'd never felt anything like this before, the feelings he had for her, and he could barely wait for the next four weeks to fly by.

However, wait he must, and he knew this. Knew that she would be worth it. Knew that he had *had* to resign as teacher there at the same uni where she was a student, even though he would no longer be *her* teacher in the subsequent terms; it didn't matter. He knew that he had to cut all ties with his job there at the uni *first*, before he could really pursue things with beautiful Sheena. He had to do it *right*. Recently he'd been thinking back over the past few years and his behaviour with his mainly female students. He now felt like he'd done so many things the *wrong* way, that he couldn't change or undo or take back. It wasn't so much that he even regretted his actions and all those extra-curricular 'study' sessions at his house (in fact, some of the more memorable images and memories were doing a good job of helping through his self-imposed period of chastity and celibacy no end at the moment) but more like he wanted to do everything *right* with Sheena: almost as if to cancel out all the 'wrong' he had done before meeting her. He was serious about Sheena and he was going to prove it to her. So, step one was: stop being her teacher or any kind of teacher at her university. Now that this particular barrier was so close to being overcome and not being an obstacle anymore, he felt elated. Practically giddy. Any worries about what he was going to do in the future for a steady income or career just weren't eventuating yet. He felt nothing but hope and excitement. Everything in him, every fibre and cell of his being, told him that he was making the right decision. The *only* decision.

He couldn't wait to *tell* her, to be with her, to (hopefully) celebrate with her. But, no. He stopped himself mid-text to Sheena and hastily tapped at the delete button. All in good time. Surely he could be just that little extra patient for a few more weeks. What was a mere twenty-eight days in the grand scheme of the rest of their lives?

He had to share his news with someone though. And he knew exactly with whom, too.

Calling him briefly to double-check he was in fact at home before trekking on up there, Brendan then hopped on a train to go the couple of stops up to Cottesloe, and a short time later was buzzing to be let in to Scott's freshly cleaned apartment. The brothers, both genuinely so happy to see each other after what felt like an age since they'd last caught up, sat on Scott's sofa, joking and teasing each other gently about not much in particular, when Brendan couldn't stand it any longer: he had to get it out.

"So, Scott-bro, I have some big news."

He was grinning and wide-eyed.

"Yeah, Brendo?" Scott smiled back and raised his eyebrows. "I thought there might be something on your mind. You seem a bit flushed Bro – you've joined my club!" Scott teased, himself now reddening and starting to blush as if on cue. "See?"

"Yeah mate." Brendan chuckled along with him. "Yes. I think I'm in love."

Scott raised his eyebrows again, and coughed a little.

"Yes. No, make that: I *am* in love. With a student."

"Oh." Scott looked concerned. "Well, what are you going to do? Won't the uni find out? You could lose your job."

He looked genuinely worried for his brother.

"It's all good, bro: nothing's actually happened yet. And no need to worry about my job – I just gave my notice hey. As of four weeks' time I will be a jobseeker and free to see whoever I want to." He smiled warmly at his brother. "I've got a very good feeling about all of this."

Scott attempted to return his brother's easy smile but his ever-growing flushed face was giving him away at feeling awkward or unsure. Confusion had creased over Scott's forehead as he took in Brendan's words of 'nothing's actually happened yet'. This was very much not like Brendan. He told him so, then punched him lightly on his shoulder and said:

"It *must* be serious then."

"Ha-ha Big-Bro." He pulled a face back at Scott. "And yes. I reckon it is."

"Well, who's the lucky girl then? What's she like?" Scott probed, although his cheeks were now flaming red in his standard style.

"Actually, you've met her before." Brendan realised. "It's Sheena. You know, from the café that time? I can't wait for you to meet her again. I can't wait to make things official with her."

He beamed at his brother. He was about to elaborate about just how wonderful he thought Sheena was to Scott, when Scott's sudden coughing and furious flushing now alerted him to the fact that it seemed Scott too had something important on his mind. Or something he wanted to get off his chest. He knew his brother too well. Knew that these were his standard 'something to do with women' reactions. What was it? Was he simply worried for Brendan? Or jealous, perhaps? What was the matter?

"You ok, Bro?" Brendan asked him directly. "Don't you approve or something?"

Scott coughed and looked instinctively down at the floor.

"No, no." He stammered out. "No, Bro, I'm happy for you. *Really*. That's great news. I'm so happy for you." He repeated.

He didn't look that happy,

"Then what's up mate?" Brendan pushed.

"Well." He coughed some more. His face burned. "I actually, erm, well..." He trailed off.

A shrill tone and hum of vibration interrupted them and Scott quickly and gladly retrieved his buzzing phone from his pocket and started to push himself to his feet. As he grabbed his crutches from the end of the sofa where they lent, he shrugged and mouthed 'sorry bro' as he swung himself out of the room and simultaneously answered the phone.

"Hey you."

He said quietly into his mobile as he exited the room and into the relative privacy of the kitchen, away from Brendan's curious ears.

Brendan recognised that tone though. Scott was talking to a chick, it had to be! He'd never seen him answer his phone and leave a room so quickly before either.

'Saved by the ringtone, hey bro.' He thought to himself. He couldn't help but smile. Scott must have got himself a girlfriend after all!

Some minutes later, as Scott made his way back in to Brendan, extremely red-faced, Brendan gave him a knowing, wide smile and asked:

"All good?"

Scott coughed and nodded as his response.

"So?"

Brendan prompted, when nothing but silence followed.

"So?"

Scott echoed, avoiding his brother's eyes, still staring down at the floor.

"Something you were going to tell me? Before your *girlfriend* rang?" He grinned at him.

Scott's face flashed a brighter shade of red, as Brenden knew it would, and his eyes shot up in surprise to meet his brother's.

"What? How do you, I mean, what are you talking about?" He was flustered. He took a deep breath in. "Ok, Brendo, yes, actually, that's what I wanted to talk to you about." He said seriously.

"Yeah mate, you can tell me!" He was as excited as Scott was serious. "Was that what you wanted to tell me? That you've got a new girlfriend?"

Scott coughed again, and then began:

"Yes. Well, and no. It's not just that." He stopped to cough, before continuing: "Yeah bro, I have some news too: I've started seeing someone. Someone I was chatting to a lot at our party, as it happens."

His flush had settled in on his handsome face permanently now. Brendan sat patiently, waiting for his brother to elaborate, an encouraging smile on his face.

"Well, erm, the thing is." Scott continued. "Yes, I suppose you could call her my girlfriend."

He conceded seriously and unsmiling.

"That's great news bro!" Brendan slapped his back heartily. "So, what's her name? What's she like? What does she do for a living? Tell me all about her!"

His excitement was palpable.

Scott half-smiled back warily and then resumed his serious expression. Brendan thought he looked almost sad at delivering this exciting news. Perhaps it was just his extreme embarrassment?

Scott coughed and continued:

"Well, she's, erm, she's... wonderful." He stated, looking resolutely at the floor once again. "She's beautiful. She's got long hair. She's erm, she's really very pretty. Erm, we, erm, chatted at our party for hours, and erm, since then, well, we've seen each other a few more times. I think about her all the time. She's the most beautiful person I've ever met."

His serious face remained in place.

"Yeah?"

Brendan asked, a quizzical look on his face. Why did he get the feeling there was something Scott wasn't telling him? Why did he look so very *un*happy at imparting this, what should be, very *happy*, exciting news? An uneasy thought struck Brendan. The only person he had ever heard Scott actually come out and call 'beautiful' was, well, was *Sheena*. Was that why Scott looked so pained? Oh god, was Scott in love with Sheena too? Was that what he was trying to tell him? Brendan frowned at this unwelcome thought.

Scott coughed again and continued:

"Yeah. Erm, she's so, erm, amazing. She's got this beautiful, bright red hair, she's quite pale-skinned, and she's so lively and bubbly. She, erm, well, she makes me feel, erm, like, I could be in *love* with her." He confided miserably.

Brendan's beaming smile was back now, as he listened to the description and realised that, of course, it wasn't Sheena who he was in love with. But why the unhappy face? He thought Scott should be ecstatic and not miserable as he appeared right now.

"Well." Brendan had temporarily forgotten his own ecstatic 'I'm in love' news. "This is fucken *excellent* bro! I'm so happy for you!"

Scott looked away. Yep, there was definitely something more to it.

"So, what's the problem then, Scott?" Brendan knew Scott wouldn't tell him what the matter was without some of his usual prompting. "You love her, she loves you, yes? Happy days!"

He scanned his brother's downturned eyes for a hint of what he may be feeling.

"Yes, erm, that's about right. " Scott confirmed. "But, erm, well, you see…" He coughed, buying himself some more time. "I, erm, well, I'm not sure how to say this…"

"What is it bro? Spit it out! Did she used to be a man? Is she insatiable in bed? I would never judge mate, all good."

He smiled and looked imploringly at Scott, worried for his brother now, who didn't smile back.

"Erm, well, erm, I wouldn't know." He coughed and looked down. "We haven't, erm, I mean... I haven't... We haven't, erm..." He spluttered and coughed again, trailing off.

Brendan thought he got it. 'So, that was it – they hadn't done the deed yet'.

"I see mate. You haven't slept with her yet, is that it?"

Scott coughed again. Brendan waited patiently for his answer.

"Kind of."

'Kind of?' Brendan frowned. What kind of answer was that? 'You either have or you haven't', Brendan thought in bewilderment.

"Kind of?" He echoed back to Scott.

"Yeah, erm, well, you're right: we haven't slept together yet." He coughed but looked up into his brother's confused eyes now.

"But, erm, the thing is. I, erm, well, I, erm..."

More coughing. His face was its characteristic deep red hue that Brendan recognised from times of deep embarrassment and discomfort for Scott. 'Shit, what is it?' He wondered.

"I, erm... Brendo, I, erm, never have." He confided.

"Never have what?" His look of confusion remained. "Never have slept with your new girlfriend? Yeah, I got that. But what's the problem mate? Don't worry, I'm sure 'all in good time', yes?"

"No, no." Scott stammered. "Never have. With anyone. At all."

He sat back. Silent.

Brendan was also silent. Taking in what Scott was telling him.

"Oh." He said, still stunned.

Scott looked miserable. 'Quick, say something Brendan!'

Regaining his composure and attempting a reassuring smile, he told him:

"Well, ok, bro. I gotta say, I'm surprised. But what's the big drama? Don't stress mate, it's all good. Don't worry about it. I'm sure this can be taken care of very shortly, with the help of your lovely new girlfriend, yes?"

He slapped him jovially on the shoulder now, attempting to lighten the suddenly serious mood and tension that hung about them.

Scott shook his head, looking even more miserable.

"I can't tell her that! What would she think of me? Thirty-two and still, ahem, still a virgin!"

He was aghast.

"Look bro." Brendan continued. "It's really not as big a deal as you're making it to be. I'm sure she'll understand, and if she's the amazing girl that you're in *love* with, well, she'd be only too happy to help, I'm sure. Just talk to her." He assured him. "Or, even better: just go for it! Who says you need to even mention it then? Just go for it, bro!"

Scott's coughing resumed. He shook his head again.

"Listen Brendo, I don't think I can." He began.

Brendan frowned and pursed his lips.

Scott clarified,

"I mean, I *can*, nothing like that. But, I can't just 'go for it' with her, bro. I don't want to mess it up. I really don't want to lose her or scare her off."

166

Brendan squeezed his brother's shoulder. Scott continued:

"There's something I need to do first. Brendo, I need your help. I wouldn't ask, but, I don't know who else to go to, and well, the thing is…"

Brendan's look of confusion was back as he sat listening to Scott's plan and request for 'brotherly help', and he couldn't help shaking his head and breathing out slowly and deeply.

'What the fuck…' He thought, frowning and taking Scott's lead, he now stared down towards the floor.

# CHAPTER FIFTEEN

In strutted the only person Sheena knew who could pull off that wondrous, lustrous, long, jet-black hair together with her gigantic, full breasts strapped tight in a red, low-cut, v-neck bandage dress and not give a fuck about the many sharp intakes of breath and stunned, admiring looks that followed her every step. As she rolled her hips deliberately (making no apologies for her very definite sex appeal she was consistently oozing) towards Sheena's round table for two, her head held high, she flicked her long, shiny mane over her nearly-bare, bronze shoulders and let a huge natural smile cover her face as she clocked Sheena's own genuine, coy smile. Sheena rose to her feet to air kiss her approaching partner in crime for the afternoon.

"April! Hello you." She cried warmly, taking her into a quick, friendly embrace. "Thanks for meeting me."

"'Ello gorgeous." April's eyes sparkled as she flirted mildly back with her employee and friend. "Not like you to call me up outta the blue on a Saturday arvo. So, either you want to run amuck with me, in hopefully the filthiest, most debaucherous way possible – yes, please, I *will* have one or ten of these."

She gestured to Sheena's own half-drunk chilled glass of sav blanc and the remainder of most of the bottle on the table before them.

"*Or*, judging by that goofy, stupid look on your face mate: I think you've got something to tell me, hey Chick?"

She now elegantly sat down at the second chair at their small, round table, courtesy of a late-afternoon Benni's, back where it all began. It was that post-lunch time of the day, when it was gearing up to be a kind of 'classy' bar-cum-chill-out-lounge, which later on would morph into its typical, predictable sweaty, writhing mass as it aimed to become a club-cum-bar. For now though, there was a semblance of class, and Sheena went with her surroundings and as requested poured her sexy, stunner of a friend-slash-boss a large glass of wine from the chilled bottle in front of them. April air kissed her a form of thanks along with a 'mwah! Thanks Hunni.'

As she leant forward to pick up her over-sized chalice and 'cheers' Sheena's own glass, Sheena couldn't help but stare, unavoidably, at April's massive, magnificent and very obvious cleavage, pushed almost forcefully up towards her as she moved. Sheena mentally raised her eyebrows. What delicious fun it *would* be to run amuck once more with this woman. For what must have been the thousandth time, she wondered about her own sexuality. She was almost 99.9% sure that she was straight as an arrow and very much into men (and specifically, just *one* man these days) however, when she was around April and when various flashbacks of the two of them together at work pounded her consciousness, that .1% suddenly became a very big .1%.

She wondered if the wait staff there at Benni's, or indeed, the scattering of other patrons sitting nearby with their own languid, late afternoon beverages, would be able to tell her current thoughts, or could imagine that the last time those beautiful, plump, glossy lips of April's had been in Sheena's vicinity that they had inched down her naked body, trailing her tongue down her smooth, burning flesh before kissing her deeply and passionately in her own special way when she came face-to-face with Sheena's bare, wet cunt, her wicked sparkling eyes flicking back up to clock Sheena's eyes-half-closed expression caused by her expert oral assault. Could they tell that Sheena's own tongue had countless times played figure of eight around April's hard, perfect nipples, as Sheena grasped and massaged her heavy, magnificent, huge breasts? Or that, countless times, the two had put on quite the impressive show as one of them donned the shiny, black strap-on and proceeded to thrust deep into the bent over other one and pound them hard and mercilessly as she called out her stage name hoarsely and roughly?

April's perfectly manicured, soft-looking hand clasped around the fine glass stem of her wine glass and Sheena looked admiringly at those perfectly polished, red, shiny, long nails. She had another flashback of April using said nails to scratch tantalisingly slowly down one of their joint client's back as she winked and pouted up at Sheena. Mmmm. It *would* be fun for one last run around with this incredibly sexy and fun friend of hers. That is, if she wasn't so obviously hung up on Brendan. It was glaringly obvious, April thought, it seemed splashed all over Sheena's flushed face there. She said so:

"So, something to tell me? It's a man, isn't it." April asked, but moreover: stated a fact.

In response, Sheena's smile widened, if anything, caused by an image of Brendan looking down intensely at her as they lay bodies pressed against each other on the cool, evening beach.

"How did you know?" Sheena countered, still grinning bashfully.

"There *is* a man, as it happens."

"Darlie, it's plastered all over your pretty little face. Someone's in lurrrrve." She grinned too now, flicking a long, wayward, jet-black lock of hair back over her shoulders. "I've seen that look before. Usually when one of my best girls has decided they'd rather go off gallivanting with said bloke and not earn shitloads of cash on the sly anymore. Am I close?"

She shot Sheena a probing, mock-stern, but affectionate look.

Sheena blushed. She'd got it in one. Maybe this wouldn't be the long, sad, drawn-out farewell/thank-you-for-everything that she'd pictured.

"Well, now that you mention it… Yes. There is someone. I think I'm in love with him. Think it could be serious." She admitted quietly.

Almost in disbelief herself still. Since their date-like non-date/student-teacher-day-out to Rotto, Sheena had been constantly giddy, almost deliriously happy, and hadn't even *seen* him in the flesh since that day. Nothing but a couple of friendly phone calls and a fair few flirty text messages since then, but this did nothing to qualm her now obvious love for him or her recurring (and very realistic) fantasy of the two of them being together properly, as a couple. It somehow felt like it was happening, albeit slowly, but that the wheels were set in motion. All she had to do was be patient. He'd made himself clear that he felt the same way and that there was just something he had to do first. So she could wait. What did a few days or even weeks matter compared to (hopefully) the rest of their lives together? It gave her goose-bumps when she got to this part of her train of thoughts. She *knew* he was special. That this was to be serious. That they had a *real future* together soon. She only had to be patient, bide her time. She just wished she knew until *when…* Ever since she'd started to confide in Gabby, on that quiet weekday afternoon, her 'relationship-to-be' with Brendan felt somehow more 'real', despite not much really having changed. She supposed it was the difference with having voiced it out in the open and to have received the full (non-judgemental) support of Gabby along with her enthusiasm and excitement for her friend. She'd told her everything, pretty much, and about just how much she felt for this man, and how *she* felt when she was with him. Gabby had concurred and agreed with her: Yes. She was definitely in love. However, she had echoed her own impatient concerns: what is she going to do? What are *they* going to do about it?

It seemed to Sheena that such small, finer details could wait. Her giddiness and happiness that he *felt the same as she did*, was enough right now. She was a one-track thought kind of girl lately, and that thought was: Brendan. Of Brendan smiling at her. Of him laughing at one of the many strange, unexpected things she comfortably said while they were alone together. Of Brendan's broad shoulders and strong arms gripping his handlebars as he peddled hard up the hill in front of her as she took the opportunity to sneakily admire him (= perv at him) from behind. He was constantly on her mind. She was obsessed. So much so, she realised now, as she thought back to her confession with Gabby that afternoon, that is only just struck her that Gabby *too* had had something she had wanted to tell her that day. However, Sheena's news had taken over and she'd gotten so preoccupied with telling her all about Brendan, that she'd forgotten that Gabby had something, probably just as important, to tell *her*.

'How fucking selfish of me, self-absorbed much…' She berated herself, feeling ashamed and guilty now. 'Must remember to ask her when I see her next. Hope she's ok.'

She cringed inwardly: how could she have ignored her very best friend, her only really good, female friend, other than this gorgeous, sexy creature seated closely in front of her now. 'Hope it's nothing serious.' She thought to herself, and semi-marvelled that 'oh look, there you go, a thought that's *not* about Brendan!'

"Well, d'uh!" April broke her temporary reverie brightly and laughed throatily. "I'm not an idiot, Babe – it's not a shock, really. I'm happy for you. Honestly Chickie, nice one. I hope you'll be very happy together. And look, I knew you weren't in it for the long-run or anything anyway, nice thing like you, you've always had that extra bit o'class. It's been a blast working with you hey, and you will be *sorely* missed, Chick. I mean that." She gave Sheena a long, poignant look. "I totes understand, Gorgeous. But, I'm wondering if I can ask you for one last favour?"

She rested one her perfectly manicured hands on Sheena's tight, jean-covered thighs now and gave it a subtle squeeze, keeping her hand clasped there afterwards. Sheena's leg tingled and burned under April's hot touch and she straightened up and leant a little closer to April who was leaning her luscious, wet, red, shiny lips further forward towards Sheena, where she began to whisper:

"Can you do me one last favour, Chickie? For old times' sake?" She fluttered her long, thick, black eyelashes ironically at Sheena and blew her another air kiss. Sheena laughed conspiratorially along with her, drawn in as ever by her friend's confidence and overtly sexy and flirty ways. She always felt like April was the fun, sexy, loud, confidant version of herself that in another universe she longed to be.

"What is it, Lovely?"

She asked her sexy friend, who was waiting for her answer, her cleavage pushed blatantly towards her and in Sheena's face once more.

"Well, Gorgeous-face, I have these two businessmen flying in from Brissy in a couple of weeks' time. They're old-time regulars, haven't been over this side in about a couple of years but when they're here, they pay *big*, and I mean: *big*. And they're a piece of cake, truly. It'd be the easiest five or so grand you'll ever make for a pretty enjoyable time with moi and those dudes – say you'll be my partner in crime one last time, go on mate! I never make the tips I do with you and our duos with anyone else. Come on Lovey, they've already booked in, go out on a bang! Last time, and no hard feelings when we part ways after that. What do you say hey?"

She rubbed her warm hand slowly in circular motions up Sheena's thigh, squeezing her playfully as her big, sparkling eyes looked imploringly at her. Sheena could hardly say no, April knew that, and she flashed her a wide, confidant smile.

Sheena smiled back and placed her hand lovingly over her sexy friend's and returned the squeeze.

"Oh, April, ok mate. Just to help you out, this one last time. Just this once though hey!" She repeated, smiling back at April.

It sounded a breeze, and helping her friend-cum-boss out one last time made her feel less guilty about giving her notice there anyway, as ridiculous as she knew it must sound. What harm could it do? It was already booked in, and would only be a couple of easy hours out of her life and then she'd be done and dusted and totally free. She knew that with the extra money too (considering it to be an end of contract bonus of sorts?) she'd also be pretty much able to be free from her lingering, post-marriage debt too, and her smile widened at the possibility. It felt so close now. Everything was at her fingertips and within reach. Including a gorgeous, fun woman she had so much time for, and a half bottle of chilled sav blanc.

She poured each a second large glassful and raised her own towards April, saying:

"To happy endings, and new beginnings!"

April laughed flirtily and clinked her glad with Sheena's.

"Y'see? You've got that bit a class thing goin for you hey. Yep, what you said then: happy endings and new beginnings, you clever thing you. I'll miss ya, Babe. Keep in touch, won't you Gorgeous. It won't be the same without ya! Now, I have a spare couple of hours: we gonna semi run-amuck? Let's order a few cocktails and some shooters and take this arvo up a gear – you've put me in the mood to party! Or, drown my sorrows, haha!"

She squeezed Sheena's thigh again, and Sheena bit her own lower lip. 'What the hell.' She thought

"Bring it on, mate!"

Taking a large gulp of her wine and smiling confidently back at April, she still felt on top of the world. The wheels were set in motion. Might as well distract herself and have fun while she was waiting 'patiently' for Brendan.

# CHAPTER SIXTEEN

A good two hours later, Sheena emerged from Benni's into the harsh, still-bright, late-afternoon sunshine (compared with the relative dark, cavernous ambience back inside the bar) stumbling ever so slightly and squinting up at the sky, shielding her delicate eyes as she assessed her surroundings. She was most definitely fuzzy. Most definitely slightly more than tipsy. Most definitely quite flustered and jam-faced. Most definitely *not* accustomed to afternoon drinking sessions with the stunning and very sexy April, who could most definitely drink Sheena under the proverbial table in, oh, just a couple of cocktails, it transpired.

'Phew. Definitely needed this air.' She remarked to herself and she casually leant against the wall outside Benni's, slightly dazed and confused, and dizzily wondering, 'where to next?'. When really, she knew she should be taking herself safely home. Hmmm.

She briefly thought about calling Brendan and seeing if he was free for a 'casual/innocent/platonic drink' but stopped herself. 'All in good time', she reminded herself, unsteadily. She smiled broadly as his image flooded her boozy brain. Glancing through the wooden-framed windows, complete with peeling paint, of the Freo-famous real-Italian pizzeria that was next-door neighbours with Benni's at the many happy couple and families within, her smile remained in place. She had to stumble to the right-hand side suddenly to avoid crashing into the steady throng that was queuing fairly patiently along the outside wall of said Italian restaurant, such were their famed pizzas and friendly atmosphere.

'Classy, Sheena.' She was mildly embarrassed as she swerved sharply to the right and narrowly avoided bumping in to the happy couple patiently waiting there, absorbed in their own romantic bubble.

"Sorry!"

She chucked out, and then let her mouth hang wide open as she stood in shock at just who the happy couple turned out to be.

"No worries mate!"

A jovial, familiar cry sounded, and the owner of this chirpy, bubbly voice casually spun around and flicked her long, vibrant, red hair over her shoulders and her pretty, equally surprised face came into view.

"Sheena!" She cried.

"Gabs!" Cried Sheena, simultaneously.

'Brendan!' Sheena thought wildly, as her eyes darted back and forth from her blushing, giggling best friend, to who she thought was *her* date-to-be/boyfriend-to-be/soulmate Mr Goodwood-slash-Brendan!

'This can't be happening.' She thought in a panic, the cocktails coming back to haunt her now as confusion and hurt began to set in. She kept a firm smile plastered on her face as she returned Gabby's enthusiastic hug and then tried to greet 'her' Brendan.

"Brendan?"

She ventured, only with a very slight slur. Damn those fucking cocktails.

His face turned an immediate and full-on, bright red, almost matching that of her own wine-face, and he quickly coughed and looked down to the ground, as Gabby gently punched her on the shoulder and giggled again.

Relief flooded through Sheena as she realised her blurry and drunken mistake.

"Sorry, I mean, Scott, isn't it? Great to see you again. And you, Gabs! Fancy seeing *you* here!" She cried, a little too excitedly and enthusiastically.

Gabby laughed again and pulled Sheena in for another hug.

"Haha, started early did you, Lovely? Good stuff."

Her face was nearly as flushed as Sheena's though, as she attempted to joke away what was fast turning into a very awkward encounter for the two flatmates and best friends.

'But why should it be awkward?' Sheena wondered, and more importantly: 'Why didn't Gabs *tell* me?!' She wasn't so far gone or too drunk and blurry to clearly see that Gabby was here on a *date* with Scott, whose crutches were now visible to Sheena, along with his discernibly different style of dressing to Brendan's. (Yep. Definitely *not* her Brendan.) They were every inch the 'new, happy couple' and Gabby couldn't wipe her giddy, wide smile off her face. Sheena thought Scott had a similar look about him too, although she remembered his obvious shyness and general nervousness from meeting him before, so it was hard to tell.

Still smiling back at Gabby, she didn't really even need to ask *why* she hadn't told her. It was blindingly obvious to Sheena, even in her drunken state: Gabs didn't tell her because it must be *serious*. She must be in *love* with Scott.

'Of course!' Sheena felt like slapping her own forehead in a very loud 'd'oh!' motion. 'That must have been what she wanted to tell me the other day! When I was so busy going on and on about myself and Brendan: *her* new boyfriend's brother!'

Feeling slightly guilty and ashamed of herself now, for not having probed and quizzed Gabby further on that particular afternoon when she said she had something she wanted to tell her, she attempted a reassuring and mutually understanding wide smile with rapid blinking to convey what she was thinking without having to voice it and spell it out in front of Scott. Gabs would know what she meant, and she squeezed Sheena's arm back gently, as if to say: 'No worries Lovely. Gotcha. No big deal.'

Now feeling like the silence and their wide, happy giddy smiling back at each other (while Scott coughed and looked down and all around – anywhere but at the two grinning women directly in front of him) was beginning to go on for too long and was getting potentially more awkward than either of them would have imagined, Gabs broke first and asked:

"So, Sheena, did you, um, did you want to join us? For some pizza? When we eventually get inside and out of this queue, that is."

It sounded like a genuine question to any bystander, but Sheena and Gabby both knew that it was not a real invitation. Sheena nodded briefly and squeezed Gabby's arm back and delivered the expected:

"Oh thanks, Gabs, but no, I have to be somewhere. Another time though!"

She swayed uncertainly to the right again, narrowly avoiding falling into the gutter, as Gabby grabbed her arm and stopped her.

"Woah there, Sheena! Are you sure you're alright?"

Her smile faltered now as a look of concern washed over her.

Embarrassed now and realising that, yes, this was the love of her life's twin brother standing just a metre away and no doubt taking in her very drunk, very embarrassing late afternoon behaviour, though he was doing an excellent job of pretending he wasn't.

'Fuck.' She realised she did not want this to get back to Brendan. Not that she was actually doing anything wrong per se, but, well, she felt embarrassed now, knowing that in all honesty Brendan probably wouldn't even care or judge her for it, she wasn't sure *why* she wouldn't want him to know about her afternoon drinking session. She clearly didn't want him to think she'd been out drinking with other men. But yet also, and she knew this was simply out of nineteen years of habit, she didn't want people to think she was drunk or drinking, and thus part of the problem. 'What problem now, though, Sheena?' She physically had to nudge herself and remind herself that there *was* no drunken husband and abusive marriage problem of which to inadvertently stir up or provoke. No problem at all. Albeit for the problem of being hopelessly in love with the forbidden fruit of her teacher, oh and being a student with a part-time job and a fair bit of debt to her name. But apart from those minor issues, she really had no major problem to speak of, which could be connected to her being drunk on a late Saturday, sunny afternoon. She was an adult; she could do what she liked.

Although her stumbling and dizziness were key reminders to Sheena, along with her rapidly oncoming pounding headache, and general feeling of shame and embarrassment, that drinking too much, was something she definitely did *not* like. With or without her ex-husband.

Sure, she'd had fun with April, sipping their wine, and later, cocktails, flirting gently and jovially with each other, April leaning closely to tell Sheena a key piece of filthy gossip or a particularly hilarious anecdote

181

about a recent episode with a client, her full, spectacular cleavage mere inches from Sheena's flushed face. However, as ever, the initial excitement, buzz and camaraderie of drinking with someone (for fun! Not just for mid-week obliteration or just because it was a weekend day. How novel…) quickly faded when she had bid adieu to April and was left on her own with the oncoming, impending hangover and the stumbly journey home she was yet to make. Now she had the *extra* 'con' of this particular boozy drinking session that *her* Brendan might hear about her being drunk and falling all over the place, in the middle of the afternoon and on her own. She didn't want that to happen. Time to pull herself together.

She straightened up, cleared her throat and laughed at herself, telling Gabby (and the potentially nearby, listening-in Scott):

"Haha, yes, I'm fine. Although these new shoes are obviously giving me grief. Think I'll go and buy a pair of thongs, as I obviously can't be trusted to walk about in these new heels."

She stuck one foot out in front of Gabby now, praising someone up above that indeed she *had* been wearing heels on that particular day (a rare event for Sheena when she wasn't at work at Secrets – heels were usually reserved for her 'Ruby' uniform).

Gabby laughed along with her, accepting the act and her reason for her near-fall.

"Yep, they look like some serious killer heels, Missy! Get thee to a shoe-shop, immediately! Can't have you tripping around Freo in those little numbers. Although they are *gorgeous*! Where did you get them from?"

Sheena was just about to launch into the no doubt very boring (to Scott

182

anyway) details of her recent shoe purchase, but luckily (for all three) the queue began moving forward and gave them all the chance to end their little awkward meeting.

"Oh look! Looks like you'll be heading in next, so I'll love you and leave you both. Enjoy your dinner and I'll catch up with you both soon!"

'Wow, look at me, already calling them a 'both'.' Sheena marvelled.

"Gabs, I'll probs see *you* sooner though, although maybe you'll be together, who knows, none of my business, ok I'll shut up now, so, anyway Gabs, I'll give you the shoe details later Lovely, better go now!"

Sheena finished digging herself deeper and deeper and rambling a very tipsy goodbye to the couple, one of whom's blushing had now returned in full force at Sheena's not-so-subtle implication that she may be seeing him at her flat when he was no doubt going to stay over to give Gabs a good seeing to.

'Good one, Sheena. Way to make that one very awkward goodbye!' She berated herself, feeling her own flush growing again now.

Gabby simply laughed it off and kissed Sheena's cheek, telling her:

"Get home safely lovely, and take those heels off Sheens – go barefoot, it's a lovely day. See you at home, Darl."

With that, the queue mercifully moved forward again, having acquired a life of its own, and Sheena stepped back and headed off down the street, once more alone with her confused, blurry thoughts. They were a mixture of: well, *that* was awkward, good one, Sheena / wow, Gabs is in love! That's awesome / yum pizza, I could really go a large Hawaiian right now / and: oh god, I think I'm going to throw up – fuck, where's a bin?...

Breathing in deeply as she slowly walked-slash-stumbled-slightly down the street, she managed to control her nausea and managed to *not* vomit. 'Yum, pizza' seemed to be the winning, predominant thought however, as she found herself nearing her local take-away/pizza delivery shop. 'Hmmm, food first, maybe texting or calling Brendan later...'

# CHAPTER SEVENTEEN

Brendan led the way, reluctantly. The wind had picked up on this otherwise balmy, Fremantle night, almost as if a sign for them to turn back now.

'This is a very bad idea'. He thought to himself, as they continued on in silence. He'd said his bit back at Scott's apartment, and it seemed Scott's mind was made up: he was adamant this was the only option he had.

Brendan had shaken his head continuously as he'd poured them both a very stiff drink each. He needed something to get through what would surely be an awkward, seriously unsexy and ultimately *not* fun night. Handing his brother's drink to him he had tried valiantly, just as he'd done the week or so before when Scott had initially broached the idea with him, awkwardly and red with deep embarrassment, of course.

"I think you're making a big mistake, bro."

He had stated. Scott immediately turned his focus to the safety of the floor.

"I mean," Brendan had continued. "Why not *try* talking to her first? Just think how she'd feel about this plan! Wouldn't that fuck things up worse than if you just *talked* to her?" He had pleaded.

Scott had joined him in rapidly shaking his head, his face red.

"I can't tell her about this. I just can't." He looked sharply up at Brendan now, a fresh look of panic on his otherwise handsome face. "And what do you mean? Why would she ever find out? You wouldn't tell anyone about this would you, bro?"

Brendan had placed a strong, reassuring hand on his arm, and steadied his slightly shaky (obviously extremely nervous) twin.

"Of course not, Bro. This one's going to the grave with me. And it should with you too. In fact, let's just not go, then there's nothing to tell and we can just go out together and have a relatively normal bro's night out, yeah?"

He'd been hopeful, so hopeful that Scott would see what a ridiculous plan it was.

Scott had dashed his hopes with his:

"But bro, you're always telling me there *is* no 'normal' and that everything's been conceived of and done before we've even 'thought' of it or decided to do it, so, in a way, I've already *done* it somewhere in an alternate version of this universe or reality…."

He trailed off and looked at Brendan, half-smiling now. Their drinks had slightly taken the edge off Scott's extreme nerves and Brendan's extreme sense of dread and trepidation.

Brendan had smiled back. Using his own philosophy material *against* him in a persuasive argument? 'Well played, Scott, well played.' He thought admiringly, however he rolled his eyes playfully at his brother, again adding to the slightly lighter, less tense atmosphere:

"Don't do as I *say*, do as I do!" He tried. "So you *were* listening to all my years of ramblings then? Or you've read through my teaching notes? Anyway, that's just all theory, that never *really* helps with your actual everyday and personal life – shhh, don't tell my students though. They might think I'm a fraud."

His eyes twinkled with the irony.

"Look Brendo." Scott had turned uber-serious once again. "I

know how you feel: you think this is a shit idea, and yes, you think I should talk to Gabby instead. But listen, I'm going to do this. Then I can forget all about it and get on with things with Gabs, and she'll never need to know that I was a lame, thirty-two year old virgin. But if you're going to help me, like you said you would, please stop telling me what a shithouse idea it is and how much of a mistake you think I'm making. I'm fucking nervous enough as it is. I need your support not your head-shaking. Please, bro. Just a couple of hours out of your life and then we'll never mention it again."

He had resumed looking at the floor, his face burning and the tips of his ears also aflame, as Brendan was temporarily silenced. His brother had a point, he knew. He had decided then and there to do whatever Scott needed him to do that night, and would from there on keep his doubts and judgement to himself. He knew this would be one of Scott's most daunting and awkward nights of his life, and he also knew just how hard it must be for him to be talking about such intimate details of his sex-life. Or, non-sex-life, as was the current case.

So he had smiled back a broad, genuine, warm smile at his red-faced, mortified twin brother, and placed his hand back on his arm, giving him another reassuring squeeze.

"Ok mate. No more negative shit from me. Promise. But I'm mixing us another few drinks then. God knows I don't want to be sober for where we're going. You in?"

Scott's eyes raised and met their mirror images looking lovingly back at them, and he tentatively returned the contagious smile.

"Yeah, go on then, Brendo. Not too strong though, hey."

They'd temporarily relaxed and spent the next few hours drinking, talking, laughing, and apparently not remembering where they would be heading in just a few shorts hours. Intentional short-term amnesia perhaps. Or a fraternal truce. Brendan definitely didn't mind this portion of the night. It felt as if it had been much too long since they had properly spent time together and caught up on each other's lives. He had genuinely been enjoying his previously dreaded Saturday night now. That is, until it really had been time to leave, time to head to their appointment (well, his brother's only, really – Brendan was just going with him for moral support and to help him through doors and along dark, unfamiliar corridors without stumbling).

They walked past a few local pubs lining the dark, windy streets, and Brendan thought to himself for maybe the tenth time that night, that wouldn't it be great if Scott suddenly and magically changed his mind and said 'hey Brendan, let's go in here for a few quiet pints instead'. As they slowly made their way past though, with Brendan looking longingly at said drinking establishments, it appeared this get-out-of-jail option would *not* be the case and they carried on with their clandestine journey, onwards to where, well, Brendan wasn't quite sure what to expect or what he thought they'd see when they got there. He was quite sure Scott hadn't a clue either: the entire booking procedure had been conducted over the phone and with the end result of an anonymous text message being delivered post-phone call briefly stating the exact address and the time for his appointment.

Brendan huffed to himself and drew his corduroy jacket tighter around him in a bid to protect himself from the wind's harassment.

'This is seriously unsexy.' He thought again to himself.

Where they would soon find themselves was completely new territory for him. He'd never entertained a desire before to ever visit that sort of place, and he felt slightly rattled and a fair bit pissed off with himself (and his brother, of course) that he would have now lost that particular claim to fame. Reminding himself that he was doing this for *Scott*, his dearly loved, do-anything-for twin brother, who needed him now, he quickly squashed down and swallowed his feelings of annoyance and his bruised ego. Literally swallowing his pride, he now glanced at Scott, who hadn't uttered a peep since leaving his apartment. He had a look of quiet resignation about him, as if he'd been chastised or told off. Looked like he wasn't finding their fast-approaching destination exciting or glamourous either.

"You alright, bro?"

Brendan asked, his face creased with worry, although the dark evening did a pretty good job of hiding this feature.

Scott coughed.

"Yeah, bro." He assured him, as confidently as he could. "Umm,

it's just up here on the right mate."

They both slowed their, already nearly an amble or slow stroll, pace as they neared a fairly non-descript, wrought iron gate that enclosed a fairly average looking, dark, large townhouse. There was no sign or plaque indicating that this was indeed the place.

"You sure, mate? Looks pretty dark inside. You sure they're in?"

Hoping, still hoping that there would be some giant fuck-up with either the address or the time/date. 'Maybe we've come on the wrong day?'

He thought hopefully.

Scott fumbled in his back pocket for his phone and swiped through a few of his messages.

"Yep." He said uncertainly. "This is definitely the place. Look:

number fifty, Harkin Avenue. Press buzzer for assistance."

He didn't move to press the buzzer though and simply looked down to

the ground again.

'Christ, do I have to everything myself?! This had better not be the case

when we're inside.' Brendan fumed to himself. Sighing audibly, but

quickly trying to calm himself down and not let on to Scott how he felt

(after all, he said he would help and not judge him, so what good would

it do to make him feel shit and even more embarrassed now they were

already here?) Brendan reached over and pressed the buzzer gingerly.

"Name and appointment time." Came a brusque, official voice.

"Erm, 10 o'clock, Scott Goodw-, ahem, Scott Smith." Brendan

had a mild panic and apparently chosen the most unoriginal

pseudonym he could think of. "And his brother-slash-escort,

Peter Smith."

"Sorry bro!" he whispered to Scott, who simply shrugged back at

him.

A loud, deep buzz from the door was emitted and a loud click indicated

that the gate was now open. Brendan pushed the gate and it swung

open easily. They made their way up the four large, marble steps to the

black front door, and seeing it was open, twisting the door knob,

Brendan pushed it wide open and held it back for them both to enter

the seemingly dark hallway inside. The door shut heavily behind them.

Both brothers held their breath. Soft candlelight lined the long hallway

where they found themselves in, and it took a few moments for their

eyes to adjust to the light (or new lack of). When they regained the ability to see they both noticed a large ornate mahogany desk just to the right of the door. Behind it stood a tiny, all but 5 foot of her, beautiful Asian-looking girl, in her, at a guess, early twenties, her jet-black hair falling in stern straight lines over her bare, pretty, delicate shoulders. Brendan was startled to see that she was topless, save for some kind of corset contraption with the breasts cut-out, having the effect of cupping this beautiful young woman's tits and holding them forward to welcome them both. Scott would have been startled too, had he not been staring so intently at the plush, deep red carpet that lined every inch of the heavily gilded decorated hallway. Brendan coughed now, embarrassingly enough almost choking as he fought to regain his composure.

The woman behind the desk stopped looking through her paperwork on top of the desk and looked up and smiled mischievously at them both, her small, deep cherry red lips twitching and smiling as if she was in on some kind of private joke.

"Ahh, the Smith brothers, I presume?"

She flicked her long, glossy black main of hair over her shoulders now, and stepped out from behind her mahogany shield of a cubicle. As she did so, Brendan, and now Scott, who had raised his eyes to her when she spoke to them, both breathed in sharply. Her black leather, cut-away 'top' (if it could be called that) ended just above her tiny and taught, olive-brown midriff and her prominent, pointy hip bones led their eyes down to the rest of her outfit: barely there tiny leather underwear (or so they assumed) and nothing else but some black leather chaps and some extremely pointy, towering fuck-me-shoes. A mini black whip was attached to her right hip by the means of a bright red holdster, and in her hand was a black walkie-talkie, reminiscent of some kind of covert, secret op.

She stood there for a moment, sizing the two brothers up. Neither of them dared move. Then, slowly rolling her hips she strode over to them. Standing before them with her little hands on her petite hips and that smirk on her cherry red, glossy lips.

"Now, let me see." She said pensively. "You must be Scott, is it?"
She had turned slightly towards Scott as he, in response, stared hard at the floor and his face flushed crimson. He coughed and nodded.
She twisted quickly to look directly at Brendan now, hands still firmly in place on her hips.

"And you must be Brendan, Scott's 'supporter' for the night, yes?"
Brendan attempted a casual, breezy smile back.

"Yes, that's right."
His eyes flicked around the hall, noting the many erotic posters and nudes that lined the corridor, amidst many a phallic statue and a few giant marble, erotic sculptures and paraphernalia. A heady, vanilla scent pervaded his nostrils and the hundreds of candles flickered behind this mystery diminutive dominatrix hostess. If it looked dark and uninviting from the outside of the large townhouse, the interior was an extreme opposite: decadently inviting and clearly designed to be both calming yet arouse all of the senses at once.

Nobody moved or spoke for a moment. It seemed like many minutes to both Scott and Brendan but in reality could only have been a few seconds. The girl chuckled again, clearly enjoying the tension and their apparent awkwardness. She flicked her long, shiny hair over her shoulders again and spun around suddenly, revealing her bare, and perfectly toned, tiny, round arse cheeks sitting atop her tight, leather chaps, as she strutted purposefully back over to the desk.

"Now, don't you boys worry about a thing. You're going to have the time of your life here. That's a 'Secrets' guarantee." She winked at them. "Now, Scott, is it? I just need your signature on this release form and either some good old, hard cash for your deposit, or your credit card, whichever you prefer. We can sort out the balance at the end of the night, as we discussed on the phone."

This girl was all calm and efficient and very much a business woman now. She handed a clipboard with some papers on it to Scott, whilst simultaneously flicking her eyes back and forth between these two, still a bit too sober for this joint, brothers.

"Now, I take it neither of you have been here before," She assumed, "So let me run through a few house rules we have here – don't worry, there really aren't many! Now, before we begin, (and then, yes, Scott, I'll take you through to meet with Melanie, your own personal hostess for tonight: I can see you're eager to get started!) can I get you two fellas a tasty beverage? You sure do look like you could do with it! What'll it be? Bourbon? Beer? Vodka? Whisky? Name your poison, sweethearts."

Brendan knew Scott would leave this choice up to him too, and quickly called out:

"Bourbon, thanks!"

"My pleasure, Handsome. Now you two just head on into that parlour room just on the left there and make yourselves comfy.

I'll be right back with your drinks, and a few dos and don'ts about this fine institution."

She was off again, rolling her hips and striding past them into one of the many darkly stained oak, closed doors that lined the vast corridor. The townhouse was something of a tardis: it looked unremarkably average and medium-sized from the outside, but was anything *but* average inside, and it was huge. The brothers glanced over to the open door about ten metres away that she had indicated, presumably leading to the 'parlour room' they had been instructed to go and wait in.

"Well, bro, this is it yeah. You sure you're sure about this?"
Brendan could only hope and give him one last chance to change his mind.

"Come on Brendo, let's go and have a drink in there. We're here now."
Was Scott's staunch reply.

'Well, I guess he's really going through with this then.' Brendan thought.

"Ok, bro, lead the way!"
He tried to sound cheery as Scott started to pull himself slowly across the large, red-lined hallway on his crutches. As they slowly made their way towards the door, a clicking sound alerted them both to the fact that another door, back over by the gleaming mahogany reception desk, had now opened, and a procession of about fifteen stunning women, all in various states of undress, breezed past them, rolling their hips and blowing kisses at them both, some smiling provocatively as they sashayed around the two temporarily stunned and frozen in place brothers, now enveloped in an intoxicating mist of different scents and

perfumes.

Scott's coughing increased to something of a coughing fit and Brendan, glad for the distraction turned to his brother to thump him helpfully on his broad back. As he did so, a horrified pair of darkly lined eyes caught his as he flicked his eyes to his left. Now definitely frozen in place, he stared at Sheena, who was momentarily floored and also frozen in place, staring back at him.

'What the actual fuck?!?' Brendan's mind whirred at a hundred miles a minute, wildly confused as to why Sheena was magically caught in the middle of this harem of premium prostitutes currently sashaying past them as they attempted to make their way into the 'parlour room'. He felt bile rise up in his throat. He thought he was going to vomit. His heart raced. His skin felt clammy. What. The. Actual. Fuck.

His face drained of colour. All he could do was stand and stare at her, his jaw hanging open in horror and his brow still creased in confusion.

Sheena was quicker to regain her composure, and equally white faced and horrified, all but ran (tottered really, given the ridiculously high stilettos she had on) down the hallway, and seconds later the brothers were alone, and still frozen in place, Brendan breathing heavily and Scott now being the one to look at his brother with concern.

Brendan stumbled back and grabbed the side of the desk for support as he tried to catch his breath and think clearly. What. The. Actual. Fuck.

"Let's get out of here."

He stated, and not waiting for Scott to reply or even start to mention that 'by the way, isn't that your Sheena?' he was at the heavy-set front door and soon would be plunging out into the now welcome, safety of the cool, dark night.

'What the *fuck*!?' Was all Brendan's mind could manage right now.

# CHAPTER EIGHTEEN

"Come on, Ruby-love, get a wriggle on: it's sashay-o-fucking-clock already! Time to look the part!"

A soon-to-be-ex-colleague, Tiffany (if that was her real name, Sheena could never be sure at Secrets) annoyingly-cheerily instructed her. She was taking her self-appointed role of 'Team Leader' *way* too seriously. Didn't she realise she was a hooker in a brothel, for fuck's sake?

Sheena grimaced and sighed loudly, impatiently. She didn't know why she had to even bother with this fake 'I'm for hire' advertising bullshit anyway, the old parade in front of the new clientele and see if he likes you to earn a bit more cash that night (Secrets was big on promoting from within its organisation, and the entrepreneurial spirit and such). She wasn't officially 'working' there anymore anyway: she'd officially given her notice and left the week before, having only come back for this very specific, very personal duo appointment with the luscious, sexy April, purely as a personal favour to her mate (and again, soon-to-be-definitely-ex-colleague). There was no fucking way she'd be interested in picking up any extra punters this evening. A quick game's a good game and all that.

Still, she rose from the vintage make-up table with spotlight mirror and nearly threadbare, dusky-pink velour, gold-studded stool, thinking that this last faux-for-sale-sashay past the penultimate client she'd ever have to vaguely set eyes upon (she most definitely would *not* be chucking out her 'come-hither-and-fuck-me-eyes' at them, that's for sure, why bother?) might help to pass the time until these 'important' businessmen finally showed up (April and her duo appointment guests for the evening were annoyingly held up or hadn't bothered turning up

197

yet – Sheena hated waiting and was not keen on being stuck with her own thoughts within the walls of this place she'd come to absolutely detest.)

"Alright, Tiff, take it easy Love. I'm not even meant to be here really, ya know. Oh well, yup, I'm ready, give us a sec, ok...."

The fourteen other beautiful women (some naturally so, and Sheena always thought: far too beautiful to be working here – they must be even more fucked up and desperate for cash than *she'd* been, and others, make-up-ly enhanced to give the impression under the dim, cosy lights of the brothel that they were also genuine stunners, and helped by the fact that they had some very large and distracting features at about chest level) amid a mixture of sighs, grumbles, and a couple of coughs, plastered on their best actress smiles and one by one left the communal changing room to go and 'wow' the couple of customers out there, aiming to floor their jaws (and ease their potential wallets open) just as they were heading into the temporary waiting area, supplied with ample porn mags, price lists, and wall-to-wall, giant erotic canvas paintings, all in a suitably dim (romantic?) light, of course.

Rolling their hips one by one, the group enveloped the pair of shell-shocked, near-identical men standing there mid-attempting to make it across the corridor and into the room.

"Yum. *Twins*...."

Purred Angela, a slightly rough around the edges, heavily made up, buxom redhead with a raspy, throaty voice at the front of the escort-group.

Sheena stopped mid-sway, suddenly feeling as if she may vomit violently. She felt the blood drain away from her face and she stood feeling the full force of sheer horror as she clocked who these twins were. Breaking out in a clammy sweat, she wrenched her eyes away from one pair of theirs and did her best to walk off without collapsing to the floor, where it felt like her heart and guts already were. She couldn't breathe. She couldn't think straight. She felt sick and shaky-as-fuck. All but running back into the room she'd just strutted out of, she ran into the toilet cubicle and slammed the lock shut, just making it in time before she retched violently into the chipped, off-white, porcelain bowl. She kneeled there, heaving a few more times, her mind reeling and her body shaking.

'What the fuck!?! What the fucking fuck was *Brendan* doing there?!'

It was definitely him, although her mind was seriously struggling to take this information in right now. *Brendan?* At *Secrets??* With his brother *Scott?!?* Gabby's new love of her life??

She retched again, nothing but green bile coming out now, and she heaved again and again, until she was dry-retching, spent and exhausted. This couldn't be real. This couldn't be happening. *Her* Brendan?! At a brothel?? Oh god, she was suddenly struck with a fresh wave of horror, processing the now obvious thought that Brendan had seen *her* there too. As one of the girls for rent. He would think she was a fucking prostitute! Indignant, outraged and ashamed, she was struggling to put her own thoughts in order. She didn't even *work* here anymore: this was all behind her, she was only here for a one-off, favour to April, she wasn't an escort anymore! Why oh why the fuck was he there on this night?? Or at *all?!* Her thoughts rushed wildly at her, clamouring to be heard:

'So, all that bullshit of 'wanting to do things right' and of 'waiting until the right time' – what the fuck was that??' She fumed, hot tears now breaking free from where they had been building up and threatening to spill over and out, now the initial shock had slightly abated, and she sat back on her heels, letting her sobs escape in a wail, not caring if anyone else was out in the dressing room or if they could hear her (fucken hell – the amount of angst and despair and crying that took place behind the scenes here, it's not as if it would be anything unusual to hear someone in a bad way in the toilets). She gulped and tried to catch her breath, wiping away what salty tears she could from her now mascara-stained, blotchy face with the back of her hand.

'So, he'll fuck a whore, but he didn't want to fuck me?' Sheena felt so hurt and wounded, even though logically she knew she had no right to. It wasn't as if he was even her boyfriend. Maybe she'd imagined their deep connection this whole time. Or why the fuck would he be there in a *brothel*?!?

She felt winded and completely blindsided, trying desperately to catch her breath and her thoughts, which were still spinning wildly out her very confused, very hurt mind. She didn't know what to do. What the actual fuck. Was he really there, about to pay one of her (on the whole) skanky colleagues for the pleasure of their flesh and time?? It was incomprehensible to her. Had he been there before? Oh god, she was going to be sick. Again.

She turned and heaved into the toilet once more, her frail shoulders heaving until she sat back exhausted once again. She couldn't decide if she was outraged and furious more than hurt and devastated, and the two differing emotions were fighting for centre stage in her throbbing head.

'Oh my god.' She paled even further. 'What must he think of me? That I'm a fucken prostitute?' She'd never forget his own look of shock and horror, equal to, if not more intense, than her own. Amazing how much shock and horror could be conveyed through simply a look. No words spoken between them. As if she'd ever be able to even *find* the right words. This was surely it then. It had to be all over now, before it even began. How would she even *begin* to explain what she was doing there? And even if she could, what about *him*? Why the fuck was *he* there? With Gabby's boyfriend? His own flesh and blood twin brother?? Her sick, disgusted and outraged feelings returned in full force now.

She saw immediately that he would no doubt never be able to find the 'right' words either. It was hopeless. Surely if either of them were to ever mention it to the other, it would be mutually destructible – each giving away their own 'dirty secret'. She couldn't very well bring it up and ask what the hell he was doing there, any more than he could reproach her for being there herself on that night. They were both mutually and equally 'caught out', it seemed to Sheena.

The unfairness of her situation came back to her once more, that she wasn't even supposed to *be* there that night! Or any night now. She didn't even work there anymore! Then, she supposed, if she hadn't come back in for one last shift, she may never have found out about Brendan and his apparent penchant for visiting whorehouses with his own twin brother.

She thought about being sick again. It was all so horrendous. And confusing. She had no idea how to compose herself, choosing to remain on the cold, slightly gritty and dusty toilet floor, dimly lit with one lone, hanging, flickering lightbulb.

She had no idea if he was even still out there. Hoping that his shock and horror had in fact caused him to lead his brother promptly back out of the large front door. But *she* was still in here, she reminded herself, and about to go and 'party' with sexy April and those two rich, outer-state businessmen and get up to all sorts of depraved and filthy acts. Brendan must be imagining all sorts about what she was doing in here right now. That is, if he was even going to give her a second thought now, or had immediately struck her from his mind and life. She wished she could call him. Even just to apologise.

'For what, Sheena?!' She scolded herself again. 'Sorry I caught you picking up whores in the brothel where I work?' She slumped her head back into her hands and resumed sobbing. It was hopeless. Mutual devastation and destruction. No good could ever come from speaking to or seeing Brendan again. An immediate and all-encompassing sense of grief enshrouded her and weighed her down. She couldn't yet move with the weight and pressure of it all. Hopeless. She sobbed. She'd lost him. Just when she'd *found* him.

# CHAPTER NINETEEN

Brendan was vaguely aware of Scott opening the heavy door (for him, this time) and holding it whilst aiming to urge him through it, back into the crisp night air. He couldn't recall if he managed to get his credit card back without any trouble, or even if Scott went to sort that out, which he assumed his (usually) level-headed, organised bro would surely do. It was all a bizarre sped-up blur to Brendan. He was in a semi-trance state, looking at the ground. Saying nothing. Feeling: nothing. Nothing but numbness. Shock was a funny thing. He knew his body was going through the motions of walking slowly down the pavement alongside his crutch-wielding brother Scott, and then he assumed they must have side-stepped that dickhead drunk group of guys who were loudly ambling their way. He guessed that after that they had, in mutual stunned silent agreement, sought out the closest pub they could and were now sitting in its quietest corner (or the quietest corner they could find, this being the usual raucous Saturday night in Freo) each with a pint in hand, each silent, save for their occasional sips and Scott's ubiquitous coughing. But, he had no memory of what thought process had got him there. He supposed some sort of auto-pilot, defence mechanism had kicked in and brought them to a place of safety, but he was stumped as to any finer details after that life altering moment when he'd clocked Sheena (*Sheena*, of all people!) parading around her wares as a potential hooker for them for the night. It was so inconceivable a notion to Brendan that his brain really hadn't caught up with what his eyes had told him, and he sat in that sort of trance state, pint in hand, and heart pounding in his throat. Scott was equally silent and shocked, save for his coughing. Either for his own fears and potential outcome of how this may play out, given that his girlfriend's best mate and flatmate, had just seen him in a brothel, or due to his empathy and hurt he felt for his brother and what he must be feeling. It seemed for both brothers the best thing to do at that point in time, was simply do nothing. At this stage anyway. Surely the answer would come to them and make itself apparent after a few more much needed, calming sips.

Scott continued to cough beside him. Glancing his way, Brendan noted his signature deep red blush, and again, even amid his own confusion and trauma, felt an immediate sympathy for his brother. What were the chances! What a nightmare for him. After all that stress, deliberation and the fair bit of planning involved, it had all come to nothing. Worse than nothing. It now seemed both brothers' love lives were now in a definite crisis. Everything had changed in an instant.

It was Scott who spoke first.

"D'ya think she'll tell her? Gabby, I mean? Did she *definitely* see us?"

His eyes flicked up and looked up into his brother's now, frantically searching for a sign that everything would be ok, that no, of course she hadn't even recognised them.

Brendan had to let out an ironic chuckle. 'Ever the optimist, eh bro?' he thought. He took a huge gulp of his beer now.

"Oh yes. She definitely saw us." He stated grimly. "No idea if she'll tell her mate. Am guessing not."

A silence fell back upon them again. Scott's coughing resumed.

"Did you know she worked there?" Brendan asked him.

Scott spun around to face him again.

"What?! What the fuck! Of course not. I would never have meant... I mean, I wouldn't have booked... I would have told you, bro!"

He was aghast, and spluttered his defence wildly.

"Nah bro," Brendan reassured him, "It's all good. I believe you. So, am guessing her job's probably pretty private, so no, I don't think she'll tell Gabby that she saw you there."

Another quiet lull.

"But then, you never ever know! Anything's possible, I'd say tonight's proved that."

Brendan couldn't help another ironic guffaw from escaping his lips, just as Scott coughed to show his dismay and unease.

Brendan, for all his open-mindedness and philosophical teachings, always having had something to say about pretty much everything in the past, was, for once, stunned into silence again. He literally did not know what to say, or think right now. So he said nothing. Scott continued to burn up and splutter beside him, and Brendan knew that it was his unspoken duty, as protective, reassuring, 'older' brother to at least try to say something calming, soothing, and at least *positive* about the turn of events. But he just couldn't find it in him. It was more than enough for him right now to muster up the hand to mouth coordination of simply picking up his pint repeatedly and bringing it close to his lips, given his confused state of mind, which now swinging somewhere between frustration and anger at Scott for dragging him there in the first place, and then anger at Sheena for quite literally being a lying *whore*. Then he'd instantly change his tune as he'd remind himself that, wait, she hadn't actually *lied* to him (although it seems apparent she may indeed be a whore, yes) she just hadn't told him about it, and then his mind would remind him of the very real love he had for both Sheena and his brother, instantly dissipating his previous anger. Her look of horror and her pale, blood-drained, distraught face as she locked eyes with him back in the chop-shop's foyer was repeatedly coming back to haunt him now, and his heart lurched, wanting to wrap his arms around her and hold her close, *never* wanting to make her look that way again.

'Oh shit'. The thought returned to him now of what she must be thinking of him. He had to clear *that* up. Can't have her thinking the very worst of him. But what could he say? That his brother dragged him there, kicking and screaming?! As if anyone would be likely to believe *that*.

'I knew it was a bad idea.' He mentally kicked himself for agreeing to, hands down, Scott's worst idea in the history of their thirty-two years of brotherhood.

But what about *her*?? His mind had tugged him back the other way in confusion again. She was a prostitute! Shouldn't that somehow change how he felt about her? He got the feeling that, if anything, he should probably be *more* outraged, if anything, than he actually was. Sure, he was shocked, and feeling confused. But, if everything he'd been led to believe, courtesy of growing up with songs such as 'Angel is a Centrefold', by now his blood should have been running cold and he should have been completely repulsed. As, in this case, 'Angel' isn't even just a centrefold model in a men's mag, she's a hooker. Takes money from random strangers and gives them head or fucks them. As it happened, one of his overriding feelings, after his shock and general confusion, was one of arousal. He was confused: why was he so turned on, or so intrigued, by this 'new' Sheena, when *she* was clearly horrified at his discovery of her. He could clearly see this was not her ideal job, and that she must have been working there due to some hard times ('why didn't she tell me? I could have tried to help.' He thought instinctively) yet the image of her with those anonymous men and those deep, red, shiny, full lips of hers, well, it was a striking one. His mouth had curved upwards into a natural smile thinking about her.

It dawned on him now that the mysterious vibe he had gotten from her, far from being the innocent, damaged introvert he was (now he knew) hopelessly in love with, but must have been due to her having a mysterious, covert 'other' life and role to play. Oh, he wished she had just *told* him. She had often seemed on the verge of being about to tell him something more, but he'd assumed it was more stuff to do with her ex-husband and more ways that he'd damaged and hurt her. Then, he supposed, maybe her choice of work *was* due to being damaged by him: she clearly wasn't doing it for fun. Or not on that particular night anyway, by the look on her face.

'Shit!' He repeated to himself. She must be thinking the very worst about him. He almost laughed at the ironic timing of the situation: there he was, about to tell her that he had quit the very *one* obstacle that was keeping them from being together: his job as her teacher, and confess his strong feelings for her, when bam: there she *was*. In a brothel that his *stupid* brother had implored that he go into with him for his *stupid* idea of getting laid before he was able to sleep with his girlfriend: *Sheena's* best friend and flatmate. How would he explain all of this to Sheena? Would she even *want* his explanation? She obviously

207

thought that he was there on pleasure and of his own accord, why would she think any differently. And that he was visiting with his *brother* too. God, she must be horrified.

But then, he mused, if she did know more about his recent past, maybe she really would be horrified. After all, Brendan had been no angel, and up until his recent new-found love and infatuation with Sheena, what was so different about what he had been doing with a fair number of his students? The only difference being that he wasn't giving them actual cash (only higher grades or exemptions from assignments) but it was still a trade-off and he knew it. As much as he would wax lyrical about there being no original thought or 'new' idea and that everything was to do with sex, he *knew* that what he had been doing was wrong, very wrong, and it now did not sit very well with him at all.

'So much for my spouting all that bullshit about nothing in this world being original, and then *still* being surprised to see Sheena doing probably what thousands of other students before her have done – why am I so shocked?' His thoughts drifted again. He sipped his pint again, realising that this, his shock and amazement, was making him smile. It felt refreshing to be able to be surprised, as he'd thought he had seen it all, thought nothing would shock him these days.

'Sheena, my darling, you never cease to intrigue and amaze me!' His smile was back in full force now, as his tender feelings won over any lingering angry ones.

He thought of her now, in the get-up he'd just clocked her in: a sexy little number consisting of a black, leather corset-type-thing with a midnight blue g-string and black suspenders, her beautiful breasts (the first time he'd really seen them in any good measure) spilling forth from the teeny-tiny, too tight leather cups, and her long, toned, black-stocking-clad legs led his eyes down to her bright blue, sky-high, stripper-esque stilettos. He compared this image with that of the last time he'd seen her, when he was pressed up hard against her on the beach, her face free of make-up, her hair wild and loose around her pretty face, and her body, fully clothed, as she smiled knowingly with him and they both shared that moment. Or so he thought. Was *that* the real Sheena, that day, on Rotto? Or on any of the countless afternoons that they had spent together talking over coffee, Sheena sitting there in jeans and a casual white singlet. Or was that woman he saw tonight her 'real' self? He guessed not judging by her look of absolute horror at either having been seen or of seeing him there.

Should he feel ashamed that he had found hooker-Sheena to be so attractive? Did he find her more attractive than former-student-woman-I'm-in-love-with-Sheena? Or were they one and the same, he pondered.

A sudden horrifying thought struck him. More horrifying than realising the love of his life, who he had just quit his job for, is a prostitute. Brendan wondered if she had been acting with *him*? Was she simply pretending that day, or on any of the many days they'd spent together, putting on a show of having these similar feelings for him? Could he believe anything she had told him? About her ex-husband, his drinking years and her abuse, what if it were all fabricated? He physically shook his head free of this thought and reminded himself that she hadn't actually *lied* to him. No, moreover, he hadn't ever *asked*. Why would he? Plus, it's not like she was even his girlfriend. He was not in a relationship with her.

'Yet.' He corrected himself. But did she really know how he felt or what he was planning? He was kicking himself now for not having made himself clear about his intentions. 'Instead of giving her a vague 'all in good time' spiel, why didn't I just *tell* her?!' He tormented himself. However, realistically, he wondered whether that would have made a difference. He had no idea whether this was a new venture for Sheena, or whether she was a pro. Well, in more ways than one.

In all honesty, to him, she didn't quite seem that convincing, seemed quite nervy or stand-offish, so perhaps this was her very first night there? His mind was coming up with all sorts of stories and solutions and explanations yet none of them were really helping him figure things out. Again, he saw he standing there, her beautiful, large breasts thrust out towards him, and a horrified, open-mouthed, shiny red pout, her full, glossy lips hanging open in shock as she saw him staring back at her. How would that have played out: could he have chosen her? Called out to her, perhaps?

His vision of her now ran her hand through her shiny, chocolate-coloured, bouncy waves and her pout turned into a mischievous smile, stretching all the way to her heavily made-up, smoky, dark eyes, her amber irises sparkling back at him. She raised one finger to her mouth and gestured that he keep schtum, whispering a gentle: "shhhh!" his way. He stood there silently, as she rolled her curvy hips towards him and stopped about an arm's length away, her breasts pushed up so close towards his face now.

"Hello there." She drawled in a seductive, husky, low voice. "I'm Bella. I'll be your hostess tonight. Follow me."

She reached down and took his hand, leading him down the dark, musty, heavily incensed hallway and into one of the many closed doors that lined it. Once inside she firmly shut the door, and pushed him, still completely silent, down onto the waiting black-satin-covered-bed. She forced his legs wide apart and stood within them looking directly into his bemused and excited eyes.

"Well well, Mr Goodwood. Fancy seeing *you* here." She teased.

"Such a coincidence too. I've been thinking of you. Wanting you. Wanting you *here*." She touched her neck softly, to show him where she meant. "And here…"

She moved her hand down to her waist, gliding it around her corset-strapped body impatiently.

"Here."

She uttered, more coarsely this time, and her hand rubbed down her body and firmly over the small blue, flimsy material of her g-string, bending towards him and pushing her breasts firmly against him. His hands went to her body now and he ran them over her firm arse cheeks, squeezing her tightly, drawing her closer towards him and simultaneously squeezing his own legs shut, effectively trapping her between them. He slapped her playfully yet still firmly on her arse, and told her:

"You dirty slut, Sheena."

"Tsk, tsk, tsk." She shook her head reprimanding him. "It's *Bella*, Mr Goodwood. And yes, I've been bad, Sir. Punish me!"

He felt his cock stiffen and he squeezed her buttocks tightly again. He slid his hands slowly up the sides of her body, cupping her breasts gently, and then continuing up, roaming around her slender collarbones and neck. He squeezed her neck firmly, almost choking the flirtatious smile off of her, and he repeated:

"You dirty slut, *Bella*. What am I going to do with you to punish you."

Somehow he was immediately naked (well, this was *his* daydream after all) which worked well, as he moved one hand to place it on the back of her chocolate-coated head and applied just the right amount of pressure needed. 'Bella' took the obvious hint and wasted no time in kneeling down before him, looking him straight in the eyes, before slowly enveloping his engorged cock between her shiny, red lips, taking him fully into her mouth and throat, as he groaned in pleasure.

"Why are you so happy? What is there to smile about?"

Brendan was rudely shaken out of his enticing reverie by a still very flustered and panic-stricken Scott, who had now finished his drink and was back to coughing and wondering out loud what would happen next.

"What should I do? Maybe you could call Sheena and tell her we left? That we were only there to meet a friend? Oh God, what if she tells Gabby!"

Scott was getting near hysterical. As much as he was talking and couldn't stop, Brendan was silent, and just couldn't bring himself to reassure his brother. He was still very much at a loss for any (helpful) words, his own thoughts still swinging wildly between being outraged and turned on. It was all he could do to shrug his shoulders back at Scott, however he did manage to remove the bizarre smile that had formed on his mouth.

Scott coughed.

"Brendo. This is fucked, I know. Please don't say 'I told you so'."

More silence. Brendan would never have said that to Scott, even if he was definitely thinking it.

Just as he was about to offer something trite and reassuring and as philosophically wise as he could about the situation, something along the lines of 'life is a mystery' or 'life's just a ride', or 'things happen for a reason', Scott spoke again.

"Maybe *Sheena* has a twin?" He asked rhetorically and hopefully.

Brendan lost it. That was it. He knew how desperately worried Scott was (and indeed he himself was desperately *confused*) but he just couldn't help himself. He thought Scott's idea was hilarious. He started laughing, as Scott looked on in horror.

"What's so funny…"

He tried to ask him, hoping Brendan would shut up. Brendan couldn't stop. The irony and apparent enormity of the situation left him speechless, and hysterical, it seemed. He lost it and broke down into massive fits of laughter. The whole thing was fucked. They were fucked. She was fucked. She was very possibly *being* fucked right now, as they sat there trying to make sense of it all. The whole thing was so very fucked, and all Brendan could do was laugh on, a look of pure insanity on his face.

"Brendo…" Scott pleaded.

"Bahaha… Good one, Scott." He finally managed. "Maybe she does have a twin. That would fix everything!"

His laughter subsided a bit, but his confusion (and Scott's obvious dismay) remained. He didn't know what to think. All he knew right now was that he *had* to talk to her.

# CHAPTER TWENTY

"Come here, babe."

A rough hand jerked Sheena's messy, just-been-fucked head of hair closer towards the owner of the demanding voice's naked body. He pushed her head slightly forcefully down, and, although mentally grimacing at his use of the nickname 'babe' and feeling repulsed at both his manner and his slightly off, sweaty, stale booze stench, she obliged, and sank to her knees in a much practised, almost auto-pilot fashion. It just seemed easier to go along with it. Easier to just get it over with and then this mystery man, who wouldn't stop calling her 'Babe' and acting like he knew her, would hopefully take his cue and exit her bedroom.

She glanced around at her immediate surroundings. She knew where she was and felt a glimmer of relief that she was actually in her room, her own room (usually and used to be her private sanctity, her safe haven). But as to who this fumbling, forceful man in front of her was, she was completely and blurrily ignorant.

Her head pounded and her mouth felt as dry as she imagined her pussy must be, which is probably why he had given up his attempt at fucking her and instead had stood up and manoeuvred them both so that she was now taking him fully into her mouth instead, as he rammed himself as far down her throat as he could, all the while clumsily and painfully grabbing and pulling on her hair as he attempted to guide her head to his own rhythm.

She'd 'come to' as he was lying heavily on top of her, trying desperately (it seemed) to guide his stiff cock into her as, she realised in horror, she was writhing away and attempting to help him. He had fucked her a bit, as much as he could, for a short time, before she could have ever thought to protest, as what could she have suddenly said:

"Excuse me, but who the hell are you and please stop having sex
with me and leave."

When she came to, as it were, she realised that she had seemingly been
getting into it, and enthusiastically moving her body with his as he
gruffly spoke her name:

"Oh yeah, Sheena, you like my hard cock, don't you, you want
me to fuck you harder with it, don't you, Sexy Sheena." He had
drawled in her ear.

She kept moving in time with his painful, sore banging of her, but in
her head was thinking 'fuck, well, he knows my name, so I've obviously
invited him in. Easier to just get it done and get him to leave.'

When the dry-ish fucking had seemingly become too much for this still
half-cut, heavy-set man that she'd found herself pinned under and he'd
released her, only to beckon her over and ram his raw, red knob
roughly into her mouth, the same thought kept coming back to her:

'It's easier to just do it. It's easier to say nothing.'

Surely he would finish soon and then leave her alone with her
mounting hangover and blank spaces.

It wasn't as if he was even paying her for this repulsive time either. She
knew logically that she could stop having him thrust into her throat and
could get up off her knees and tell him to go, but it just seemed easier
all round to remain in place. It had been easier lately to just go along
with all kinds of things, once she realised what was happening and she
'came to' and found herself in various compromising situations and
positions; always surprising herself not least by how much of a good
actress she must be, seemingly enjoying herself and putting on a very

good act of being into whatever she found herself doing. The men she had inevitably found herself riding hard, or who were thrusting deeply into her, amidst her loud, appreciative cries and groans and moans complete with the right amount of writhing and grinding, must have been none the wiser. She assumed she must have been equally enthusiastic in her inviting them back with her or in her going home with them, for the later encounters to even been occurring (and it wasn't like she was passed-out, motionless drunk: just not at all there – her body was off without a rightful owner or mind) but she had no way of recalling that, and probably never would, such is the mystery of the drunken black outs. For those first few, initial moments when she would 'come to' she always found it extremely interesting and curious that she could be seemingly *so* into what she was doing and yet have no memory or even inkling as to the events which led up to it. So she would continue doing just that for a few minutes more, as if she had body-snatched another person's role. This wasn't her, *Sheena*, who was currently grinding herself theatrically and sweatily into this mysterious, dark, overweight, rank stranger, no, it was as if she had been placed directly into a movie and was both watching herself on screen but knowing it was really being played out in some reality. The whole experience was bizarre at first, and then the disgust and horror set in and she would inevitably decide it was easier to just go along with the proceedings. After all, maybe she had initiated them? And really, the less fuss made, the better, and surely he would then go?

It wasn't as if it was technically *rape*, as she definitely seemed to be giving her consent. But that's what it felt like. Rape. Had she raped her own mind, via booze? She wondered sketchily, and thus allowed her body to be unexpectedly raped too? Although unbeknownst to, let's call him 'Adam'. No, wait, she mused, as he plunged his hard cock even deeper down her dry, sore throat, while grabbing her hair tighter and roughly with his big, clumsy hands, and her eyes watered and widened in response. He's more of a 'Greg' or a 'Shane', she decided, willing him to near his finish so this would be over: he'd leave her alone to just crawl into her bed and shut out the world. That was all she wanted to do right now. Her head was pounding in time with her face being pounded by 'Shane', and she felt as if with each thrust she might finally break. She felt lightweight. She felt everything and nothing, all at the same time. Shane ploughed on regardless.

"Sheena, Sheena, Sheena."

He had something of a mantra going that indicated he was building up to something.

'Please.' She begged in her mind, but did nothing, just let him fuck her face and wreck her already much wrecked, just-been-fucked hair. Tears sprung from her eyes now, where they had built up due to gagging on Shane's substantial girth and long, hard cock being forced down her throat, and quietly rolled free down her flushed face. She made no move to wipe them away or hide them, doubting this less-than-gentleman would even notice, let alone care, with his ever quickening liturgy of 'Sheena, Sheena, Sheena', and rough-handling hands on the back of her head.

Bile rose up in her throat and she fought back the urge to retch and vomit, as mercifully he grabbed her head tighter and closer now and shot his plentiful load directly down her throat.

'Thank fuck for that.' She thought, relieved.

He finally released her and she fell back shakily to her carpeted, once a safe-haven, bedroom floor, her head pounding with fresh vengeance and her face a mascara-smeared and stained blotchy version of her former self. Her gentleman companion predictably wasted no time in pulling his jeans back on and miraculously procured a crumpled, black shirt from the corner of her room and bade her a hasty, but cheery farewell:

"Thanks Sheena, darling, see you again now."

She shuddered to herself as she closed the door creakily behind him. She most definitely would *not* be seeing him again. She was sure of it.

Stale booze pervaded her nostrils and every sense and she sat there bemused at how her life had too quickly become this: sad and depressed and frequenting various local bars by herself only to get hammered and consequently picked up by any of the less than favourable (scummy) men at said bars, more often than not, feeding her lots of the said drinks that got her hammered in the first place, alcohol doing their job for them and making the transition from bar to bedroom oh so easy.

She didn't even *like* drinking too much, or the feeling of being too drunk, she reminded herself, sitting there shaky, spent and slightly broken. Yet lately, that was all she seemed to be intent on doing. She sometimes wondered if her ex-husband's alcoholism was contagious and that somehow she might have caught it from him. She knew this wasn't really 'her' or who she was, but she just couldn't stop. She could see what she was doing and yet was powerless to stop it: almost like she was having an outer-body experience, knowing and watching herself spiral down and further into that abyss, but yet being paralysed and helpless to actually do anything about it. A similar feeling to when she 'came to' and would find herself enthusiastically riding some hairy stranger, or being spit-roasted roughly by two equally hairy equally strangers to her (although they always gave her some clues that earlier in the evening they must have all had a good chat, or at least knew each other's names, calling them out roughly as they went at her, or, more usually, as they hurriedly left her room, with a 'Cheers, Sheena', or 'See ya, Sheena').

'So much for always being true to yourself.' She shook her head in shame. She had never felt so *far* from being her true self. Not even when she was effectively doing the same thing for a living working at Secrets. At least she was sober then and in full control of what was happening.

The pounding was back again. Or perhaps it had never gone away, but now it definitely seemed up a notch, intensified somehow. It took her a few more seconds to realise that this newer, more urgent, quicker banging, was actually her door. Someone was knocking on her bedroom door. Panic gripped her. Oh god. He wasn't back was he? Sheena's stomach lurched, fearing he had meant what he said when he'd uttered those sickening words about seeing her again. The knocking stopped and was replaced by a gentle:

"Sheena? You in there? You ok, Love? Can I come in?"

Sheena drew in a huge breath of relief and her body relaxed back into her position of being curled up on the floor. *Gabby!* Thank god.

She made a move to stand up now, and ever so slowly made her way over to sit gingerly in the corner of her messily, destroyed bed, calling out as loudly as she could manage:

"Yeah, Gabs, it's open."

Her head hanging naturally down in a mixture of defeat, shame, and extreme dehydration. She was hungover and shaky, and dusty as fuck, but welcomed seeing Gabby at any time. It struck her now that she hadn't actually seen Gabby for weeks now, such was the result of her newfound binge-drinking, bar-propping-up, status: she was never usually in at home during the evenings anymore, and she felt a sudden pang of guilt re: not having even known if Gabby had been away or not. She had been talking some weeks back about going back to visit her folks inland at Kalgoorlie. In fact, she'd been talking about taking her new boyfriend Scott there to introduce him to her family, so maybe just as well Sheena hadn't managed to see her in the meantime. As much as she had been trying to banish the horrifying memories of seeing Brendan and Scott together, as clients of Secrets, through her bouts of daily self-flagellation, her routine of getting blind, getting laid, and then hiding in self-loathing until the inevitable hangover subsided, the memory still came back to haunt her, far more regularly than she would have liked, and it was best that she, in no way shape or form, *ever* let this be known to Gabby – fuck, how would she even begin to tell her?! Her mind could not even fathom. Better that she just keep avoiding that whole scenario. So, she realised now, that she'd been inadvertently and subconsciously avoiding Gabby altogether. Her best friend. She was mortified and full of even more self-disgust and shame. Suddenly Gabby was wrapping her warm, comforting arms tightly around Sheena, squeezing her close. Not seeming to care about the stale stench surely pervading from her every pore.

"Hey Stranger."

She squealed, squeezing the slightly frail Sheena even tighter, causing her to smile despite the shocking hangover and lingering guilt over being a shit friend.

"Hey you!"

Sheena responded, as brightly as she could manage. She suddenly broke out in a fresh wave of heavy perspiration and felt herself growing flushed as a weirdly awkward silence fell over the pair of should-be best friends. Gabby simply kept her arms hugged tightly around Sheena, enveloping her with herself but not saying anything.

Sheena broke the awkward silence first.

"So, umm, did you just get back then Gabs?" She clumsily extracted herself from her friend's tight embrace and made her excuses: "Sorry Gabs, feeling really sick hey. Few too many drinks last night."

A wave of nausea rolled over her as the dusty memory clamoured for centre brain stage. She thought she might vomit right there and then, but the feeling passed and she breathed a long, shaky, slow breath out, feeling Gabby's watchful, concerned eyes burning into her.

"No." Gabby started but then paused, looking at Sheena with even more concern now. "No, I got back last week. Don't you remember? I saw you briefly the other night, when you were with, what was his name again, Mark, was it?"

Sheena had no memory of this. Silence was her awkward response. It seemed Gabby's question was rhetorical anyway and she continued.

"Yeah, haven't seen you much lately though mate – I miss you! What's been happening?"

She asked as cheerily and optimistically and as Gabby-esque as ever.

Sheena had a brief and sudden urge to reveal all to Gabby, to tell her exactly what had been happening right down to her being a worker at a brothel and witnessing the very-real-love-of-her-life having been caught out there with his brother (who she assumed was Gabby's boyfriend still, again feeling a large pang of guilt of being a shithouse friend again, who didn't even know if they were together or not anymore) but the enormity of the situation crushed her. She opened her mouth ready to tell Gabby something vaguely positive instead, or a lie about what had been happening, and aimed to plaster on a fake smile too, thus giving credence and weight to her 'everything's been great' faux-story she was aiming to give, when instead a choked sob surprised her and escaped her mouth. That was it. She cracked. Crumbled. Broke down. Utterly.

Something had shifted and some kind of emotional floodgate had opened up and the tumult of all her pain and pent up emotions burst free. Gabby simply resumed her position and placed her arms back around Sheena and held on tight. She didn't seem at all surprised by Sheena's emotional deluge. Didn't try to ask what was wrong or what had happened. She said nothing. Just held on tightly.

Sheena's hiccupping and near hysterical sobbing continued for quite some time. She feared she may not actually be able to stop.

Eventually, after quite some time, Sheena did stop. Just as suddenly and dramatically as she had started. She drew in a gargantuan breath and attempted to paint on the original smile that she'd tried to before, the one that inadvertently had triggered her break down. She managed it this time, and faux-grinned sheepishly at Gabby, who hadn't moved from her all-too-close (by anyone else's standards) position, and continued to silently hold her friend close.

"Phew."

Sheena breathed out again, still shaky from her self-administered alcohol poisoning.

"Don't know where that came from!"

She admonished herself.

More silence from Gabby. This wasn't like her, Sheena thought. But then, she supposed, *she* wasn't like *her* usual self either, whatever that was. She wasn't quite sure she even knew herself these days. Why though, did this feel so *different*, to Sheena? Why did she suddenly feel awkward and unsure in front of *Gabby*, her *best* friend? Was it the secret she kept, weighing her down, that she'd seen Gabby's boyfriend (or then-boyfriend; she didn't know if this was still the case) in a brothel, or the larger secret about *herself*, that she had been working in that particular brothel? Or the fact that she had somehow become the sort of person she had strived so hard *not* to, the kind who regularly and easily lied to her best friend (a woman who she loved, respected and admired) and to herself, and who regularly took herself out to get blind drunk and take away the pain of losing Brendan by being taken home by any random manly-enough stranger who would fuck her or whom she would fuck until she 'came to' and became fully conscious again and could then let the true self-loathing begin, and she could then have a bonafide hangover and a reason to wallow and stay in bed all day.

But how could she tell all this to Gabby? When there seemed to be a gulf between them, a strange distance and gap, despite Gabby literally clasping Sheena tight to her bosom and there being physically no space between them and it was hard to tell exactly where Sheena ended and Gabby began. She knew they hadn't properly seen each other for weeks, but surely that shouldn't make things this, well, *weird*, between them? They were best friends after all. They could spend months apart and then surely it'd be just like old times when they *did* meet up. Usually anyway. So why did Sheena get the feeling that something was different. She thought maybe she was imagining it. After all, these hangovers lately left her feeling very paranoid and confused; unsure of what she had said or done during the previous evening or last few hours. She wondered if she had behaved atrociously to Gabby last night and hence that was the reason behind the silence and the weird awkward vibe she was getting.

"Umm." Sheena broached tentatively. "Did I do anything to upset you or piss you off last night, mate? My memory's a bit sketchy."

She flashed a small, apologetic smile and looked up at her friend.

Still more silence from Gabby. But she did at least hug her tightly again. Feeling somewhat comforted, Sheena's eyes pricked with tears again. Gabby was so good to her, and all she could do was lie to her and then lie again. She hated herself right now. Had never felt lower. Just as she was about to start apologising profusely and begging Gabby's forgiveness for a being a shit friend (she still had no idea of how to broach the greater problem, which was: the whole 'I was working as a hooker and in walked your boyfriend and the love of my life') when Gabby finally spoke again, effectively taking Sheena off the hook.

"Look Sheena. I wasn't going to say anything or intervene. But I have to now. I'm worried about you. What you're doing. You're not yourself"

The embrace got even tighter if that was possible.

"What's wrong? Why are you doing this to yourself?"

Gabby fixed her with a stern look.

Sheena wasn't used to this version of Gabby.

"What, umm, well."

She started, with no idea of what she was going to tell her. She could feel that familiar lump in her throat and those tears rising up, threatening to break free again and spill onto Gabby's neck and cleavage once more.

"The thing is."

Sheena began and then stopped herself. She just couldn't. She couldn't tell her. She didn't know how she could even start. Her body threatened to give herself away again and threatened to crack and crumble once more.

Gabby asked her again, with that stern, direct, probing voice of hers:

"Sheena, why are you doing this? Tell me what's wrong."

Sheena looked down, drew in a long, deep breath, and made up her mind. She would tell her everything, right then and there. Maybe Gabby even had a solution?

Just as she was opening her mouth to speak, Gabby continued.

"Is this to do with that place you've been working at? The gentlemen's club?"

She asked, clearly and directly, but with no surprise or judgement evident in her voice.

Sheena all but choked on her own tongue and flicked her eyes back up to meet Gabby's own eyes, filled with concern.

"What are you talking about?"

She asked, her confused hangover self not sure if she was hearing this correctly.

"I know where you've been working, Sheena." Gabby stated calmly.

Sheena's mouth dropped open, aghast. Gabby squeezed her tighter. Sheena's mind raced. What the fuck? Scott must have told her! She was outraged.

Gabby continued:

"I don't care, Sheena. I'm just worried about you. Look, I followed you one evening, when you were made up to the nines and not at all yourself. I'm sorry, it was really none of my business, but I was just worried about you and where you might be going dressed like that. This was a few months back now. Anyway, I wanted to check you were ok, so I walked behind you and saw where you went into. A little bit later, when I went in there after you, I put the two and two together."

Sheena was still horrified. Gabby had been in there too! She felt a little sick now.

"But look mate – I don't care that you work there. Geez, don't ever think that you can't tell me things like that, I'm your best friend, Sheens!"

Sheena's tears threatened to escape again as she felt the depth of her best friend's love and concern envelop her. If anything it made her feel even more shithouse. There she was, beautiful Gabby, extremely concerned about her, and completely non-judgemental and uncaring about what Sheena was doing in her private life, and Sheena couldn't even bring herself to tell her about Scott and Brendan. The reminder of

Brendan and her loss of him thudded through her guts again and she looked down, biting her lip and sighing deeply. It was hopeless.

"But look, Sheena, I don't know if anything happened there that's upset you, or that you want to talk about, but what you've been doing lately: the drinking, the different man each night, then shutting yourself away all day – I'm really worried about you Sheena."

She kept up her assault of the tight hug, and silence filled the room again.

"I know Brendan is too. Worried, I mean."

Gabby's final attempt to get an answer out of her friend.

Brendan?! How would Gabby know about Brendan! Scott must have talked! And why would Brendan be worried about her? What, worried that she was going to spill his and his brother's dirty secret? She was even more confused now, her eyes darting about in confusion.

Gabby put her out of her misery and elaborated:

"Scott says that he's been trying to call you for weeks but you won't answer your phone or return his text messages?"

Sheena nodded. This much was true.

"I don't know what's happened Sheena, but it seems you're desperately unhappy. And why won't you speak to Brendan?"

More silence.

"Look, you don't have to tell me. That's cool. But, please talk to him mate. I'm sure everything can be fixed and sorted."

She reassured her. She was so hopeful. Sheena felt slightly better.

Was there really hope after all? Did Gabby know something that she didn't?

Gabby placed a soft, warm hand over her own still shaking one, and urged her, more kindly and gentler this time:

"Please just talk to him, Sheena – whatever's happened. Just see what he has to say. I'll love you just the same, and I'm sure it's the same for him. Talk to him mate, please."

Those sobs finally broke free again and Sheena surrendered this time, thinking of Brendan and of what he might have to say, and of her beautiful best friend's unconditional and unwavering support and love for her, and she let go and sunk into her friend's welcoming arms, loud sobs echoing far into the corners of their small, shared apartment. Could it really be that simple? She wondered, dustily.

# CHAPTER TWENTY-ONE

Sheena's phone vibrated urgently in her tight dress pocket, alerting her to what she assumed was another text message from Gabby. She half shook her head, but smiled broadly as she retrieved the phone and indeed saw the word 'Gabs' printed cheerily across its screen. Yep. Just as she'd thought.

"Just another reminder that today is your SPECIAL DAY! Happy birthday to the most amazing chick I know! And don't forget – 4 o'clock at the corner of Church Street and Marine Parade."

As if she could forget. This was Gabby's third enthusiastic birthday message so far today. Sheena smiled again, thinking of her soul mate, her 'person', her amazing Gabby, who she didn't know where she would be without her. She'd been nothing short of amazing, especially during these past few months, when, incredibly, life seemed to have gotten relatively back to 'normal', whatever that was supposed to be for Sheena, anyway. At least, life had seemingly moved on somewhat, and the pain was becoming less and less each day. She'd thankfully managed to stop her downward spiralling path of self-destruction anyhow, she knew thanks to Gabby's support. They had embarked on a 'health kick' or 'detox' that was usually doing the rounds in those early January, post-festive days, them only being a month or so late. Better late than never, she'd supposed.

Gabby had initially been the driving force behind this, making oh-so-subtle suggestions for the pair of them going out for juices and herbal teas and trying new 'healthy' veggie restaurants that had popped up and appeared almost overnight in Fremantle, and asking her to join her on various yoga sessions on the weekend. Sheena had gone along with her at first, mainly in a bid to please her and to stop her from giving her that look, or from even mentioning that Sheena might want to try talking to Brendan to sort out whatever mess she thought she was in. Mercifully Gabby had gotten the hint that Sheena really didn't want to talk about it, and after quite possibly the vaguest, shittiest explanation from Sheena, along the lines of "he found out about the job I used to have there" (she didn't dare go into detail about how, and probably never would), she hadn't mentioned his name post that initial, intervention-esque afternoon where Sheena had literally broken down onto her. Sensing that the way forward instead might be to focus on getting Sheena out and about and into some positive, healthy activities instead, to both clean her up and take her mind off things, that is exactly what she had done. And by jove, it was working. Sheena was smiling more, slightly more, and had almost got her old glow back, albeit being a dull shadow of its former vibrant self. At least she seemed to be eating meals now and keeping 'normal' hours again, and seemed to have pulled the plug completely on her mission to get absolutely obliterated every night (or on any night). Gabby supposed it had a lot to do with the fact their term at uni had started again and so both friends were now back into full-time lectures and classes, not to mention the money involved in her blotto missions (although more often than not, these would usually be funded by the less-than-gentleman in question who would be essentially guaranteed a companion for later that night) but Gabby was thrilled none the less, to see Sheena restored, *almost*, to a version of herself again.

Sheena took her friend's unfaltering, unwavering support and decided that if Gabby wanted her to stop going out and getting trashed and going home with different men each night (or bringing them home to theirs) then that is what she'd do. She didn't want to hurt Gabs. As a side bonus, she then realised just how much it *wasn't* helping her anyway and just how miserable it had been making her. So instead, she joined Gabby for all the tea, juice, and 'healthy food' dates that she offered. She downward-dogged with her in yoga like a champ. She allowed her to hug her and hold her close and to be told that everything was going to be ok and she listened politely when Gabby told her that, over *time*, things would start to seem better. And while she was waiting for that 'better' feeling for things not to hurt anymore, she got back to throwing herself into her studies and taking every and any extra shift at Café Noir that she could. Gradually, oh-so-slowly, Sheena came to agree with Gabby. She started to smile, genuinely, again. She started to, sometimes, forget how upset she was. Brendan was still in her thoughts, daily, of course. But she was gradually coming to terms with the fact that she wouldn't be seeing him again, and was *trying* to forget about labelling him 'the one' in her head (and in confidence to Gabby). The distraction of her mountains of uni work was helping anyway. Some days she didn't even cry at night alone in her room. She knew she had mainly Gabby to thank for that.

So when Gabby had suggested, or declared rather, that this birthday of Sheena's this year would be *epic* and would definitely by a cause for celebration, and that they would go out and paint the town that proverbial, figurative red, Sheena had half-smiled, half-grimaced and knew she had no choice really: she had to do it, for Gabby's sake.

If left to her own devices she would have happily ignored her upcoming 36<sup>th</sup> birthday, her not being at all a fan of celebrating birthdays, least of all her own. After years of dreading any social occasion and what should in society's eyes be a 'celebration', which then every time, during her long marriage anyway, predictably turned to shit: any would-be fun and happy time marred by her ex-husband's need to get as trashed as possible as quickly as possible, using any 'celebration' as yet another excuse and reason to do so. So Sheena had developed a general dislike of celebrating her birthday and most other occasions too, choosing instead to forget about the day altogether, or brushing it aside completely, not really seeing a need to celebrate her 'special day'. She had never fully understood this anyway – people were born every single day; it wasn't unusual. It wasn't like she had done anything special that deserved a special mention of a 'party' (i.e. a bonafide reason for her ex-husband to drink on her behalf, or even more so on his, when his 'special day' rolled around). This general aversion and distrust of birthdays had stuck around after she'd left Peter too, and as much as Gabby was excited and enthusiastic about it (Gabby was very much a 'birthday' person, explaining patiently to Sheena that it was a 'special day' as it was intended to celebrate that particular person and be grateful and excited that they had been made and appeared within the universe) Sheena knew she was really just placating her best friend here and agreeing to celebrate with her for her birthday, but moreover just to keep the peace and to please Gabby and to thank her (or go some way to, anyway) for all she had done for Sheena lately: the literal picking her up off the floor, fixing her life, making her smile again, making things seem 'normal' again and allowing Sheena to be hopeful that things really *could* be better in the future (and that the past is the past: both her ex-husband and her regrettable choice of part-time job induced by debt). It was the least Sheena could do to show up and appear to be happy and excited with Gabby about herself turning another year older. She felt she owed her. Plus, the more she saw or made Gabby smile, the more Sheena realised she was mirroring her and smiling too, almost by some sort of osmosis. Gabby was so good for her, despite her ongoing heartbreak.

When she realised that by throwing herself into her university studies and distracting herself at work (mercifully the café was crazy hectic busy these days thanks to term being in full-flow again and late-summer tourists flocking to Fremantle in droves) she was, most days, able to forget about the dull ache and gaping hole in her heart that was the result of 'missing Brendan'. So when Gabby had arranged this 'surprise-secret-birthday-celebration-for-Sheena' night out for her, Sheena had had no choice really. She'd slipped on her best 'I'm ok – I'm happy – I'm keen' smile and agreed. How could she *not*?

Gabby was being extra elusive and mysterious about the particular details of her 'birthday extravaganza', as she called it, to which Sheena had rolled her eyes in an exaggerated fashion and crossed her arms over her chest.

"Please just tell me we're not going clubbing or out to some hideous nightclub!"

She pleaded with her friend, although knowing that Gabby would more than likely be well aware that this was in no way Sheena's style anymore, if it ever had been.

"Don't worry, Sheena." She placated her. "You'll love it, I'm sure. Just a quiet dinner and drinks for the two of us – no big surprise party I promise. You sure you don't want to invite some of your other friends though?"

Sheena had thought about that for all of one second. Hmmm. She had kept herself to herself so much this term she wasn't sure if she had any other 'friends' to speak of. She was, of course, polite and friendly, to a point, with her Café Noir colleagues, but never hung around after her shifts there, never joined them on their occasional night outs, and never gave too much away about her personal life. She'd brushed *April* completely, seeing her in a different light now. She felt a mixture of hurt and anger if she allowed herself to think about April. She had genuinely thought they were great friends, even underneath their strange 'professional' relationship. But April seemed only focused on whether Sheena was coming back to work for her yet, and when Sheena thought about it, *really* thought about it, she ended up realising that April had preyed on her in her most vulnerable of times and she felt cheated and used and spat out. Sure, she accepted her own part to play in her hideous and ridiculous job she'd somehow suffered through, but April acting as the glamorous bait and coaxing her into the lifestyle and job amidst a pretence of being her good friend too, well, it sickened her now to think of it, and she felt the bile rise up as she pictured the beautiful, sexy and determined (won't take no for an answer) April approaching other lost, skint and broken young women around Fremantle. So, the few times her phone had flashed up with April's name (which was getting less and less frequently – April must have been getting the hint) Sheena had simply pressed 'reject', feeling a little bit more empowered with each press of that button. She knew she should probably just block her number altogether but some reason she didn't.

She wondered if it was for the same reason as that she hadn't deleted Brendan's number either – did she want a reminder of that past year? Or was she not ready to let go completely of his memory yet? She wasn't sure, but she left him there in her phone regardless. A harmless numerical entry.

"No." She affirmed to Gabby. "No one else I'd rather be forced to celebrate my day of aging with, haha, than *you*, Gabs! Let's just keep it small hey, just you and me. "

She had smiled a genuine smile back at her friend now, feeling that familiar warmth and love for Gabs spread through her. She didn't know what she would do without her, quite honestly.

They held each other's gaze just a moment longer than usual. Sheena broke first:

"But what should I wear? You won't tell me where we're going until the day, ok that's great, but will you give me a heads up about the dress code? Or will that give the game away too much?"

Gabby giggled and half hugged her in closer.

"Nah, that won't give it away!" She grinned. "Just be yourself. Dress however you like!"

Sheena grinned back. Well that helped, she thought ironically. That wouldn't be hard though. She felt like she'd been nothing *but* herself lately: no make-up, no hair-styling, definitely no fuck-me-heels. Almost like she was the anti-Ruby. She found it hard to even conjure up the character of 'Ruby' anymore and the memory was becoming less and less real for her. But she was definitely a fan of the 'au naturelle' look these days, and had never felt freer, or more beautiful and confident, for that matter. It obviously suited her and was no doubt helped by her natural brunette good looks. She was infinitely more beautiful by just 'being herself' than she ever was or felt when she was made-up with foundation, and thick, black mascara, and that ruby-red lipstick – she couldn't fathom how or why she had done that to herself, although she realised it had served as a good mask for her when she needed to transform into that secret other persona and job. Maybe that's why she found any kind of make-up particularly abhorrent and ridiculous now. So Gabby's instruction of 'just be yourself' sat very well with her, and wouldn't be at all hard.

She'd swapped her usual shifts at the café for that weekend and written her to-do lists for her assignments she had on the go to get done on Monday, so had effectively given herself the whole weekend off. Gabby had something to do elsewhere early on, so she'd told her (sensitively leaving out exactly what she was doing and where she was going – Sheena assumed she must be meeting Scott early on but was kind enough not to say so. Sheena was fairly certain that Gabby was very much still seeing Scott, but miraculously she had yet to run into them again. She sensed that Gabby was being extra conscientious and sensitive about not bringing him round when Sheena was there and hadn't mentioned his name, or explicitly asked: "oh, who are you meeting up with?" Which was a rare occurrence, the two friends respecting each other's privacy more than ever.) So Sheena had the whole apartment to herself to leisurely get ready in.

She'd run herself a hot bath, complete with vanilla scented bubbles and lit the scattering of coconut and lime scented candles that lined the tub and windowsill. Soaking in to the glorious hot water that enveloped her naked body hungrily, she felt her whole body smile. Life was great. Everything would be ok.

She sat back and rested her back against the cold shock of the bath's surface, relishing its cool, hard contrast with the slightly too hot, almost scalding, bath water. Half-closing her eyes and sighing in satisfaction, and wait for it, what was that feeling that she thought was slowly creeping back? That's right: *pleasure*. She arched her back, allowing her full, large breasts to be thrust out as she slowly ran a hand leisurely up her taut and soapy left thigh, switching unhurriedly to continue its ascent up and over her exposed breasts now, her nipples hardening in response. She closed her eyes completely and ran her other hand down in the opposite direction now, keeping it tightly squeezed around her right thigh now as she brought her left hand back down to underneath the bubbles. As she stroked her thigh with one hand she slowly rubbed her other hand back and forth ever so slowly over her submerged tiny, taut stomach and every so often dipped her hand down further and teased herself gently. She arched her head back now and to her side and an image of Brendan kissing her bare, exposed neck while he massaged her thrust-out, full, wet and soapy breasts burned into her thoughts. Her eyes flicked open again and she mentally kicked herself. Damn. Not so over him nor had banished him from her thoughts as she strived to be. Work in progress, she comforted herself. Feeling the ache and need for him all over again, raw and fresh. She just missed him, and wasn't quite done with her grieving for what she felt she'd lost or what might have been. Putting that thought aside and literally brushing herself off, she'd then got out of the bath and set about getting ready and psyching herself up to be visibly 'happy' for Gabby.

She'd massaged some shea butter carefully and lovingly all over her bronzed, trim but with all the right curves in all the right places body, paying particular attention to her inner thighs and breasts, feeling that strange and long-forgotten feeling of pleasure creeping back and reminding herself that she might not be completely broken after all, and then towel-tried her naturally wavy, thick, glossy, chocolate-brown hair. A light, fresh moisturiser, and her favourite, go-to, little-black-dress (like a slightly oversized, fitted, cotton, simple t-shirt or long singlet, yet hugging her in all the right places) completed her very simple 'getting-ready' routine, in under twenty minutes, and then she had set off to the agreed meeting place, eager to see Gabby's smiling, beautiful face.

Sheena walked slowly to the meeting spot, her head held high whilst she enjoyed the late afternoon sun shining on her bare face, her skin with its natural, signature bronze glow, and the shea butter with a hint of her vanilla-scented bath from earlier wafting around her as she strolled. Her phone vibrated again and she shimmied it out of her dress pocket.

"Change of plans sweetheart. Meet me there at the restaurant instead. I've reserved us a table at Eat Drink Lounge, under your name, Lovely."

Sheena smiled and sighed. Oh Gabby. Reserving a table at the newly opened wholefood restaurant-cum-bar that they'd both been eager to try since it opened in Freo a couple of months back. She knew where it was, having a great spot down by the water and next to the famous

Little Creatures brewery-cum-restaurant-cum-pub. What a good choice. Nice one Gabs. She was so thoughtful: knowing that Sheena had been wanting to check it out for a while now, but had either been too busy with work and study, or too poor. Usually it was the latter. Feeling extra gratitude that Gabby had demanded that Sheena would not be paying and that this was very much Gabby's treat, she pushed open the heavy, rustic-looking oak door, taking her into the dimly lit (very much going for 'mood lighting') restaurant.

A super-smiley, typical 'Bondi-hipster' (more like Freo-hipster then, she mused to herself) beard adorned adonis of a maitre-de complete with man-bun/top-knot, sleek black tie resting upon his crisp, starched, white shirt, and black apron tied neatly around his dark, denim, equally starched and pressed jeans, greeted her with gusto from the small teak desk to the right of the dark entrance.

"A very good early evening to you Madam, do you have a reservation?"

His dark eyes twinkled and sparkled as he spoke and his perfect, white teeth flashed brightly at her, waiting for her response.

She returned the smile, a little hesitantly.

"Umm, yes, it's for Sheena? Table for two?" She glanced around, hoping her eyes would adjust soon to the dim lighting. "My friend's meeting me here." She confirmed.

The male-model-esque man ran his finger up and down a large, leather-bound reservation book as if in deep thought and then clicked his thick, manly fingers and smiled again.

"Ahh yes, of course. Here it is. Sheena, please follow me. Right this way."

Sheena's eyes now adjusted to the uber dim, romantic lack of lighting as she weaved her way amongst the empty make-up of tables and chairs, following her enthusiastic host, she realised there were no other patrons in the joint. In fact, it didn't seem to be open at all. The dim lights, she now realised, were not exactly the romantic soft-lighting she'd assumed at first, but most of the lights just weren't switched on yet. She immediately felt for Gabby – poor Gabs: finally reserving a table for them and arranging this big 'surprise' and she had got the time wrong. Hmmm, Sheena had thought it was odd that Gabby had mentioned they were going for dinner but to meet her at the too-early sounding time (even for them!) of 4pm. But then, why were they expecting her and welcoming her in? Why not tell her 'oh sorry, we're not open yet'?

"Here you are, Sheena. Oh, and a very happy birthday to you!"
Her gorgeous male escort snuck a brief but hot kiss onto her confused, burning cheek and gestured that she should shuffle into the secluded, private booth that he'd led her to. 'Oh my': a vaguely horrifying but enticing thought struck her. Had Gabby arranged some kind of private, sexy, 'heady' rendezvous with this veritable sex-god that was here before her? The two had often discussed a similar fantasy that they shared, namely that of a handsome, sexy stranger waiter or driver or barman or something along those lines, leading them to a secluded, 'secret' although at the same time very public place, such as the corner of their bar or restaurant, or the back of their limo or taxi (with or without tinted windows) blindfolding either Sheena or Gabby (whichever one was relaying her particular version of this standard fantasy) and then proceeding to give them the best headjob of their

young lives just before anyone else sees them or shows up. Sheena gulped, suddenly nervous now. Shit Gabs, that was only a daydream! She was only half joking around. Although she felt relieved for the second time that day that maybe she wasn't completely broken in that regards after all as she felt that familiar ache and tingle in her groin as she smiled back at her waiter-male-model apprehensively.

As he stepped back to allow her to slide in and onto the deep red, high-backed, leather sofa that made up one half of the booth, and then promptly nodded and walked away, leaving her to gather her thoughts and smile again to herself at her wild and preposterous thought that Gabby may have arranged a sexy, male prostitute for her birthday (as if she *would* really, considering Sheena's recent revelation) she breathed a sigh of relief and shook her head, gently chuckling to herself. 'Of course that wouldn't be the case!' She berated herself mildly. Feeling only slightly disappointed.

Some lights nearby now flickered on. Oh, maybe they were just running late with opening this evening? Still, it remained eerily empty.

Sexy-male-escort-man reappeared out of nowhere bearing a shiny, turquoise large round cup containing some kind of steaming, caffeinated beverage.

"A double-shot, skinny mocha for the birthday girl – extra hot and extra chocolatey – just the way you like it!" He asserted confidently.

What the? Sheena smiled quizzically at him. Wow. Gabby had really been paying attention. She'd got her coffee order down pat and everything. She'd obviously planned this birthday surprise down to the finer details. Oh Gabs: she never ceased to amaze Sheena.

Adonis had mysteriously left her to it again, and Sheena brought the steaming, inviting hot drink closer to her lips, breathing in its intoxicating, heady aroma, and smiled, wondering where Gabby actually was. It wasn't like her to be late.

Music started in the many small speakers that she now saw lined the large, oak rustic beams that cross-crossed the ceiling and framed every inch of the large, cavernous restaurant. Seconds later, Sheena let out an audible, loud giggle of surprise as 'Morning Train' began to blare out. As her namesake Sheena (Easton) reminded her that 'he works all day to earn his pay, so we can play all ni-ight!' Sheena shook her head, a huge grin upon her radiant, beautiful face now. Gabby really *had* thought of everything. Where was she though? She needed to give her a very big hug and thank her for going to all this effort for her.

She settled back into the comfy, giant sofa that effectively dwarfed her, as tall and curvy as she actually was, her flowing, curvy mass of chocolate waves contrasting beautifully with the cherry-red leather. Male-model-escort-dude ('ok, he's definitely not an escort', she reminded herself, smiling bemusedly at her earlier mistaken, brazen thought) went about his duties of finalising setting the rest of the place up, she assumed for other customers, when they were officially 'open'. He glanced at her every now and then with a broad, knowing smile and an extra cheeky wink thrown in for good measure. She started to relax. This wouldn't be so bad after all. Who cares that it was her 'dreaded birthday'? Well, Gabby clearly cared, and that was a-ok with Sheena, she realised. But where the hell *was* she?

A figure suddenly caused a shadow to fall over Sheena and she looked up about to jokingly ask Gabs exactly that question of

"Where the hell have *you* been? You sure took your time!"

when she was stopped mid 'Where…' in her tracks, her mouth gaping open in aghast and shock. Quickly remembering to close her mouth, she then cleared her throat and swallowed nervously. She wasn't expecting this.

'Gabby – I'm going to *kill* you!' Was her first thought, still expecting Gabby's heart-shaped, pale, luminous little face to be popping up behind this extra surprise figure in a bid to explain or offer some sort of "sorry mate…".

No one else appeared. Sheena's eyes darted all around the room. No one else was coming.

Brendan finally spoke.

"Sheena. Hi. It's so good to see you."

\*\*\*\*\*\*\*\*\*\*\*\*\*\*\*\*\*\*\*\*\*\*\*\*\*\*\*\*\*\*\*\*\*\*\*\*\*

Sheena's heart had seemed lodged in her throat for a good few minutes, her eyes locked with Brendan's own bright, sparkling eyes looking intently at her. She must have glanced furtively behind him, scanning the empty space for Gabby's rightly guilty-looking face, as Brendan hurriedly explained:

"Oh, she's not coming. Well, not just yet anyway. Sorry for the rouse, and for essentially tricking you into meeting me here."

She said nothing. Just closed her still gaping, surprised mouth (which must have gaped back open again). Yet she smiled back at him warmly, in spite of her mild annoyance of being ambushed. As her namesake finished the song and a none-too-awkward slight silence settled over the pair, they just smiled at each other, as if caught in a stupor. Again, Brendan broke the comfortable silence by asking:

"Do you mind if I sit down? Please hear me out, Sheena. I really am sorry for surprising you like this, but I didn't know what else to do – I've been needing to talk with you, to explain about that night, for so long now. You wouldn't return my messages or answer my calls. Please don't blame Gabby for this. This was *all* my doing. Oh, and happy birthday, by the way."

He smiled tentatively, but looked unsure if he should indeed sit or remain standing there.

Sheena shook her head and laughed lightly now, putting him out of his misery by gesturing with her outstretched hand that, sure, he could take a seat.

"Well, you've done well then, Mr Goodwood: the location, the perfect coffee, Morning Train playing just for me, I assume."

She teased him now, but her broad smile remained annoyingly in place, despite herself.

"*Brendan*, please." He frowned now, looking to destroy the light-hearted mood she'd somehow set. "Seriously Sheena, please hear me out."

He slid into the high-backed, leather seat next to her, his leg accidentally brushing against her own bare thigh where her casual, black dress had slightly risen up. She readjusted herself now and shimmied slightly further along the seat, aiming to give him some more room, and needing some space to get her breath back after a slight, inward gasp had escaped her involuntarily after the electric jolt of feeling Brendan's leg pushed against her own once again.

She needed to focus. He obviously had something important to say to her. She should stop reminding herself how handsome and rugged he was, how she'd forgotten how just being in his presence made her feel this way: tingly and giddy, and as if she wanted to rip his clothes off roughly and ravish him then and there at the dimly lit table. Focus, Sheena. She instructed herself, trying to force herself to remember that the last time she actually *saw* this man was during her last ever, ominous shift at that brothel where she mistakenly spent her time for a while, and all the subsequent anguish and heartache that followed that chance encounter. But she couldn't seem to recreate or conjure up those feelings now, instead feeling nothing but excitement and joy at seeing him again.

"Will you hear me out, Sheena, please?"

He repeated ardently, looking deeply and seriously into her sparkly, amber eyes once again.

She already knew that, of course, she would. That was evident to both of them, otherwise she would have simply gotten up and left by now. He was just being polite and overly cautious. She supposed he'd planned this moment in his head, however original or unoriginal, and this serious speech or confession or getting something off his chest was a part of his plan.

He nudged his knee against her own again, sending that fissure through her whole body once more, and smiled now: his broad smile suiting his handsome face much better than his serious look, and whispered:

"You're looking beautiful, Sheena."

Another nudge, making contact with her leg for slightly longer this time.

"I've really missed you."

She returned his knee-nudging, playfully, and asked him:

"What did you want to tell me then, *Brendan?*"

She emphasized his name and smiled, genuinely and calmly back at him (although inside was a very different story and her heart was just about ready to burst out of her chest). She was surprised at how nonchalant, and well, *normal*, this felt, sitting here with Brendan, having not seen him for almost two months and having tried to forget all about him and that he even existed. She realised she really had missed him too. She would of course 'hear him out' and listen to what he had to say.

"So many things."

Was his simple, concise answer. But he pressed his leg against hers, and leaned towards her and just smiled.

"But, please, finish your coffee first, Sheena. Then maybe we can

go somewhere more private and I can really explain."

Male-model-adonis-waiter did seem to be popping up all over the place, straightening table cloths and cutlery, so Sheena could understand Brendan's reluctance to talk about what was surely a very delicate and intimate topic. Her leg burning from where the heat of his own leg was still pressed against it, she bit her lower lip, thinking, in spite of everything, that she really *would* like to go somewhere more private with him. Focus, Sheena, focus!

"But, here goes, in a nutshell: it wasn't what you thought – when

you saw us there, that night, I wasn't there for…. I mean, that

was a big misunderstanding…"

She had looked down suddenly, her face now burning with her own personal shame of remembering why *she* was there on that particular night, a fact that couldn't be so easily dismissed as a 'misunderstanding'. Sensing her discomfort, he continued:

> "And quite frankly Sheena, if you're thinking about that you were also there that night? *Don't*. We all have things in our past we regret or aren't that crazy about. I don't care what's in your past, Sheena. I just care about *you*. These past few weeks have been meaningless without you in them. Listen, ok, you don't have to believe me, but I really wasn't there for the reason I'm assuming you thought I was there for. But, a few home truths about me that I am not particularly enamoured with, and would change if I could are: I'm no angel. I've done things I regret. I've taken advantage of way too many attractive students and I've abused my vague position of power."

Sheena's eyes widened at this confession, but she just nodded and gestured that he should continue.

> "But, believe me when I say: that all stopped when I knew I had serious feelings for *you*, Sheena. Since we began our regular coffee dates, and then our trip to Rottnest…"

He trailed off, remembering the feel of her body underneath his own on the sand. Her eyes widened again and her stomach flip-flopped as she thought of his hard, strong, muscular body pinning her down in the sand on that dusky, early evening in Rotto.

> "I was in Secrets that night for *Scott*. Against my better judgement. And we left anyway, as soon as we saw you. Now that's his business, which he has since heartfeltedly and honestly been able to sort out with Gabby – she's wonderful: she really is a godsend, that one."

Sheena nodded in agreement. Oh, *Gabs*.

"But the point is: that really wasn't my thing, nor has it ever been, to be quite honest. Never found it a turn-on. Now, I'm not saying I've been completely innocent, as I said: I have a past that I'm not at all proud of. But that's all it is: it's in the past, Sheena. It has been for ages now. I have put it behind me, just like I've put *your* past there too – no need to dwell or explain why you were there Sheena. We've all been through hard times, I get that, but *please*: I've been going crazy with missing you."

Waiter-model nearby coughed now to remind them of his presence. Sheena was about to return Brendan's sentiments re: missing him and also to tell him that there was still their logistical and legal dilemma of being teacher and student, but Brendan spoke again:

"Come on, drink up. Let's get out of here. I've got something I want to show you."

She hid her coy smile with her coffee cup as she drained the rest of its contents, thinking playfully to herself, that 'I bet you do'.

Allowing him to take her hand to help her out of the booth after him, she wondered if he felt the same palpable sexual tension that she'd been aware of mounting that now enshrouded them, almost thick enough to cut with a blunt knife. His stare into her eyes and similar coy smile to that of her own told her that he sure did.

"Don't worry." He joked, breaking the tension with a low chuckle. "We are actually coming back here later to eat though. Your amazing friend Gabby has our reservation for 8 o'clock tonight. I hope you don't mind me and Scott joining you two lovely ladies?"

Some quick calculations in her head told her that gave them just over three hours of which to continue their talk and catch-up (or confessional?) and plenty of time for Brendan to show her that 'something'.

'Stop it, Sheena, focus. He seems serious.' She was finding it hard to focus on anything except how good and easy it felt to be in this man's company again, or how to look away from staring at his manly, lightly hair-covered, tanned forearms, that led her eyes up to his broad, manly chest, pulling his crisp, black shirt taut across said chest. Any previous anger or embarrassment that she thought she would have felt upon seeing him again simply didn't eventuate. She felt foolish now for her strict 'no-Brendan' rule she'd imposed on her life. Every cell in Sheena's body was currently reminding her that she had missed this man like she would miss one of her own limbs.

They walked in comfortable silence in the now early evening, light dusk, casually still hand in hand (he hadn't thought to let go after being a gentleman and helping her get up from the table). He led her through his cheery, bright red front door, and then down through the smaller, pseudo-covert-cupboard-like-door under the stairs, which she remembered only too well as leading down to his well-stocked wine cellar and quiet sanctuary. She wondered briefly now just how many attractive students he may have also led down here and her smile faltered, a frown now replacing it. Sensing her hesitation or perhaps struck by the same thought, he turned his face up to look back at her and smiled broadly, giving her a reassuring wink.

"You're safe down here with me, Sheena. I promise."

'Damn.' She thought to herself, realising that if she was being honest with herself, she knew she didn't want to be 'safe' in his company. Maybe he really did have something to show her after all.

As they reached the bottom step and her eyes adjusted to the lack of light down there, she looked around and gasped. The full racks of bottle after bottle were nowhere to be seen, save for a couple of solitary bottles adorning the expansive, dark, wooden benchtop, the very same one that featured in her frequent fantasy of being passionately taken by Brendan in this wine cellar, which now seemed to be less 'wine' and more just cellar. A few still-open boxes remained at the foot of the stairs, with about two thirds of the space filled with bottles. Disappointment sunk through Sheena's guts. He was leaving.

"Looks like you're moving then."

It was all she could do to state this fact whilst choking back the sob that was now threatening to escape. She forced herself to breathe normally. Why bring her here? To show her this? The sofa, at least, remained in place. She quickly moved to the right and sank down mercifully, her fall cushioned by the firm leather upholstery. She tried smiling back at him reassuringly. She failed.

"Moving?" He frowned. "Well, no, well, yes and no. Maybe…"
Her turn to frown now.

Brendan quickly joined her on the sofa, his leg comfortably pressed up against her own again, and his arm brazenly snaking around her bare shoulders, pulling her tightly towards him. She could smell his own signature brand of manly 'Brendan' mixed with some kind of masculine-sports shower gel remnant.

"Sheena." He began again. "I thought I'd better start packing up this space so that if you and I choose to sell this house to buy our own place *together*, well, that you might have some ideas for down here."

Sheena's heart had stopped, she was sure of it. Time seemed to freeze. What the actual fuck?! She wasn't sure she had heard him correctly. He mistook her stunned silence for displeasure, and he continued hurriedly:

"Look, you don't have to decide today. It was just a thought, just one of our options. Another one is: we stay put, in this house, and again, you might have your own ideas for this space down here. Look, I understand, about your ex and your past: and that's exactly where all your worries and pain should stay – in the past. If you need, or would like, a life without alcohol in it, then that's fine by me – whatever you need Sheena, just say the word. The wine bottles are almost all gone – I've been selling them over the past couple of months. Incidentally building up a nice little extra savings fund that I thought could come in handy for a bit of a romantic elopement and honeymoon soon…"

She couldn't contain the giant grin that burst across her face now. What. The. Actual. Fuck.

Brendan returned her gargantuan grin and pulled her closer in to him. She finally managed to break her stunned silence with a:

"Wait, what?! Brendan! But, but…"

Her mind raced wildly. This was crazy. This was too much. This was…. Somehow, kind of perfect. Finally, her 'sensible', *logical* mind remembered something.

"But, you're still my *teacher*."

Her hand had found his thigh and she squeezed it affectionately. He leaned closer and kissed her slowly and deliberately on the cheek.

"Not anymore."

He whispered, the hand of his arm that was wrapped around her rubbed her bare shoulder gently in smooth circles.

"Yeah, but it's still not allowed. You'll still get sacked for it, Brendan." She shook her head, sadly.

"No, I mean: not anymore. At all. I quit teaching at the university. About a month and a half ago. I'm officially and definitely *not* your teacher anymore, Sheena, and I'm very much, completely, and unequivocally, head over heels, in love with you. I need you back in my life, Sheena. So, we can choose our own path, make our own destiny and truth. What do you say, Sheena?"

He looked at her uncertainly now, and close enough to her face she could have stuck her tongue out and tasted his skin if she wanted. The tension was thick and palpable once more. She burned for this man. She couldn't believe this was happening.

Running her hand gingerly and slowly up his thigh, the same thigh she had squeezed cheekily mere moments ago, she returned his steady gaze, and broke the tension a little by a playful:

"Oh, Mr Goodwood!" and a nervous laugh escaped her.

"*Brendan!*" He growled deeply back at her.

"*Brendan.*"

She repeated back to him, savouring the feel of his name on her lips and the sound of his name, the same name she'd called out so often during fantasies in her head.

"Wait." She said. "Go back to the part about packing up this wine cellar. Actually, Brendan, there is this recurring thought that I *have* had about the space down here." She pushed slightly closer against him before continuing. "It might be better if I show you rather than put it into words."

She stood up abruptly before she lost her nerve, breaking the spell of intimacy and closeness for the pair, momentarily. It was now Sheena who led Brendan, eagerly, by the hand, back over to the now almost completely bare, darkly-stained, wooden surface. As they neared the edge of the benchtop, Brendan caught on fast and wrapped his big, manly hands tightly around Sheena's petite waist and hoisted her up effortlessly, placing her on top of the hard, shiny, wooden surface, the cool wood against her bare skin where her dress had risen up yet again causing her to shudder and gasp. Brendan kept his warm hands firmly in place, while Sheena's own hands began exploring his rock-hard chest through his shirt. He had now moved his face closer to hers and his lips met hers hungrily, finally kissing her deeply and urgently. His hands travelled up her arched torso, deliberately and slowly, reaching her face and locking onto each side, as his tongue delved mercilessly into her mouth, clashing with her own furtive tongue. Her legs had, of their own accord, opened up and wrapped tightly around his muscular body, drawing him in closer to her and keeping him tightly against her as they continued to kiss passionately.

Stopping their kiss to catch their breaths slightly, they both panted, looking at each other, almost cautiously. Brendan slowly stroked his hands back down her body now, paying particular attention first to her slender neck and collarbones, before massaging and caressing her large, full breasts through the dress's thin material. Sheena groaned and closed her eyes. Brendan calmly pulled the material down now, causing the dress to cup her now naked breasts which he lowered his wet mouth to and began slowly licking and gently sucking on one, as Sheena moaned loudly now, grabbing his head closer to her and playing with his tousled, brown hair, her legs still locked around his body in a vice-like grip. Her hands found the edge of his shirt and fumbled there for a minute with the seam, before tugging at it impatiently, indicating: 'off, now!' Brendan reluctantly stopped what he was doing and near-ripped his own shirt off, discarding it hurriedly to the floor. Sheena shimmied her dress down even further in response and he moved his bare chest and body back tightly against hers, both of them groaning loudly and simultaneously with the feel of their hot skin on skin.

Sheena felt like she'd waited long enough. She had never felt this aroused before. She had to have him inside her. Now. She ached for him. Burned for him. *Needed* him. Right now. Her hands now found his belt buckle and fly to his heavy, faded-denim jeans and she confidently ripped them open, quickly releasing his huge, engorged cock that had been pushed up hard against her, straining at his seams. Feeling its smooth, firmness in her hands now, as her fingers instinctively curled around its thick shaft, she groaned, about to lose her mind with her lust for this man. Brendan got the hint in no time and pushed her dress up past her thighs now and instead of wasting any more time by removing her black g-string, he gently stroked her through its material, feeling just how fucking wet and turned on she was, before he hooked his finger around said g-string and pulled it deftly to one side, instantly replacing it with his throbbing schlong which he guided into position, resting on Sheena's hot, wet, aching-for-him pussy, as his mouth found her own mouth and he delved his tongue deeply into her mouth as an indication of things to come.

Sheena wrapped her legs deftly and quickly around his back again and urged him to thrust himself into her. She had never wanted anyone more. She needed him inside her. So, she told him so. In case there was any confusion on his part.

"I need you inside me. *Now.*"

She whispered hoarsely and breathily. Brendan groaned in response, held her small waist tightly in position, one of his big, manly hands on either side, and happily obliged: thrusting deeply and slowly and deliciously into her, filing her up completely.

"Oh!"

She must have yelled this loudly.

"Sheena!"

He cried out simultaneously, slowly pulling his cock out before slamming into her again, as she kept her legs wrapped tightly around him.

For all her many, many fantasies involving this man and this exact spot in his cellar, their coupling was over surprisingly quickly, and the pair collapsed onto each other, catching their breath, each one thinking the same thing: 'Oh. My. Fucking. God.' There would be no question that they were going to be together after this. Sheena couldn't believe they had even left it this long. As they regained their breaths and their heart rates got back to normal, Sheena cleared her throat and told him honestly:

"I have pictured that happening, just like that, so many times."

Her face was still flushed from their quick, hard, good-old-fashioned-fucking and her hair was in a similar just-been-fucked state. His strong, steady arms enveloped her again, pulling her close against his bare, still sweaty chest, not caring that they stuck together, clammy skin on clammy skin now.

"Oh, Sheena." He breathed out a long, shaky sigh. "You have no idea how good it is to hear that. I've thought about this every day for months now. Multiple times a day even."

"Not a very original thought for us both then?" She posed rhetorically and teasingly. "But then, *Brendan*," With the emphasis on his name again. "there *is* no original thought, ever, is there? And by visualising this, we have clearly brought it into reality and have essentially created it via our own thoughts and wavelengths and frequencies. Is that right, *Mr Goodwood?*"

She smiled genuinely at him. He chuckled along with her, shaking his head amicably.

"That's exactly it, Sheena. There is no original thought, *ever*. But there is no one else quite like *you*. And I'm never going to let you go, Sheena."

He kissed her again, slowly and deeply. Another of his 'teachings' drifted into her blurry, post-orgasmic thoughts. 'It *is* all to do with sex.' Brendan pulled back to finish off what he was saying, echoing her thoughts uncannily with:

"It's all sex, this life, that's for sure, but Sheena: let's create our own reality: our own truth vibrating in harmony. This isn't very original either Sheena, but then, nothing is, yes? So – I love you Sheena, more than I can adequately put into words – will you marry me and be my future?"

She answered his question with a very unoriginal squeal and pulled him in closer for another tight, hot embrace, her mind wandering again. 'It's all about sex. I honestly love this man, this person. This is where I am meant to be.'

## ABOUT THE AUTHOR

Lois Wood is a pun-loving, London-born-and-bred, now Novocastrian-wannabe (in Newcastle, Australia) whose debut novel Bacon Sleep Sex was released in 2015. When she's not traveling to/around Asia and teaching English, she can be found dispensing nutrition advice, running marathons or trail running, travel writing, working for health organisations, and of course: writing fiction, as can be seen in the fictitious tale you've just read: Ethereal. She also finds it mildly bemusing that readers often think and ask her if the protagonists in her books are based on herself, and hastens to add that no, they are entirely fictional, as is every other character in her stories (i.e. Lois Wood has definitely never been a high-class prostitute, nor a philandering philosophy professor). She resides in a quiet suburb of Newcastle, NSW, with her fiancé and free-range guinea pigs. At the time of publication Lois is on the cusp of motherhood and is about to become a full-time mum. She's absolutely thrilled about this next chapter of her life, and hopes to continue reading and writing fiction in between feeding and changing the little one. Watch this space...